PANIK

CHRIS SELWYN JAMES

ISBN 978-1-916301-0-8 (paperback)

ISBN 978-1-916301-1-5 (ebook)

Cover Design by David Provolo.

First Edition

www.chrisselwynjames.com

ABOUT THE AUTHOR

Chris Selwyn James is a writer and health economist, with a PhD from the London School of Hygiene and Tropical Medicine. Early in his career, he worked in Rwanda a few years after the genocide. This experience had a profound influence on his fictional writing, particularly in exploring mental health and trauma. He has worked in over twenty countries in Africa, Asia and Europe.

Chris lives near Paris with his wife and two children. You can connect with him via his website: chrisselwynjames.com

For Sandra

CONTENTS

I fear sleep, just like everyone else. I've taken the tablets, tried to meditate. I even joined one of those pointless dream-awareness groups. But it's all the same – there is no cure. Each night as I lie awake, I try to remember how it was before the troubles began. Back then, dreams could be beautiful, all warmth and light. Sleep would come easily and I'd wake up refreshed. The world seemed a hopeful place.

Now everything has fallen apart. Sleep-deprived addicts wander the streets; whole cities have been abandoned. Burials, when they happen, are hasty affairs. More often, the dead are left to rot. They call it the Panic, as if it were a fleeting emotion. But to me it is something deeper. Something missing from our hearts.

AT DAWN

September

1

The sun, blood red, rose above the empty streets of
Oxford. Karen Newton stared at it directly, transfixed
by the brutality of the sun's light. It left a burned
imprint at the back of her eyes.

Lightheaded, she sat down on a bench overlooking the
River Cherwell. She had already walked over half the way
home, following her night shift at the John Radcliffe Hospital.
*Only another fifteen minutes' walk and I'll be lying next to my
husband,* she thought. She pictured him turning on his side as
she entered the room, mumbling "I love you" before falling
back to sleep. A habit stretching back almost twenty years, one
that never failed to make her smile.

A bird chirped above her, waiting for an answer in the early
morning air. Karen stood up, feeling the familiar aches and
pains in her joints, pulled her coat close. As she walked, she
found herself thinking of her children, as she often did. Both
had been adopted, and both were loved as if they were her own
flesh and blood. They were long since grown, twenty-seven and
twenty-one now. She was proud of who they had become. Rosa
was a brilliant and intense woman, profoundly intuitive, filled

with a deep-rooted empathy that touched everyone she knew. Rosa was particularly protective of her brother, Nathan, who was sensitive, thoughtful and adored by his friends. Sometimes Karen thought he was too delicate for this world. But it was Rosa whom she worried about more.

Birdsong filled the air, one call answering another in the calmness of the road. Such moments of serenity before the start of the daily grind made shift work more palatable to her. As she walked, Karen glanced up at the trees lining the street, spotting a chaffinch hopping along a branch. It seemed to be staring directly at her. She stepped closer, lost her footing, and fell to the ground. The bird fluttered its wings and flew away.

Her lower back was sore, but she didn't seem to be badly hurt. Still, her heart was pounding from the shock. She removed a soggy leaf from the sole of her shoe, then carefully stood up. *I'm getting old,* she thought, brushing away leaves from her skirt. Her heartbeat felt irregular: it raced, then seemed to stop for too long. She leaned against a tree, breathed in slowly, exhaled, felt a little better.

Karen let go of the tree and continued to walk. Her pounding heart had triggered a memory, one never far from her thoughts. *Did we do the right thing?* She placed one hand on her chest and felt her heartbeat gradually resume its normal pace. Glancing up at the streaks of red crisscrossing the sky, she was taken by a familiar pang of guilt. *We had to do it,* she told herself. Better than leaving Rosa's heart condition untreated. And it all turned out fine. The surgery had been a success, and the subsequent check-ups had never caused any discomfort. Now, Rosa was a healthy young woman, and the scars on her chest were barely visible. She was doing well, with a good job in London, a decent group of friends and a brother who adored her. Perhaps one day soon Rosa would settle down, start a family, and she would become a proud grandmother.

Karen hummed a half-remembered nursery rhyme, imagining herself and her husband by their daughter's side, picking up their grandson for the first time. It will be so beautiful, the little baby gazing at them in wonder. With this image still fresh in her mind, she turned off Banbury Road and onto Cunliffe Close, where she lived. She gazed at her home – a well-kept terraced house they had lived in for years – with new eyes. They could probably squeeze a single bed and a cot in the second bedroom, she thought. Or even place a cot in the main bedroom. She looked forward to telling her husband about this when he awoke.

Her house key jammed in the lock. *That's strange,* she thought, trying to turn it left then right. But soon enough the key slid in and she opened the door. She placed the keys on the sideboard and hung her bag on the bannister. Sitting down on the hard chair kept by the front door, she took off her shoes and socks, scrunching her tired toes on the soft beige carpet. It had been a difficult night at the hospital. The palliative care unit had been understaffed because of an unusual surge in emergency department admissions. Three of her colleagues had been transferred to the emergency department for most of the night.

Worse, the patients under her care seemed to have been in more pain than usual. Potent opioid medications seemed to wear off too quickly. Her gentle kneading and massaging of their knotted limbs offered minimal relief. It all seemed so futile.

Don't think like that, she scolded herself. *That is not how I am. Stay positive; what I do helps, at least in some small way. And now the shift is over; it is time to lie down next to my husband, my soulmate for all these years, and let sleep carry me away.*

Climbing the stairs, she could already picture him, probably stirring in his sleep now, his mind subconsciously attuned to her arrival and then her presence as she lay down next to him.

She opened the bedroom door. Rays of sunlight shone through a gap between the curtains. It seemed too quiet.

"Roger?" she called out.

Then she saw him, lying face down by the entrance of their en-suite bathroom.

Slowly, almost trancelike, she crossed the bedroom and bent down next to her unconscious husband. Only then did she notice the pool of blood around his downturned face. Carefully, not wanting to see too much, she felt for a pulse. There was nothing.

———

The phone rang, pulling Rosa out of a restless sleep. Groggy, she reached for it, her mother's name blinking on the phone's screen. She glanced at her watch. It was half six in the morning.

"Mum? Is everything OK?" she asked, though she already sensed something was wrong. Fragments of a recurring dream remained in her mind: a train station, a woman wearing a bright red scarf, an overpowering sense of loss. A dream that had become more intense in recent weeks.

"Your father, it's..." her mother started, but then she was sobbing uncontrollably.

"Mum, I'll come right over," Rosa said, sitting up. "I can get there in an hour and a half if the trains are running OK."

"My darling, thank you. I'm at the police station. On St Aldates. It's awful, so awful. I don't know... Your father, he's dead, Rosa. The police think he was murdered! Don't tell Nathan, please, not yet. I'll call him later."

Rosa remained silent for a few seconds, even though she desperately wanted to scream. She mustered all her emotional strength to reply calmly.

"OK," she said. She stared at the wall. She had thought... well, she didn't know what she'd thought. That her father had suffered a heart attack perhaps, or been injured on the road. But not that he was dead.

"Rosa?"

"Oh, Mum," she said, feeling the tears well up but keeping the anguish out of her voice. "I love you so much. Stay at the police station. I'll be there soon."

Rosa put the phone down on the bed and gazed blankly at the patterns lining the carpet. *Her father murdered? Who could have done such a thing? And why? Whoever it was will pay for it, I'll make sure of that.*

No one did it, the voice told her, a quiet murmur inside her head. *He killed himself.*

"Ana, shut up!" she said aloud. But she feared the voice was right. The voice was always right.

Rosa's mind raced with images of her father sitting there in desperation before he committed suicide. *Why?* She pounded the bed with her fists, picked up a book from her bedside table and threw it across the room. She looked at her hands and started sobbing, gulping for air as the tears ran down her face.

Pull yourself together, she told herself. *What matters right now is that Mum is sitting alone in a police station. She needs me.*

Rosa stood up. She picked up her mobile phone and ordered a taxi, then scribbled a note for her housemates to let them know she would be out of town for a while. From her wardrobe, she took an overnight bag and packed a few essentials.

Looking at her watch, she noted that she still had a few minutes before the taxi would arrive. She went to the bathroom and splashed cold water over her eyes. She cupped her hands together so that the water pooled, then submerged her face.

It is easy to become complacent, she thought, *to expect life to go on happily and without major incident. Easy but naïve. This world* is unpredictable. It can be cruel when one least expects it. The sun rises and you wake from sleep, just like any other day. Even when everything has changed. Whether her father was murdered or killed himself doesn't matter in the end. The fact is, he is dead. Somehow, she, Nathan and her mother would have to deal with it the best they could.

2

The authorities were treating it as a murder case. There was no obvious sign of a break-in, but Roger Newton's eyes had been gouged out and his neck slashed. The coroner's report noted that although in theory this could have been self-inflicted, murder was far more likely. Neighbours reported hearing screaming, which suggested a struggle.

Rosa's father worked in logistics, a procurement officer in a large warehouse, and the police hypothesised a motive based on a business transaction gone wrong. However, the company made money from the practical and uncontroversial task of transporting pharmaceuticals to retail outlets, and her father was no more than a mid-ranking employee there. He was a dependable worker who fulfilled his duties promptly and without complaint, and colleagues had not noted any unusual recent behaviour. The police were still investigating it as a murder, but the trail was going cold.

Constable Daniels, the police detective leading the investigation of her father's death, had informed Rosa yesterday that he would have to close the case next week. Unless, that is, they found new evidence before then. When she pressed him on whether they normally closed investigations like this so quickly, he said he had never come across a case like this before.

She had sensed a tension in his manner, in the lack of certainty in his voice and the way in which he avoided her eyes. It worried her, particularly because up to that point the constable had been hard to read. Rosa had not told her mother about this conversation, at least not yet. She feared it would set back her recovery.

Rosa and her mother sat on a bench in the University Parks. It was early on a Thursday morning, a fortnight since her father had died. Neither had been sleeping well. Still, the fresh air and peaceful surroundings helped them feel calm. Mature trees lined the path: hawthorns, cherry trees, a large English oak with gnarled roots. Rosa and her mother held hands, sipping coffee as they gazed at the trees and watched other early risers walking through the park.

The past two weeks had been hard. Her mother spoke very little, was not eating well, and until recently had not ventured out of the house. She spent most of her days sitting on the sofa, leafing through the daily newspaper or flicking listlessly between TV channels.

"Look at that bird," her mother said, pointing at a crow. It had cocked its head to one side and seemed to be staring directly at them.

"Maybe it wants some coffee," Rosa replied, happy just to hear her mother's voice.

Her mother smiled. "You're a good person, and strong," she said, squeezing Rosa's hand.

"And you're a wonderful mother. I mean it. How you've

been with me, and with Nathan, too, since all this happened. I really appreciate it."

The crow cawed, then flew away.

"You know, I think I might be ready to return to work."

"That's great, Mum, really it is. But don't rush it."

"I won't. Perhaps I will go back part-time, at least to begin with. Helping patients will help me, I think. And I can't keep relying on you or Nathan to always be here."

Rosa looked across at her mother, and then at the trees in front of them. The leaves were just starting to change colour.

"Even if you go back to work," she said, "I'll stay with you."

"What about your job?"

"Don't worry. My boss is an understanding woman. I can do a lot of the work from home, anyway. As for Nathan, he's a student, he has loads of free time!" she said light-heartedly. "But seriously, I know he's happy to come. The train ride from Nottingham is easy enough."

"I am doing better, Rosa. I know it's been hard for you, too."

"It has been, but I'm doing OK. And Nathan's coping well, considering." Rosa noted a worried look on her mother's face. "Don't worry about us, please," she continued. "Just concentrate on your own health for now. Promise?"

"All right."

Rosa glanced again at her mother. Her face looked drawn, with dark bags under her eyes. Still, she was happy that her mother was starting to talk more freely.

It had begun to drizzle. Dark clouds hung heavy in the sky. Rosa's mother stood up and stretched out her arms. "Let's go home before we get soaked," she said. "I'll make us both something nice, maybe pancakes topped with fresh fruit. How does that sound?"

"It sounds perfect."

They walked along Banbury Road. Students on their bicycles pedalled past, cars and buses edged forward in the traffic. A woman wearing a smart suit strode by purposefully, clutching a handbag in one hand and umbrella in the other. A jogger, a middle-aged man breathing heavily and with sweat dripping from his face, also overtook them. He wore a headband and running shorts that were too small for him. Five years ago, Rosa had run the London Marathon, but she hadn't run much since.

They stopped at a pedestrian crossing near the house and waited for the traffic lights to change. An old couple was also waiting there. They were doting over their granddaughter, who was sitting in a pushchair. The young girl was giggling as her grandfather dangled a soft toy in front of her and made funny noises. In the distance, a police siren sounded. The pedestrian light was still red.

"Nee-nor, nee-nor," the little girl sang, and her grandparents laughed.

The sirens were much louder now. Rosa noticed a subtle but clear change in her mother's demeanour: the clenching of her jaw, flushed cheeks. She glanced up the road and saw the flashing blue lights. It was an ambulance rather than a police car. Cars moved to the side to let it through. The ambulance turned just before the pedestrian crossing onto Belbroughton Road, which was one street along from their house.

The pedestrian light finally turned green. Rosa's mother stopped by the intersection of Banbury Road and Belbroughton Road, and stared at the ambulance. It was parked near the corner of the road, outside a redbrick house that was partially concealed by a long hedgerow.

"That's where Professor Hinton lives," her mother said. "I hope he's OK."

"A friend of yours?"

"Jim and I used to play badminton together, years ago.

Maybe I should ask if I could help. I probably know the paramedics."

"Shouldn't we just leave them to it?" Rosa asked, but her mother was already walking towards the ambulance. They stopped by the vehicle. No one was inside. The front door to Professor Hinton's house was ajar. Rosa thought she could hear someone crying.

"Let's go, Mum."

"Wait. I think they're coming out."

A paramedic appeared. Rosa's mother recognised him.

"Greg, hi, it's Karen from the Radcliffe. Is Professor Hinton OK?"

The man looked at Karen, then at Rosa. His face was drained of colour.

"There's nothing we could do."

"You mean..."

"Yes," he replied, shaking his head.

"What happened?"

"I don't know. But it ain't the only case. Overnight there have been others across the city."

"What do you mean?" Karen asked. Her voice sounded unsteady. "It's not connected to my Roger, is it?"

"I don't know. I'm sorry, Karen, we're not meant to say nothing. I've already said more than I should. You best go home."

"But..."

"Mum, we should go," Rosa said, leading her mother away. At the corner, Rosa glanced back. The paramedic was on the phone, his head bowed. She felt a jolt in the pit of her stomach. Somehow, it was connected to her father's death, she was sure of it. She feared it was the start of something terrible.

"And now back to our main story," the BBC news presenter said. Rosa and her mother stared at the television.

"Twenty-four people died in Oxford last night, in what appears to be a spate of suicides and attempted suicides. Three more victims are in hospital, in critical condition. Reports coming in suggest today's tragedy was one in a series of incidents that have struck Oxford in the space of a few weeks. Earlier, we interviewed a local policeman, who had this to say..."

The camera panned to a man in uniform standing outside a coffee shop on Cowley Road. Police had cordoned off an adjoining street. Rosa recognised him as one of Constable Daniels' team investigating her father's death.

"Constable Atkin, can you tell us what happened?"

"I can confirm there have been twenty-seven cases overnight, with twenty-four deceased."

"And can you confirm whether all were suicides?"

The policeman shook his head. "All I can say to you right now is that we are working closely with the hospitals. We will release a statement when we have further details."

"Thank you. Were the cases in a particular part of the city?"

"No."

"But they were all in Oxford?"

"As far as we know, yes."

"And did –"

"Sorry, I have no further comments at this point."

"Thank you, Constable Atkin."

The news channel returned to the studio.

"It is not clear yet how these cases are connected," the news presenter continued. "But in a further development, two recent deaths in Oxford – until now treated as murder cases – are being linked to last night's deaths. We hope to have more information soon."

Rosa's mother switched off the TV. She leaned forward on the sofa and covered her eyes.

"What is this all about?" she whispered.

Rosa moved closer to her mother. She could see that her face was moist with tears.

"I don't know," Rosa said. "But we've got to keep strong, all three of us. Dad would've wanted us to focus on moving forward."

"How?"

Rosa placed an arm gently on her mother's shoulder. She sensed a growing depression, one that would only spiral downwards. Closing her eyes for a moment, she pictured her mother by a hospital bed, holding a dying man's hand.

"Think of your patients at the hospital, over the years," she said, looking at her mother. "After surgery, chemotherapy or some other aggressive treatment. All of them struggling with immense pain. You were the one who helped them through it."

"It's a palliative care unit. They all died in the end."

"Mum, don't sound like that. The point is," Rosa said, holding her mother's arm and gazing at the faded wallpaper in front of her. "The point is this. You made the last days of your patients better, far more bearable. You helped them stay calm despite the pain and all the medications. Enough at peace to keep on, to even laugh once in a while."

"Maybe."

"That helped them, and their families, too, when they came to visit."

"I suppose so. It's just hard to take. Sometimes it seems like there is so much wrong with this world. I just don't understand what's going on."

Karen wept and Rosa embraced her. After a minute, she said, "I know you're right, Rosa. I must try to keep strong. I'll go back to work, start seeing people again. Get on with things."

"That's good."

"And right now, I'm going to make us some delicious pancakes, like I said I would!"

Rosa smiled, but she knew her mother's joviality was forced. "I'll give you a hand."

"No, you stay put. Relax a while. You're looking after me all the time. It's about time I looked after you."

"OK, but call me if you need me."

"I will. Read a newspaper or, better still, something that has nothing to do with all this. There are a couple of new magazines that I bought just yesterday."

"Sure."

Rosa watched her mother leave the room. Even though it had been only a couple of weeks since her father's death, her mother had visibly aged in that time. She walked in slow, hesitating steps; sometimes it seemed each step required effort. More of her hair had turned grey, her skin looked drawn, and there were dark bags under her eyes. She knew her mother had not been sleeping well.

Mum will be OK, she told herself, but she wasn't fully convinced. At least Nathan seemed to be doing a little better. He had stayed with them in Oxford the first week. He hadn't talked much about how he was feeling, but he'd been great with their mother. He'd wanted to stay longer, but their mum insisted he go back so he wouldn't miss course registrations. Rosa persuaded him to leave, promising she would stay with their mum until the murder investigation was over.

Rosa picked up a magazine and flicked through the pages. Models staring vacantly, their clothes hanging limp from their anorexic bodies. *I Lost Thirty Pounds in Two Weeks* read one headline. There were before and after photos of a woman, overweight and glum before, fake smile after. Rosa thought of two friends of hers, one very thin and the other overweight. Both were unhappy with their bodies. She turned to the next page. *How I Went from Zero to Hero* was this article's headline. A middle-aged man stood outside his mansion, trophy wife by his side. The article detailed his success as a self-made millionaire.

It's true, she thought. This world we live in is really messed up. We value the wrong things. Money, appearance, climbing the rungs on society's ladder. Materialism. For how many years, how many generations, have we been like this? She sensed Ana then, murmuring something. *Shush*, Rosa whispered, not wanting to hear her voice.

Ana had not spoken to her since the day her father had died. Still, Rosa was more aware of her now than she had been for many years.

Rosa had first heard Ana's voice when she was fourteen. At least that was the first time she could recall with absolute certainty. Rosa had been old enough to know not to tell anyone, understanding that once people labelled you as insane, that was it. They would lock you up in an asylum, left to bang your head against padded walls.

That first time, it was an early evening in summer. She was walking alone in the woods, a shortcut back home from a friend's house. Ana's voice suddenly came into her head, an urgent whisper commanding her to hide. She looked around, disoriented and nervous, expecting to see someone calling to her. A friend maybe or some silly prankster. But there was no one.

Hide, the voice repeated. She ignored it but the voice grew hysterical. *Hide! Hide! Hide!* the voice screamed, loud enough to make her head hurt. Moments later, she heard real voices, drunken men's voices not far away, and she knew then she had to obey the voice. Looking around, all the trees seemed too thin to conceal her. The voice guided her towards a large holly bush. She pushed herself in, ignoring the painful sting of the spiny leaves as she crouched there and waited.

Three men staggered by, two much older than the other. One of the older men, gaunt and unshaven, was drinking from a glass bottle. The younger man started singing. He sang falsetto, some crude ditty that the third man found hilarious. They stopped not more than five metres from where Rosa hid, the laughing man holding his large gut as if it was the funniest song he had ever heard. Without warning, the gaunt man who had been drinking swung the bottle, hitting the younger man in the back of the head. This made the fat man laugh harder, even as his companion fell to the ground.

"Don't you ever sing like a ponce again," the gaunt man said, furious, standing over the younger man. "Now get up, and let's find us some fresh skirt."

A few days later, the local news reported a missing girl, and that police were looking for three men who had been seen hanging around the school. For weeks, Rosa cried herself to sleep. She didn't say anything, though, not even to her brother or parents.

From that point on, the voice stayed with her, mostly silent but always there. A presence waiting in the back of her mind. She began to call it – or her – Ana. Most of the time she tried to shut her out, tried to forget Ana was there. Rosa wanted to belong; she had an intense fear of being perceived as anything but ordinary. Yet sometimes she couldn't shut Ana out. Each of these times, Ana had said just a few words. *Hide. Stay away from her. Don't believe what he says.* As if she could sense evil. Still, Rosa was wary of her.

Her mother walked into the room carrying two plates of pancakes with sliced fruit on top.

"They look delicious," Rosa said.

"I burnt them a bit, but hopefully they're OK. There are

more if you want. Have a seat. I'll bring out the cutlery and some tea for us."

"Thanks, Mum."

"It's my pleasure."

Rosa sat down. She heard her mother humming in the kitchen. *Everything will be all right*, she told herself. *Things will return to normal soon enough, and Mum will be better, stronger than ever.* Yet deep down she knew none of this was true.

———

The night sky was clear. Rosa lay in bed with the curtains open, unable to sleep. She stared out at the stars. *Each one is a sun like ours*, she thought. Burning heat, nuclear fireballs that bring life but can so easily take it away. No wonder ancient civilisations used to worship the sun.

The rest of the day passed by without major incident, but still she felt uneasy. Her mother, though trying to remain upbeat, was clearly troubled. She seemed distracted. Once, Rosa caught her mother staring at her own reflection in the hallway mirror, pulling on her cheeks and the tired skin under her eyes.

The phone call from Constable Daniels hadn't helped. He had been insistent on seeing them that afternoon. He'd only agreed to postpone the meeting once Rosa had promised to contact him immediately if, as he put it, either of them had "dark thoughts."

Rosa thought again about the conversation with her mother after dinner. It made her uneasy.

"Last night I dreamt about your biological mother," her mother had said. "In the dream she looked different to how I've always imagined her. She had your beautiful grey-green eyes, yes, and the same slight dimples when you smile. But her skin was nothing like yours. It was blotchy and pale. She looked anaemic."

Rosa glanced down at her hands. She had always assumed one of her parents was of South Asian origin based on the colour of her skin.

"In my dreams, her features are never that clear," Rosa said eventually. "But she's always wearing a bright red scarf, waving to me from a distance." It was the first time she had told her mother about this recurring dream, though she didn't mention she had seen her biological mother – or whoever this woman was – as a child, at Kings Lynn train station.

"Would you have liked to meet her?"

"Yes. Well, I think so at least. I don't know anything about her."

"I know. I'm sorry."

"Mum, there's nothing to apologise for," Rosa said. "You are all that I need."

"Rosa, I love you with all my heart. You know that, don't you?"

"Of course I do."

"Good. It's just that..." Karen started, then stopped. She removed her glasses and patted her eyes with a napkin.

"Just what?"

"Oh, it's hard to explain."

"You can talk to me."

"I know. The tricky thing is...it's about you. Your childhood."

Karen hesitated.

"Go on, Mum. You don't need to hold back."

"I know. I've always told you the truth; Dad too. Everything we knew. But one thing we've never talked about much is the surgery you had as a young child. Do you remember?"

Rosa looked at her mother, noticed her hands were shaking. "A little, but not a lot," she replied.

"I think about it a lot. I mean, I know it had to be done, and it was a success. You've run, what, three marathons already, haven't you?" She laughed, trying to sound jovial.

"Now you're doing what you always do, exaggerating my achievements," Rosa said lightly, trying to put her mother at ease. "Maybe I'll enter the next one in London."

"Good!"

"But what about the surgery makes you worry?"

"It's not the surgery. The follow-up appointments. Do you remember them?"

Rosa glanced again at her mother, noticing the expectation in her face. She shut her eyes for a moment, tried to picture the hospital in her mind.

"I remember certain things, but not very precisely," she said. "Like these long corridors with high ceilings, the smell of hospital disinfectant. Doctors shining bright lights into my eyes and asking what I could see."

"Did they ever do anything...that made you feel uncomfortable?"

"No," Rosa replied, surprised.

"Are you sure?"

"Yes. Don't worry, Mum. You and Dad were always there."

"Hmm." Karen paused for a few seconds. "The hospital, well, let's put it this way: it wasn't like the John Radcliffe."

"Mum, why are you worrying about this now? Is there something about the treatment you haven't told me?"

"No, nothing like that. You needed the surgery, and they did it professionally. I worry only that the whole thing – all those hospital visits – may have been traumatic for you, that's all."

"There's nothing to worry about. The doctors were nice."

"Yes, but..." her mum said, looking down at her hands. She was fiddling with her wedding ring.

"But what?"

"Oh, I don't know. Nothing, I guess. I just worry about you. But I know you're strong."

―――――――

Rosa rose from her bed and drew the curtains, then lay back down. She shut her eyes and focused on her breathing, inhaling air through her nose then exhaling in a slow, controlled manner.

She felt each breath, sensed her heart beating hard and then sleep rushing towards her, like a sudden weight pulling her down. For some reason she felt nervous, her heart beat faster. Yet she could not stop sleep from taking her away. She felt herself slipping into the depths of a cavernous hole darker than the night sky, with no stars or moonlight to guide her.

> Everything is dull grey and stationary. She is standing still, watching a train approach the station. The train is the only thing moving. Rosa is just a young child, four or five years old maybe. Someone is holding her hand. A young man in military uniform. In the distance, she sees someone: a woman in a bright red scarf, her biological mother. The woman is unable to move, but is waving frantically at Rosa. She is shouting. No, not shouting. Screaming.

Rosa woke up, dripping sweat. Then she heard it again. A pitiful scream, like the sound of a wounded animal.

"Mum," she gasped.

She leapt out of bed and rushed to her mother's bedroom. The room was empty. The window was wide open, the curtains billowed in the wind. Terrified, she approached the window and peered out, picturing her mother lying motionless on the floor below. She wasn't there. Rosa exhaled, muttering to herself to keep calm.

But then she heard a new noise. A faint scratching sound coming from her parents' en-suite bathroom. Rosa rushed across the room and tried to open the bathroom door. It was locked.

"Mum, open up!"

Nothing.

"Mum, it's Rosa. Please open the door," she pleaded.

Still nothing. She put her ear to the door and heard the same scratching sound more clearly. Like paper being ripped.

"Mum," she shouted, desperate now.

There was no reply. Rosa pushed against the door, shoved her shoulder hard against it to try to break the lock. The door moved a little but still wouldn't give. She took a few steps back, braced herself, and then ran full pelt at the door. Wood splintered. Rubbing her shoulder, she ran again into the door, and this time the lock broke away from the door.

Her mother was lying on the tiled floor, nail scissors by her hands, her throat slit. Blood dripping from crude cuts around her eyes made it look like tears of blood. Her eyes open, blank, staring at...nothing.

3

The G-Cafe was a five-minute walk from Kings Cross station. Ambient techno played; graffiti was painted directly over faded wallpaper. The place was packed, as most cafes were these days. As Rosa queued at the counter, she glanced over at her younger brother sitting by the window. Nathan looked jumpy, tapping his hands on the table and fiddling with the sugar container. She wondered if he had also cut down on his sleep, as so many people had started to do. More caffeine was the last thing he needed.

It was early October. Less than a month had passed since their mother died. It was the first time she'd seen him since the funeral. In those few weeks, everything had changed. There had been close to two thousand cases, and the majority had died immediately. It was the most gruesome of maladies. People would wake in the middle of the night gripped by an uncontrollable hysteria. Screaming, they would try to tear out their own eyes with their bare hands. If they weren't successful, they'd reach for the nearest implement to hand – a knife, a razor blade, anything that was sharp. Some of them slit their own throats, as their parents had.

"Here you go," she said, handing a coffee to Nathan. "A long black, double strength."

"Thanks," he replied, pouring in a few spoons of sugar.

"How have you been?"

"So-so. You know."

"Yeah. I miss them so much. When Mum died..."

"Rosa, do you mind if we don't talk about that? Our parents. At least not just yet."

"OK," she said. She tried to catch Nathan's eye, but he was looking down at his hands. For a split moment, he seemed ancient, despite his thick brown hair and wispy stubble. An old man contemplating mortality, rather than the bright-eyed twenty-one-year-old he had been just a few months ago.

She glanced around the room instead. The atmosphere was subdued. Last time she had been in this cafe, it had been humming with life: mainly students talking about music or politics. That was a while ago, though, before the epidemic.

News outlets labelled it "mass hysteria." Tabloids were full of stories of regular people going mad. Scientists came up with the acronym SED, for sleep-induced encephalopathic delirium. Yet most people simply called it the Panic. Other countries had closed their borders to British residents until the epidemic was brought under control.

"Thanks for coming down to London," she said. "Especially for such a short visit."

"Not at all. It must've been harder for you."

"What do you mean?"

"They're clamping down on travel in and out of Oxford, right?"

"Oh that. There is a lot of paperwork, but they let people come and go. This thing isn't infectious."

"Don't be stupid," he said in exasperation. "It's an epidemic, Rosa."

"Please don't talk to me like that," she replied, trying to keep her tone calm. "Look, I know it's scary."

"Sorry. I didn't mean to sound...you know."

"I know. I'm not trying to argue, but scientists have said this isn't contagious."

"But how do they really know?"

She looked at her brother. His hands shook as he sipped his coffee. "Let's talk about something else," she said.

"What else is there to talk about?" he said, raising his voice. People stared at them momentarily, before returning to their coffees.

"Nathan," she said, reaching across the table for his hand. He pulled away. She looked at him with sadness. This was not how her brother normally was.

"Thousands have died," he muttered. "Probably many more than what the government says."

"Perhaps."

"And the few that survive don't last long. Do you know what they've been doing to them?"

"No," she replied, not liking where the conversation seemed to be heading.

"The government locks them up."

"Nathan, how do you know this?"

"They force-feed them," he said, ignoring her question. "Monitored in isolation wards, they're gibberish wrecks. Most of them die within a few days."

"I don't know. There are always conspiracy theories with these kinds of things."

"It's the truth; everyone knows it. It's on the internet if you know where to look. That's why I've got to get out. You should too, Rosa. There are ferries to Northern Ireland. For government workers and people with the right papers. But I've heard you can buy tickets on the black market."

"What are you talking about?"

"Oh, Rosa. Northern Ireland is applying to the UN for temporary secession from the UK. Yes, even with the bipartisan politics there and all the shit with Brexit. You do know about that, don't you?"

"Yes, but so what?"

"So better to get out while we can. More chance than making it to mainland Europe. They've closed the Channel Tunnel. The French and the Dutch won't let us in."

"Nathan, stop being so paranoid," she blurted out. "This thing – the Panic – they'll get it under control soon enough. Concentrate on the here and now, on your studies and friends."

"What's the point?"

"Oh grow up," she said, her voice rising. People were probably staring at them, but she didn't care.

The train edged forward then accelerated, leaving the town of Didcot behind. Rosa stared out the window. Boats moored along the River Thames bobbed about in the water.

She thought about her conversation with Nathan earlier that afternoon. His determination to buy a ferry ticket to Northern Ireland seemed foolish. Still, she regretted snapping at him. She was worried about his frenzied and paranoid state. He was clearly upset. Nathan was still the same quiet, sensitive boy of his childhood. Growing up, Rosa had been very much the big sister who eased him through the uncertainties of adolescence. Now, Rosa was acutely aware of how alone he must feel, given everything that had happened. Lecturing him as she had done would have only made him feel worse.

She wished their meeting had gone differently. She should have listened to his views more patiently. Two siblings talking frankly but respectfully, as close friends would. Maybe they could have even been able to talk about their parents.

"We will be arriving in Oxford shortly," the train conductor announced. "Please have your arrivals card completed and passports ready."

Rosa glanced around the carriage. There were only a handful of other passengers, and they all looked preoccupied. She took out her passport and stared at her photo, one taken a few years ago. She had cut her hair short back then. She looked so different to her parents. People always knew she'd been adopted – her light brown complexion was darker than her parents' pale skin, and her hair was darker, too. She had grey-green eyes, whereas her parents' eyes had been dark brown. She could have passed for Nathan's biological sibling, though.

The train pulled into Oxford station. People disembarked and queued by the platform exit, where station officials inspected their passports. It was a slow process. Rosa adjusted her bag on her shoulder whilst waiting in line.

"Please step aside," an official instructed an old man. She held his passport, having scanned it through a handheld reader. "One of my colleagues will need to talk to you."

"Why?"

"Sir, you'll need to do as I say. I'm sorry."

"But my papers are in order," the man said, his voice quivering. "I live here and I need to get home. My wife will be worried."

Other passengers in the queue watched without saying anything. A second official came over. Rosa noted he carried a gun.

"Mr Florence," this official said, looking at the old man's passport, "I'm Special Constable Wright, from the London Met Office. There is nothing to worry about. We simply have to conduct random medical checks on arrivals. It's standard government policy."

"But..."

"No ifs and buts, sir. Now please do not make a scene. It won't take long, I promise."

Rosa watched the old man being led away, his head bowed. She felt uneasy. In her trips between Oxford and London, she had never witnessed police pulling aside passengers for a medical check. The government seemed to becoming more anxious about the epidemic. She looked at her arrivals card. On it, she had ticked the box next to the question 'Have any of your relatives died from SED?' She wondered if that meant they would pull her aside, too.

"Madam, your documents please."

"Oh sorry," Rosa said, taking her passport and arrivals card out.

The station official ran her passport through the reader. Rosa noticed a slight change in the woman's expression, the way her jaw clenched and muscles tightened up.

"Ms Newton, you'll need to step aside," she said.

Rosa nodded, trying to stay calm. She didn't want to make a scene.

"Blue-green," the station official spoke into a handheld transceiver. She tried to say it in a neutral tone, but Rosa could tell that the woman was nervous.

It had already been twenty minutes. She waited in a small room, doing her best to stay calm. Blinds had been drawn over the windows. Other than a few fold-up plastic chairs and a table, there was nothing in the room. It was part of a temporary portable building located in what was once the train station's car park.

They had taken away her mobile phone. She fiddled with her handbag's strap, wondering what she could do. Constable Wright, the same official who had earlier led the older passenger away for a medical check, sat opposite her. Early on, he had made it clear he couldn't answer any questions, only saying that a colleague would soon arrive to explain everything.

She thought she heard a car pull up outside, then car doors opening and closing. Constable Wright's expression remained inscrutable. She held her breath and listened. People nearby seemed to be conferring in low voices. Then she heard footsteps approaching, and someone climbing the steel stairs.

A man opened the door. He wore military uniform and carried a briefcase. Constable Wright stood up as he entered.

"Thank you for your patience, Rosa," the man said. "I'm Andrew Shaw."

"Are my papers not in order?" she asked.

The man looked familiar. Light blue eyes, a nose that was slightly bent, sandy-brown hair. He was probably in his early fifties.

"Your papers are fine," he replied. "I'm here because of what happened to your parents." He unfolded a chair and sat down. "Craig, thanks, I'll take it from here."

Constable Wright nodded and left the room.

"What's all this about? Did I do something wrong?"

"I'm sorry. As you know, these are not normal circumstances. However, I can assure you there is nothing to worry about. I work for the government. My job is to help monitor the SED situation. So I have a few routine questions. After that, I'll be able to tell you more. But first, can you confirm that your full name is Rosa Lilly Newton?"

"Yes."

"And your parents adopted you when you were six months old?"

"That's right."

He opened his briefcase and handed Rosa a photograph. "Who is this with you?"

Rosa looked at the photo. It was an old picture, slightly

faded, from when she was about seven or eight years old and Nathan was still a toddler. "How did you get hold of this?"

"Rosa, could you confirm who is in the photo with you?"

"Nathan," she said quietly, handing the photo back to him. "Whatever this is about, please keep him out of it."

"Thank you. Don't worry, this isn't about Nathan. The photograph is simply a further check to avoid any issues of mistaken identity. Medical records from twenty years ago sometimes have errors. Now let me explain. I know that as a young child you had surgery for a rare condition."

Shaw paused, closing his briefcase. Rosa waited for him to continue, but he remained silent.

"What's that got to do with anything?" she asked finally.

"Maybe nothing. We don't know yet. But it is possible that your illness as a child has some similarities with SED."

Rosa stared at him, incredulous. "How?" she asked. "I had surgery for an abnormal heart rhythm. How can that have anything to do with the Panic?"

"We're not sure yet. All I can say at this point is that we think you may have something in common with the few SED survivors we've been able to monitor. But it's hard to know with any certainty. Our scientists' hypotheses are based on your old medical records."

"Sounds like you're clutching at straws."

Shaw shifted in his chair. "There's not much else we can do. SED has killed over two thousand people. Many more will die if we fail to act decisively, explore every avenue. That is why we would like to monitor you more closely. You can help us better understand this illness."

Rosa glanced around the room. Her heart was pounding. *What am I getting myself into*, she wondered. *Not that it's like I have a choice.* Even if she managed to sidestep Shaw, there would be people waiting for her outside.

"What if I say no?"

Shaw shook his head. "These are my orders. Rosa, let me reiterate, there is no need to worry. The monitoring won't be intrusive, and you'll be well cared for. I can guarantee you that, as I'll be the one overseeing it."

"OK," Rosa said, doing her best to appear calm despite feeling like her whole body was shaking. But then she pictured herself in a cell, banging her head against a padded wall. *Christ, they are going to lock me up!* She shuddered. *Got to do something fast. But what? Fuck, I don't know, I've got no fucking idea. Ana, Ana! If you can hear me, tell me what to do. Now!*

Silence.

They both stood up. She could tell Shaw was alert, ready to move quickly if needed.

"Thank you, Rosa," he said as he led her outside. "This is for the greater good."

She walked slowly down the steps, Shaw by her side. Constable Wright was there, a few feet ahead. She panicked. Without thinking, she broke into a run.

"Rosa, please," Shaw said, calling after her. "There's nothing to be afraid of."

She dodged past Constable Wright. But there was another policeman ahead. He grabbed her, held her still. More police officers came over.

"Help!" she managed to scream before they covered her mouth. People were staring at them. They dragged her back and bundled her into the back of a car. One of the police officers entered the car after her.

Shaw was already in the driver's seat. "Please try not to worry," he said, turning around. "We're not going to hurt you. I promise."

PEDDLER

November

4

Nick Parry hadn't slept for thirty hours. One sleep in two nights. That was his routine and he stuck to it with steadfast dedication. Unlike most people he did this without taking anything stronger than coffee. For now, at least. He pulled up his sleeve and stared at the needle marks on his arm, still visible underneath the tattoo of a blazing sun.

That was long ago, he reminded himself. *Long before this epidemic. I was young, hurting, weak. A different person from who I am today. Back then, heroin seemed like the only way out. One year of my life, then I got back on track, didn't I? Now it's a different situation completely. These new drugs are medicine – they help people. They are nothing like heroin.* Yet with each passing day, it became harder to convince himself that the benefits of these drugs outweighed the costs.

He pulled his sleeve back down and glanced at his wrist-watch. Twenty past five. Even if he walked slowly, he was going to be early. With his hands in his pockets, he shuffled from one foot to the other, willing the sun to rise. He glanced at the trees lining the streets. Without their leaves, they seemed brittle and old. He shut his eyes for a moment and tried to picture something positive, but nothing came to him. He sighed. It felt like spring might never come.

The journey into Oxford had been exhausting, especially with all the bureaucratic checks. Nick had taken the government bus in from the small village of Nuneham Courtenay. It was the only way into Oxford, unless you were in the military. Trains no longer alighted at the city, and the ring road around Oxford had been closed off to regular traffic. Nottingham, where he stayed when not on business, seemed far away.

To Nick, the government was paranoid, and believing that such control points would make any difference just seemed idiotic.

He started walking again. The passing houses and concrete quickly became one brown-grey blur. After a few minutes, he came to a small park. The grass was overgrown, the small playground there had been vandalised.

PANIK

The single misspelt word – spray-painted in bright red across a wall – dug into him, made his heart pound. *Be cool*, he told himself. *It never takes you when you're awake.* He wrapped his arms tightly around his torso, walked at a faster pace, concentrating on speed and motion. Yet still he felt a panic rising up.

"Hi, Nick," she said, appearing in front of him like an apparition.

"Kiyoko," he mumbled, hiding his nervousness as best he could.

"Are you OK?"

"Yep, all good."

"You're near the end of a thirty-six-hour day, aren't you?"

"It's that obvious?" he said, trying to sound light-hearted.

"Yup."

He looked at her in the gloomy light. She wore navy-blue leggings and a faded denim jacket. Her black hair was cut short. He wondered, as he always did, how her eyes could seem both confident and gentle at the same time. She smiled at him. Already he felt calmer, simply by her standing there and smiling. *In another life, perhaps we could have been lovers*, he thought. *Not in this one, though. No one has any appetite for romance now. Anyway, I prefer to sleep alone.*

"You managed to get hold of the full amount?" she asked.

"I did."

"Good. Then let's go to Bishop's Cafe just off Cornmarket Street. Looks like you need a dose of caffeine even more than I do."

"Are you sure it's safe?"

"It's fine. Deals go on there all the time; the owner doesn't care. You know me, I do my research."

The street was quiet, and the two of them walked without saying anything. Sturdy trees lined Abingdon Road, their vitality contrasting with the abandoned homes and boarded up shops. Oxford's population had emptied out early in the epidemic. Thousands had died from the Panic, and most of those not struck by the illness had fled the city if they could.

That was in the early days of the crisis. Now, new legislation made it much harder for the remaining Oxford residents to leave, and all telecommunications had been cut. Callow soldiers who had never fired a gun outside the training grounds monitored those who stayed. The two universities in the city had shut down; the centre of town was all but deserted. Nothing but a few grimy cafes and corner shops selling their products at extortionate prices. People were increasingly reliant on government handouts, distributed once a week. Exhausted residents would queue for hours, waiting for the convoy of armoured vehicles to arrive with their meagre supplies.

It was different in Headington, a suburb in the east of the

city. Restaurants and gastro-pubs, even a well-stocked super-market, catered to the health professionals living there. Pharmacists, nurses and doctors, particularly those with specialities in neurology or psychiatry, were paid substantial bonuses to work in Mantle Hospital. They lived on-site, and they guarded the hospital closely.

FRJ, a pharmaceutical company, funded the research undertaken there. Internal documents leaked to the media suggested that the corporation believed the epidemic had potential to go global. If they could produce a blockbuster drug, they would make billions for their shareholders.

"Are you going to sign up?" Nick asked her, breaking the silence.

"For what?"

"Mantle Hospital. Easy work, free food and board."

"No, not while I can make ends meet with my work. There are still enough people paying for my services, and I think I'm helping them. I hope so at least. Although my reputation is nothing like Rosanna Day's, it is good enough to keep me going. How about you?"

"Nope. I get by, shuttling between here and Nottingham. Though I have stayed there before."

"You did? When?"

"Beginning of October. In the early days, before things got so fucked up. I only stayed a couple of nights."

Nick glanced across at Kiyoko. "It wasn't bad," he continued. "Well, other than having to wear one of those caps with wires. That and the scientists with their beady eyes."

He remembered one of the scientists waking him in the middle of the night, prodding his skin, then shining a torchlight into his eyes. The bed next to him was empty. It used to be where Gary Young slept. He was a gentle man, had lost his family, too. They had shared stories about their lives before the Panic. Nick even told him a little about his mother's losing battle with cancer many years ago. How he'd been mature enough as a teenager to help her during her illness, yet not so mature that he could deal with the loss when it came.

"I know a few people who are still in there," he said, wondering what had become of Gary.

"How are they–"

A piercing scream interrupted their conversation, reverberating through the neighbourhood of terraced houses. Nick glanced at Kiyoko nervously. For a moment he felt like screaming as loud as he could, giving in completely. Instinctively, Kiyoko brought her hand to his, squeezing it hard. They hurried along, neither of them daring to look back.

After a few minutes they had crossed over the Thames and were on St Aldates, walking by the ancient stone walls of Christchurch College and onto what was once the main shopping area. A few people were milling about in the afternoon mist, watched nervously by soldiers. They all looked like they hadn't slept for days. Kiyoko let go of his hand, motioning in the direction of the cafe.

A tinny bell rung as they entered. The smell of caffeine helped to calm them both.

"Two coffees please. A regular for me and a large one for my friend."

The waiter nodded without looking at them. He turned around to make the drinks, pouring in the black liquid from a large thermos flask. "Sugar and powdered milk are on the tables," he said, his voice a dull monotone.

Kiyoko paid and they sat at one of the far tables. Only a handful of other customers were around, each sitting alone, not quite asleep but barely awake. None of them looked like they were in any shape to make a deal. A television in the corner of the room was playing MTV or some other music channel, the volume set low. He stared at the singer on the screen, hypnotised by her bland voice and weird robotic dance.

"You OK?" Kiyoko asked.

"Yeah," he replied, looking away from the TV and at Kiyoko. "You?"

"I think so. More people are dying, aren't they?"

"Officially it's close to thirty thousand. They say the epidemic has slowed, now that most people limit their sleep. I don't believe it, though. People are still dying all the time. Not just here in Oxford or nearby. I've heard rumours that there have been loads more cases, all over. Certainly, people have died in Nottingham, and in London, too. And who knows what's going on in other countries. Everyone I meet is scared. The government denies it all, of course."

"It's crazy. It scares the hell out of me. Some reports say as many as half a million are dead. It can't be that high. But everyone I talk to here in Oxford seems to have known someone who's died."

"Me too. I want to run, but I don't know where to go."

She sipped her coffee, added in two teaspoons of sugar. "At least you can leave Oxford when you want," she said, staring at the black liquid twirling around in her cup. "People here hang on to the hope of Rosanna Day coming. That somehow she can teach us how to fight this illness. Maybe she can."

Nick glanced across at her. The first time they had met, he had felt an immediate connection. Ever since then, they had always got on well, even if it was in a cautious, slightly guarded way. A friendship constrained by their business transactions. Despite still being attracted to her, he was careful not to overstep, not to allow himself to imagine their relationship developing beyond that.

But that scream. Somehow, it seemed to have brought them closer. At least that was how he felt. He wanted to squeeze her hand, to tell her everything.

"Kiyoko," he said, "I don't know about Rosanna Day. Maybe it's true, I hope it is. What I do know is I can get you the papers.

No charge, nothing like that. You just tell me when and I'll work it out."

"I appreciate that. But it's OK. I wouldn't know where to go. I've only ever lived in Oxford since moving to the UK, and there's no way I could return to Canada now. And anyway, I'm doing all right."

"OK. But promise that you'd tell me if you wanted out."

"I promise. The thing is," she said after a pause, "every day I watch the news, and it's always the same. The politicians ramble on about how they regret the situation, that they have no choice."

"Easy for them to say when they're watching from Scotland."

"Exactly. They never use the word 'quarantine'. Out of the corner of their mouths, they stutter that SED isn't contagious. They blather on about the heightened security only being precautionary. That it's temporary and will be cancelled soon," she said, rolling her eyes.

"It doesn't make any sense. People should be out on the street, demonstrating."

They talked about why there weren't more demonstrations. Nick said it was because of PureForce, how their riots made others too scared to speak out. People would have seen in the papers the severity of the government's response. He also thought it was because life was still bearable, outside of Oxford at least. There were curfews and other rules, but people continued to work, socialised, spent the night with their families.

But Kiyoko wasn't convinced. She thought it was something far simpler, more primal. "It's because people are scared of large crowds," she said. "Of the mob mentality and a panic building up out of nothing."

"I hadn't thought of it like that," Nick said. An image of a deranged crowd, all bulging eyes and spittle, flickered in his mind. "But I think I know what you mean. I avoid crowds when I can. I don't know why, but I do."

"Not that anyone would catch it that way," Kiyoko said. "Even though the Panic probably is contagious, no one has ever caught it while they're awake."

"That's what they say. But how can they know for sure?"

"What do you mean?"

"The final stage, when people, you know. Sure, that seems to happen after sleep. But maybe SED victims were already sick."

Nick glanced around the room. Nobody seemed to be paying them any attention.

"Let me put it this way," he continued. "No one knows how long it takes for this thing to develop. Perhaps the sickness was already inside them."

"Maybe. A girl in the room next door to mine died from it before they closed down our college. That scream! It was... it was as if she'd lost her soul. Everyone staying there on that hallway must have heard it. I called the night porter, as others did, but we were all too scared to leave our rooms. The night porter was braver than we were. But he wasn't able to break down her door in time."

"That's awful."

"It is. How about you? What was your first brush with the Panic?"

Nick stared at his coffee, thinking about the question.

"Don't answer if you don't want to," Kiyoko continued, glancing at him for a moment, then down at her cup. "We haven't ever really talked about this stuff, have we? And I never know whether I should ask people these things."

"It's good to ask. I haven't seen the Panic, not directly at least. But my father witnessed my sister...he saw it all here in Oxford, right in his own home. I spoke with him on the phone soon after, and he was a total wreck. He died the next night."

"I had no idea, I shouldn't have... I'm so sorry," she said, reaching for his hand across the table.

"You don't need to apologise," he replied. "You know, my sister was going to start a PhD that very week. She was intelligent, much brighter than me. Years ago, when she was only thirteen, she was the one who'd dissuaded me from dropping out of school," he said, wanting to tell Kiyoko about the drugs and the shoplifting but knowing it wasn't the right time. "Her thesis was going to be in philosophy, something to do with ethics and the work of Kant. She tried explaining it to me more than once. Not that I ever understood it, but god, she was so excited!"

He paused to keep his voice steady. He didn't want to cry. "At least they both died early enough in this epidemic to have a proper funeral. I had them buried next to my mother."

"It isn't fair," she said, pushing a loose strand of hair away from her eyes, then returning her hand to his.

"It's not. But it's no one's fault. At least I hope and pray it isn't. How about you? Have you lost anyone close to you?"

"Friends, yes, but not family. I told you before about my boyfriend. I try to imagine him alive, even though I realise it's unlikely. He would've made contact by now, if he could."

"Maybe. It's hard to get into Oxford. And the internet is closely controlled; the phone lines were shut down early."

"True, but he could have found a way. An old-fashioned letter, they still allow those. And you're able to get in and out of Oxford, aren't you? He could have found a way. Either he is alive, but has not tried hard enough to get in contact, or he's dead."

"Things aren't always straightforward."

Kiyoko let go of his hand, adjusted her chair slightly. "Sorry, I know how it sounds. It's not that I don't care."

"I know."

"Thanks. Anyway, at least I know my family is safe in Canada and Japan."

"Have you heard from them recently?" he asked. "I know it's not easy with the government controls."

"About a month ago. They have been trying to get me out all this time. But you know how it is. Obtaining the necessary paperwork took forever. They put me on a waiting list that never cleared. Governments all over are incredibly cautious. It's ironic, don't you think?"

"What is?"

"How this country is the one that's been cut off. I mean, politicians have been pushing so hard to keep out foreigners these last few years. Anyway, a couple of months ago I took my name off the waiting list. My parents were understandably livid, but what they don't realise is that I want to stay here now. I'm helping people, and that's more important than anything."

Nick nodded, took a long sip of his coffee. He felt incredibly tired. He dropped his head down so he could breathe in the coffee and the steam. He shut his eyes for a moment, and already his mind was wandering. *I could sleep for a thousand years*, he thought. *I'd find my sister and father in my dreams; we'd sit out in the garden and have a barbecue. My mum would be there, too. She'd marvel at how we'd turned out, especially after all the shit I'd put her and Dad through, and we'd all hug her tight. It would be a bright, sunny day, warm but with a soothing breeze. Perhaps we'd be throwing a Frisbee about. And Kiyoko would be there with us. She'd get on with them so well. She understands how it is to feel like you're on the outside looking in. We'd chat about light, easy stuff, like books and music, all sorts of things...*

"Nick? You can't sleep here. We'll get in trouble. Nick!" she said, shaking him.

"Huh? Sorry. I'm so tired."

"I'll order you an espresso. More effective than what they put in the thermos."

"No. They're too expensive."

"I insist. You're not on any of the drugs, are you?"

"'Course not."

"Good. I'll be back in a sec. Stay awake."

"Right."

He watched her walk over to the counter, felt his heart beat a little faster when she turned back to smile at him. *Stop it,* he told himself. We're only friends, nothing more. He glanced at the three other customers in the cafe. One of them was trying to read a tattered newspaper; the other two were staring stonily at their mugs of coffee. They all looked like they had lost someone.

"Here you go."

"Thanks," he said. He drank the espresso in one go. The caffeine registered. "That helped. In Nottingham, even the espressos seem watered down."

"Are you leaving Oxford tonight?"

"Tomorrow. I've got to stock up in Headington, and my contact at the hospital is only free from eight."

"Right. You have somewhere safe to sleep?"

"Yep. Normally I find a spot up in Summertown. Most of the rich people have left Oxford. It's easy to locate an empty house."

"No, you shouldn't go. The squatters up there, they've become more organised now, and they're territorial."

"I'll be OK," he said, not telling her that squatters had also taken over his old family home in Botley.

"It's not safe," she repeated. "Stay with me. That's a more sensible option. Number 7, James Street. It's much safer, even with Cowley Park nearby. My clients tonight have only booked me from six to nine. A young family living near my house. After that, I'm free. I can watch over you. It'll help you rest better, and I'll sleep once you've settled."

"Are you sure?"

"Of course. There is lots of space. Teresa and Sarah, who used to rent the place with me, they've long since left Oxford." Kiyoko paused. "We're more than business associates, aren't we?"

"We are," he said. "Thank you."

She smiled at him, a gentle smile filled with empathy and kindness, one that belied her tender years.

I must not fall in love with her, he thought. *She probably doesn't see me that way anyway. I am a good six or seven years older than her, after all. Perhaps we can become close friends. I should stop selling her the drugs, then. Maybe after tonight I will. It's not so bad, though; they aren't for her.*

"You'll need some tablets for your six p.m. clients, I suppose," he said. "Do you want the whole set now?"

"Sure."

He discreetly took a small carton from his jacket and handed it to her. The manufacturer and brand name were clearly visible on the tablets as well as on the packaging: GreenShoots, manufactured by FRJ. Kiyoko's clients would never buy the unbranded versions, even though equally effective generics were now being smuggled in.

"Twenty sets of four uppers plus one downer. Remind your clients of the difference. Small ones up, big one down."

"They know; but yes, I will."

"Kiyoko, I sell these pills everywhere. Not just in Oxford. They're easy enough to get if you have the contacts, and I think they can help. But the more powerful ones, like Wake and Rest, although the government has approved them, I would never touch the stuff myself. I only sell the first-gen pills. So please..."

"Don't worry, Nick. I appreciate your concern, really I do. I like... I've enjoyed our chat today. It feels as if, I feel..."

Kiyoko paused, looked at Nick directly for a moment. Her light brown eyes softened the harsh lights of the cafe. Nick felt his heart jump.

"You know, I tried W&R once," she said, biting her lip. "It was terrible. In the early days, I tried all sorts of things, not only the drugs and the sleep suppression. I even tried dream-awareness programmes, discussion groups, you name it. But I keep it simple now. Coffee and tea. I meditate, too, and I think it helps. As does good chocolate and a sugary Pepsi. I sleep every night if I can. Very occasionally, I take sleeping pills, regular ones. But never anything stronger than that."

"I'm glad."

Nick glanced around the cafe. The TV was playing the same music video as before. Some new customers had come in, three men discussing something in low voices. He wondered if they were making a deal. Certainly, they looked more alert than the other customers there.

"Here you go. That's four hundred pounds," she said, handing Nick a wad of twenty-pound notes. "You should count it."

"It's OK. We know each other well enough, don't we?"

She smiled again, but this time he saw the weariness in her eyes. *One day it'll be over*, he thought, *and when it is I'll take Kiyoko on a trip to the coast. If her boyfriend returns, the three of us will go. I wouldn't mind. We'll find a quiet spot and sleep right there on the sand, the sun beating down, the waves lapping lazily against the shore.*

5

B onfires lit up the park; a mass of drumbeats filled the air. It was six p.m. When they had left the cafe a few hours earlier, Kiyoko warned Nick of the latest troubles in Cowley Park. The soldiers had long stopped trying to maintain order there. But it was the only way into Headington if you didn't have an official permit – via the Tonge building in the abandoned Oxford Brookes campus, where one could pick up forged documentation for fifty pounds, and then onto Gipsy Lane. Once you had made it that far, Headington almost felt like the normal, unassuming suburb it used to be.

Nick kept his distance from the small groups dancing around the bonfires. The drummers were relentless. Everyone in the park was high on one drug or another, most likely crack or meth. It was an unpredictable place. He didn't need caffeine to feel alert.

A reveller stumbled by, oblivious to Nick's presence. He wore a lurid orange jumpsuit. He was waving his hands up and down like a bird, making loud croaking noises as he lurched towards the next fire. Nick exhaled slowly, trying to calm himself. But his nervous adrenaline had turned into anger.

What a bunch of wasters, he thought. *They have given up already. All they care about is the next hit.*

He knew, though, that he had no right to be so self-right-eous. After all, he had been an addict once, too. He knew exactly how strong that craving was, the way your heart pounded and your hands, your whole damn body, shook, and how a voice in your head said it's OK to take it just one more time.

On top of that, the drugs they took really weren't so different from those that he sold. Stronger, maybe, but still designed to do the same thing – numb the fear. The drugs he shifted were almost as hard to obtain, despite being produced by the reputable FRJ and sanctioned by the government. Officially, one had to find a government-approved outlet to purchase the drugs, but those shops were usually out of stock, especially here in Oxford. So people turned to drug peddlers like Nick, paying over the odds to suppress sleep. If they didn't have enough money, they would buy 'Outreach' or one of the other unofficial generics, which Nick also sold.

"Mister, you dealing?" a young woman asked, prodding his jacket. He hadn't seen her coming.

"No."

"Mister!" she said, grabbing his arm. The girl was barefoot; her clothes were torn and dirty. She looked no older than eighteen, and he feared she was younger. "I don't mean those drugs," she said, nodding towards the nearest group of revellers dancing around a bonfire. "I want W&R, Outreach, Green-Shoots. Anything will do. I need to stay awake."

He shook his head. For a moment, he saw his sister in her. Maybe it was in the way she tied up her hair.

"I've got money. That's not all. I'm pretty, aren't I? Look at me. Let me touch you. You can do things to me if you like, there in the bushes. I just need one upper."

"I don't have anything."

"Homo! Dumb faggot!" she screamed, the whites of her eyes visible even in the dim light. She punched him feebly. Her fists were like feathers, she was so exhausted and weak. He pushed her away as gently as he could, yet she still fell to the ground.

"I'm sorry," he said, walking away quickly, the heat of strangers' glances burning his back.

She'll make it through the night, he told himself, even though he didn't believe it. He felt guilty, but he knew he would have felt as bad if he had given her a tablet. With each passing day, he was less sure of the drugs he sold. Still, he knew he had become far too mixed up in the business to safely navigate a way out now.

Nick looked grimly ahead. Less than a hundred metres of darkness to clear before the last few bonfires at the top of the hill. Drumbeats reverberated around the park. He clenched his fists, shifting the metal keys round in his pocket so that they protruded between his fingers. The metal would do its job if he needed it, one quick punch to the hand or face enough to stall any would-be mugger. It wouldn't be the first time. He glanced around, desperate not to have to use the keys again.

He had just made it past the final set of bonfires when he heard a sudden loud yelp behind him. Turning around, he saw two men attacking a third man. One of them held the victim while the other punched him hard in the face. He slumped to the ground, and they took turns kicking him, harder and harder.

They were only fifteen or twenty feet away, between him and the fire. The junkies nearest the flames started groaning in some kind of drugged reverie, then pounded their drums as hard as they could.

Nick knew he should just keep walking, that it would be dangerous to intervene. *And then what*, he thought. *Continue to be a coward who always takes the easy option? It's one thing to sell these drugs; it's another to let a man be beaten to death.*

He turned around and quickly scanned the ground, looking for a weapon – a branch, a brick, anything solid. There was nothing.

"Fuck it," he muttered. He ran towards the fire, making sure the two men couldn't see him. Then he tackled one of them from behind, punched him in the back of his skull, two, three times, the keys between his fingers. He knew he needed to move quickly if he were to have any chance. But before he could do anything more, the other man came at him, punched him hard in the ribs, pushed him to the ground.

"Scum," the man shouted, his eyes bright and manic. Scars criss-crossed his face. "I'll kill you."

His hands were around Nick's neck, strangling him. He tried to push the attacker's hands away but wasn't strong enough. He felt a sharp pain in his throat and chest. The air suddenly seemed too thick; the drumbeats had become muted and slow. *I can't breathe*, he thought. *I'm going to die.* The man's eyes floated in front of him, two black holes of nothingness. Each drumbeat seemed to last an age, reverberating in his head. Somebody or something howled. He started to fade.

Smash – glass shattering. His assailant crumpled to the ground. Suddenly he was able to breathe.

Nick gasped for air, then retched.

"Leave now, while you can," said a woman holding a broken bottle top in her hand. The bonfire lit up her features: wavy grey hair, crow's feet around her eyes. She looked too old to be there.

Nick nodded, standing up unsteadily. "Thanks," he mumbled, glancing down at the two men he'd attacked and the third man they'd been beating. None of them was moving.

"They'll be fine," she said, pulling a patchy blanket over her shoulders. "When they come to, they won't remember any of it."

Nick shrugged, unsure of what to say.

"You saved that man's life," she said. "Thank you for being brave."

6

"Blue is the new purple," Harold Stone said with a nonchalant wave of his hand, enunciating each syllable in the manner of someone accustomed to being listened to.

It was eight o'clock. Nick gingerly touched his sore ribs. Not broken, probably just badly bruised. Only an hour or so ago he had been in Cowley Park – a place that could not have felt more different from Harold's plush apartment in Headington.

Harold tapped his cigar in an ashtray balanced precariously on his armrest. "LC+. One course of these blue pills can keep you awake for ninety hours," he continued. "Think how easy that would be to sell! One sleep a week. A rather effective marketing pitch in my book."

"Side effects?" Nick asked, rubbing his eyes, finding it hard to concentrate. He desperately needed some shut-eye himself.

"Yes, though nothing much to worry about. Light-headedness, blurred vision. Oh, and they're diuretic."

"Diuretic."

"That's right. In these doses, they make you go to the loo, a lot. Customers should ensure they keep themselves well hydrated at all times."

"Nothing else?"

"Nothing else as far as I know," Harold said, pushing his blue-rimmed designer glasses back to the bridge of his nose. "We've trialled them in the hospital for four weeks now, and there haven't been any side effects more adverse than what I just described."

Nick looked at Harold, then at his own hands. They had a slight tremor. "What about longer-term effects?" he asked.

Harold sighed. "The rules are different today," he said. "In an ideal world, yes, we would have more time to test and to monitor, to do rigorous randomised clinical trials. The reality is we simply do not have that luxury, with the SED epidemic as it is. Four weeks is, in my experience, more than long enough to establish the key details. In fact, I am already working on the successor to LC+. That drug is still stuck in the pre-clinical stage. It's ready to trial, but medical doctors and nurses are always more conservative than us chemists. They've persuaded FRJ to hold off testing on people for now."

Nick sat back on Harold's leather sofa. The apartment had, with its oversized furniture, wood panelling and classic artwork, a 1950s decor. It was spacious enough to make the styling work, with high ceilings and large bay windows. *Harold must be raking in the money*, he thought.

"Before we do this, tell me how you've been."

"Huh?" Nick said, surprised. Harold and Nick met once a week, had been doing so for the past couple of months. The deals always went smoothly, but it no longer felt like they were anything more than business associates.

"You look like you've been in the wars."

"I told you it was nothing."

"How about a little something to keep you awake?"

"You know I don't take any of that shit, Harold."

"And very sensible that is, too. You wouldn't want to shit where you eat, isn't that the saying?"

"Something like that," Nick replied. The phrase sounded preposterous in Harold's posh private school accent.

"I have a copious supply of energy drinks. Or plain old tea and coffee if you prefer."

"I suppose I better have something. I'll have a coffee, then. Thanks."

"Black, no sugar, isn't that right?"

"Yep."

"Good. I'll make a strong brew."

Nick stood up once Harold had left the room. His mind kept drifting away; he was worried he might fall asleep if he stayed sitting down. He went over to the window. Spotlights lit up the apartment block's small communal garden. The lights were powerful enough to spot any intruder. A plump rabbit, unperturbed, chewed the recently mown grass. The place created a tempting illusion of calm. Standing there, he could almost imagine Oxford as a city no different from any other. Almost as if it were a regular night, a night in which parents would be happily tucking their children into beds, and then a few hours later sleeping restfully themselves.

He turned away from the window and looked around the sitting room. On one wall hung a large oil painting. Something about it caught his attention. In the foreground was a man's head on a platter carried by a young maid. Her expression was one of pride mixed with fear.

"An unusual Renaissance piece," Harold said, carrying in a silver tray with a French press, two cups and jars containing sugar and cream. "Fifteenth or sixteenth century. The hospital removed it from the Oxford Town Hall for safekeeping. Must be worth a few bob."

"Gives me the creeps. I wouldn't want it hanging on my

wall. Still, this place is much nicer than your old digs at the hospital."

"Why, thank you," Harold replied, putting the tray on the table and sitting down. Nick sat down, too. "And don't worry," he continued, glancing proudly around the room, before adding a dash of cream and a heaped spoon of sugar to his coffee. "This apartment is equally secure. They monitor Beech Road twenty-four hours a day. Same with all the other streets adjoining the hospital. FRJ has invested heavily in security."

"FRJ, Fucking Ridiculous Junkies. They just want to protect the goose that lays the golden eggs, don't they?"

"Nicholas, do you actually *want* to do business tonight?" Harold asked, visibly annoyed. "We may be friends, but I could easily find other dealers."

We have never been friends, Nick thought, staring at Harold's receding hairline. "Yes," Nick said, sipping his coffee. It had a grainy, bitter taste to it. "Harold, you know I don't mean you or Mantle Hospital. I just mean FRJ."

"I know you don't mean it," Harold replied, calming down. "Still, I find your comment irritating and lazy. Because it's really not so simple. It's too easy to critique Big Pharma, to reduce the equation to profit plus shareholder return."

"That's not what –"

"Nick," Harold said, interrupting him, "we haven't known each other that long, have we? But I've been a chemist for, what, fifteen years or more. I've had to deal with prissy executive directors, people who have lost touch with the beauty of chemistry and focus only on the numbers. I'm not pretending FRJ is faultless. They fly in by helicopter when the rest of us are stuck on the ground. And yes, I've heard the rumours about cases in other countries. But none of us really knows what's going on beyond our borders, do we?"

"I guess not."

"All being said, FRJ is better than those manufacturers who

produce Outreach and other poor-quality copies. At least they are regulated by the government."

"True."

"Think about it this way. Without FRJ, more people would have died. The drugs are, I admit, a stopgap solution. As I think you know, one of the few things we have learnt is that people only die from SED when they are unconscious. It's true we still don't know how long this illness resides in the afflicted before it manifests itself, or whether it's even contagious. But people like us, who adhere to the thirty-six-hour day, or even the 1-to-3 schedule, are much less at risk."

"Are they really?"

"Of course! Better advice than those early government advisories not to panic, to sleep normally, or even to take sleeping pills. What a disaster that was! As for all this talk on the streets about Rosanna Day, how can she teach us to fight off SED? Like it's that easy."

"They said she had the illness as a child."

"Wishy-washy spiritual stuff," Harold said, adjusting the glasses on his nose. "Who dreamt her up? No one even knows what she looks like."

"There are grainy photos of her on the internet, back when she was a child. Supposedly the government has her locked up."

"You don't believe it, do you? It's just another conspiracy theory. Fake news."

"Maybe. I don't know," Nick replied, leaning back in his chair.

"We are still far from knowing what causes SED, let alone finding a cure," Harold said, sipping his coffee. "So all we can do for now is suppress sleep as much as possible, and make sure sleep is as deep as the ocean when it does come. LC+ excels in that task."

If they are so good, why don't you take them, Nick wanted to ask him, but he bit his tongue. He knew he had to stay on good terms. He added some sugar to the coffee Harold had made. It still tasted bitter.

"I think I'll stick with the old tablets for now," Nick said at last. "Fifty sets of GreenShoots, as per normal."

"You don't want to buy the new drug? I understand why you're reluctant to deal W&R, what with its strong side effects. But LC+, it's..."

"No thanks, Harold."

"Why not?"

"I don't know," he replied tiredly. "I just don't understand how a drug with such a long up wouldn't have a deeper down."

"That's the beauty of it, Nicholas!" Harold said excitedly, wiping sweat from his brow. "The 'up' pills are more than the normal mix of caffeine tinged with amphetamine. We've added a new active ingredient, codenamed LC, or 'latent consciousness'. My marketing term, I'm embarrassed to say."

Harold paused, as if he were waiting for an approving comment. Nick didn't say anything.

"So," Harold continued, "after the initial adrenaline spike, LC+ helps the body to control the stimulants. They only become active when the body is close to losing consciousness."

"Harry, I'm sorry, but I'm too knackered to get what you're saying."

"Let me see," Harold said after slurping down his coffee. He took a lighter from his jacket pocket and lit another cigar. "It's like this, more or less. Normally one's body reaches a point when it really must rest. It doesn't matter who you are, at some point you will have to sleep. It is at this precise point that LC+ takes effect, and it does so intelligently. LC+ releases just enough medication to keep someone awake, but in a state that requires minimum energy."

Like mindless zombies, Nick thought. He looked at Harold surreptitiously as they drank their coffee. The man had aged noticeably over the last couple of months. The wrinkles on his face seemed deeper; his bald patch had spread. *How often does he sleep*, Nick wondered, *and how easily?*

The second or third time they had met, Harold had earnestly told him about the hospital's attempts to find a cure. It hadn't been so long ago – late September, about a week or so before Nick had stayed in the hospital. Back then, it seemed like they could have become good friends. However, they were both very different people in those early days.

Harold had confided to Nick that he suspected SED was not purely psychological, that there may be an organic factor contributing to the hysteria. After a few too many whiskeys, Harold had muttered something about transmission being related to GM crops and the water supply, though he didn't explain the basis of his suspicions.

"Listen," Harold said, tapping cigar ash into the ashtray, "why don't you take a set – on the house. Sell them to one of your regulars. Although they'll go for seventy or eighty pounds a pop in accredited outlets when the government finally gives them the green light, you could easily charge one hundred, maybe even one fifty, on the street. Then, next time we meet, you can decide if you want to buy more."

"And so W&R will go the way of the earlier drugs?"

"Indeed, they will! From what I've heard, LC+ is selling supremely well already. Customers never disappoint, do they?" he said, clasping his hands together in delight. "They always want more."

LAB RAT

December

7

R osa awoke with her fingers grasping at the sheets. Her heart raced from a dream she was unable to reassemble. All she could remember were the drab colours and a feeling of immense sadness. Keeping her eyes closed, she tried to calm herself before the questions began. She pictured her childhood home, her parents laughing as she performed a magic trick, the one where she pulled a silver coin from behind her brother's ear. She knew, though, it was a moment in time firmly torn from the present, a sepia-tinged image.

Electrodes were taped to her forehead; a clip attached to her left index finger monitored her pulse. She sensed someone was in the room and she could faintly hear Ana murmuring her name. Ignoring the voice as best she could, she breathed in deeply, then exhaled, repeating this six or seven times. The slow, steady sound of her breathing helped ease the fear. Carefully, not fully trusting her senses, she opened her eyes.

"Are you awake? Rosa? Rosa, what did you dream?" the man asked, peering at her from behind a sanitary mask.

Rosa stared blankly at the middle-aged man. "Who are you? Where is Lillian?"

"It's me, John. John Okoro. Lillian will be in later."

"Oh, right," she sighed, recognising him now. *Why had I forgotten that? And what was the point of this endless monitoring?* It was almost two months since they had taken her from Oxford and locked her up here. Christmas was two weeks away. *In all that time, what had they learnt?* At least they hadn't yet tried any more invasive techniques, though she supposed it was only a matter of time. Soon, perhaps, they would have her tied down, metal bolts fastened around her wrists and ankles, as they dug in with their scalpels. She'd probably spend her thirtieth birthday here at Cloxham Manor, in an induced coma.

"Rosa, try to remember. Colours, shapes, sounds. It is always possible to remember something."

"Nope."

Silence.

"What do you mean?"

Part of the dream came back to her then, a dream within a dream, the one she never shared. Bird wings fluttering, then guttural moans and frail hands clutching at her feet. On the horizon, a huge wave of smoke and rubble approaching, and the realisation there is nothing she can do. She'd described her other dreams to them, but never this one. Just as she had never told anyone about the voice in her head.

"Rosa?"

"You're a scientist, John. Why do you care about my dreams?"

"You know why."

"I want to hear it again."

John Okoro rubbed his temple. "Fine. There are three reasons, Rosa. First, the patterns of your brainwaves during sleep are nearly identical to those who have been struck by the epidemic. High amplitude theta waves lasting for hours on end.

Second, we think you had the illness as a child. Third, you haven't clawed your eyes out."

"It doesn't make any sense," she replied, thinking about when she had been sick as a young child. *How could that be connected*, she wondered. Although her abnormal heart rhythm had been serious, the open-heart surgery performed on her was successful. Nothing more than routine check-ups every few years following the surgery. Still, something about it had clearly bothered her mother. Rosa thought about the conversation they'd had hours before her mother killed herself. Again, she wondered if her parents had been hiding something from her. Perhaps it had something to do with her biological parents? No, it wasn't possible. Her parents had always been completely honest with her, she was sure of it.

She remembered her mother gently tracing the faint scar on her chest with her finger and saying, "I love you, heart."

"Is my heart strong enough now?" Rosa had asked her. "Of course," her mother had replied.

That was a long time ago. Now, the scar was barely visible. In all the years since, as the scar had gradually faded, she wondered if her heart had become harder, unable to let anyone in. She thought about her brother then, hoped he was safe.

"Look, Rosa, this isn't an exact science," John said. "That's where you come in. To help us learn more about what's going on. Now, please, could you tell me whatever you can remember about your dreams from last night?"

"What does it matter? It'll come for every one of us in the end, anyway."

"No, it won't. We just haven't identified the specific cause yet. But if we understand it better, we can find a cure."

"You've been studying my dreams for two months, and it doesn't seem to have made any difference."

For a moment, Rosa considered asking when she would be released. But she knew there was no point. She looked at what she could make out of John's face: a pair of tired, watery eyes behind rimless spectacles, his delicate nose covered partially by the sanitary mask.

None of this was his fault, she realised. He had always treated her with respect, unlike some of the other scientists. She wondered if he missed his family as much as she missed hers. At least his loved ones were safe, back in their hometown near Lagos, thousands of miles away from the troubles here in the UK. That is, assuming the epidemic hadn't spread beyond the island. It was impossible to tell. Other countries had been quick to isolate the UK early on, so no one really knew what was happening in the rest of the world.

"Why do you need to wear that thing over your mouth?" Rosa asked. "I'm not infectious."

"It's standard protocol."

"Whose protocol?"

"You're right; it doesn't matter," John said, untying the mask to reveal a patchy beard covering a slightly recessed chin.

"Have you always had a beard?"

"It's grown since I started this ridiculously long shift," he sighed, an attempt at a smile appearing more like a grimace. "Now, Rosa, please, just answer my questions. I can then tell you about the director's new proposal. But first we need to do this properly."

"If Shaw's got such an exciting proposal, why can't he tell me directly?"

"Rosa, you know it doesn't work like that."

"Fine. Then let's get this over with."

Rosa watched Dr Okoro with his clipboard at the ready, surveyed the sparsely furnished room, and considered what exactly she was going to tell him.

Since she had been interned at Cloxham Manor, running was Rosa's one effective coping mechanism. She would set the gradient on the treadmill to a slight ascent and run at a comfortable pace for an hour or more. When she'd first started jogging, she had worn headphones, blasting dance music or heavy rock songs. Now, though, she preferred to run in silence, concentrating on her breathing so that she could empty her mind of wandering thoughts and attain some inner serenity.

Sweat dripped down her neck. Images of her parents came into her mind. They were smiling at her brother's incredulous expression after Rosa had shown him the coin that appeared from behind his ear.

She notched up the running speed to nine miles per hour, aware of her feet pounding against the rubbery surface and the loudness of her breath. The memory faded away. She looked around the small, windowless room that functioned as a gym, then back at her reflection in the mirror, at her grey-green eyes, her light brown skin, at her nose and mouth inhaling and exhaling the musty air. A couple of times her mother's face came into focus; each time, she pushed the image away.

Staring into the mirror, she noted her slender but well-toned legs, a natural fluidity to her movement. *I'm not very strong*, she thought, *but if I were ever to escape, I would at least be able to keep running.* She brushed a loose strand of hair away from her face. She knew she was pretty quick, too, fast enough to get away from most people. *You are much more than that, Rosa*, the voice murmured. She closed her eyes, focused on her breathing, each intake and release of air, and Ana slipped quietly away.

The digital display reached the sixty-minute mark. She reduced the speed and incline until her jog became a fast walk, and soon she was motionless on the treadmill. Wiping the sweat from her brow with a small towel, she checked her pulse before carefully stepping off the machine.

They called Cloxham Manor a "safe house," but it felt to Rosa more like a cross between prison and laboratory. Her living space was monitored around the clock; the front door separating her apartment from the main building was permanently locked, and the veranda door to the back garden was locked at night. Still, she knew that there were worse places to be interned. She had access to a wide selection of books and movies, the food was reasonable, and she could run more or less whenever she wanted. In addition to the gym and the room in which they monitored her sleep, there was an open plan living and dining room, and beyond that a veranda leading to a small, well-tended garden. Colourful pansies had been recently planted, offsetting to some extent the brick walls lined with jagged glass and barbed wire.

She could just about see over the wall if she stood on one of the garden chairs. Fields of rye had been left to grow wild, and beyond that was woodland, separated from the fields by a long mesh fence that seemed to surround the grounds.

She would often sit in the garden and think back to her childhood. Gazing up at the sky, she would try to recall the fondest moments, blocking out recent traumas and ignoring the voice inside her head that called for her. Sometimes she caught a faint whiff of the sea, which would help bring back family holidays on the coast. She would carefully cultivate those images so that they lasted a little longer: her parents lounging in deckchairs, dozing in the sunshine, her little brother digging his small feet into the wet sand, watching in fascination as the tide drew the sand around them.

Nevertheless, Rosa always remained acutely aware of her lack of freedom. It wasn't only the physical restriction of the place; being cut off from news about what was happening in the real world was just as bad. There was no internet, no live TV or newspapers, and of course no visitors. Two months had passed without any contact from friends or her brother, and she agonised over whether they were alive or dead.

Some of the scientists she spoke with at the laboratory did tell her a little about the spread of the epidemic. Lillian had been the most forthcoming. She had shared as much information with her as she was allowed, maybe more, showing Rosa the government reports that justified her incarceration and illustrated the gravity of the situation. These documents detailed how the illness had recently started to appear in several locations around the country. Most deaths continued to occur in Oxford, but there had been cases reported as far away as Windsor and Milton Keynes.

Initially, scientists assumed some kind of viral or bacterial infection was causing people's brains to deteriorate. Conspiracy theories included failed military experiments, profit-obsessed pharmaceutical companies or some combination of the two. People believed you could catch it simply by being within the vicinity of someone struck by the Panic. However, months of intense research had failed to identify the cause, nor how the illness could be contagious. Lillian believed the Panic was fundamentally psychological, as did other university-based scientists, and her theories were given increasing consideration by her colleagues at Cloxham.

Rosa left the gym and stood by the bay windows. She glanced at the flowers, then at the brick walls topped with broken glass and wire. She touched the window in front of her. *Most likely reinforced glass,* she thought. *A chair, or whatever else I could throw at it, would probably bounce right off.*

She thought about her brother. She regretted how she had been with him the last time they met. She tried to convince herself that he was OK. That Nottingham University's leafy campus would provide a reliable shelter from this crisis and his friends would be looking out for him. She liked to imagine he had a girlfriend there, someone gentle but strong who could keep him from withdrawing too far and help him cope with all that he had seen. But she recognised she was being overly optimistic. Probably life on the outside was much worse now than when she had still been free. And as they had come for her, it meant that they may well have come for Nathan, too.

The government didn't seem to be taking any chances with the epidemic. Lillian had recently told Rosa that the government had shifted many of their key London-based staff to offices up in Edinburgh. When this was leaked to the media, the spokesperson described the move as a precautionary measure. They insisted that London was not at risk, and they did their best to dispel any panic by making carefully staged appearances in the capital.

8

"I want to show you something," Lillian said to Rosa.

It was a crisp, sunny morning. They were sitting out on the veranda, drinking coffee. The pansies had been dug up and new flowers planted: pots of purple heather. Rosa exhaled and stared at her breath hanging in the air. *How much longer will they keep me here*, she thought. *And how much longer can I bear it?*

"Remember your recurring dream of the woman with the red scarf?" Lillian continued. "The same woman who when you were a child called out to you at Kings Lynn train station."

"Yes. She kept calling me Ana."

"We've been looking for her and have put together a list. Twenty women who might be the one you saw at the station. It was a painstaking process, but your sketches helped a lot. Here they are."

Rosa took the leather folder, unsure if she wanted to open it.

"You can look at it later, in private, if you prefer."

"No, it's OK." Rosa ran her fingers over the elasticated band holding the sheets of paper together. "Do you really think it's possible she is my biological mother?"

"I don't know. What do you think?"

"Yes. I'm not sure why, but I do. We have the same eyes and nose, or at least that's what I like to remember. But it's more than this. It was the way she looked at me. I know this sounds silly, but it was as if she really knew me, deep down. Like she..." Rosa stopped, not finishing her sentence.

"Like what?"

Like she knew about the voice in my head. "Oh, I don't know, it's stupid."

"It doesn't sound stupid to me, not in the slightest. The maternal link is a powerful thing, something well known but easily underestimated."

"Maybe."

Rosa undid the clasp holding the papers.

"We've compiled a short dossier on each of these women," Lillian said. "Photos from about twenty years ago, when you think you saw her. More recent photos, too. Also, brief descriptions of their life histories: whether they had jobs, children, husbands, and so on."

Rosa opened the folder and scanned the faces on the first page. There were four different women, each staring at the camera at three different times in the past. None of them was the woman with the red scarf. She looked at the second sheet of paper. *The lady at the bottom of the page, could that be her?* Her heart raced. She had green eyes, and her hair was bundled in a familiar way. But no, her nose was different.

The same thing happened on the next page and the page after that, a momentary quickening of her pulse as she stared at a woman's long, wavy hair or green eyes or some other half-remembered feature. Yet none of them was the woman from Kings Lynn train station, and after that she was scanning the sheets of paper without expectation, no longer confident she could identify the woman even if she saw her. She handed the folder back to Lillian, shaking her head.

"Could you look at the last page again? The team who put this folder together said these three women did not match your sketches as well. Yet from what you've told me, I personally..."

"Lillian, I've looked at all of the photos already. She's not there."

"There's one woman in particular. I researched her background and she matches up well. Edith Dubois. Her hair was cropped short, nothing like your description. That's why it may not be apparent straight away."

Rosa turned to the last page.

"As with all the women in the dossier, Edith gave up her daughter for adoption around the time you were adopted," Lillian said. "She'd named her daughter Anna, as did the other women on this last page. But more importantly and uniquely, Edith had escaped from a secure hospital."

"Why would my biological mother be in an asylum?" Rosa said, struggling to control her voice. "And how's that significant anyway?"

"I wouldn't call it an asylum," Lillian replied, "though Edith was there as a mental health patient. The reason it's relevant is because Edith was obsessed with her daughter's safety. Her medical records at Hailstone Hospital indicate she would say, repeatedly: 'Anna be safe, Anna be safe, Anna be safe.' Like a mantra, the same phrase you heard at the train station."

"Where is this Hailstone Hospital?" Rosa asked. She felt both scared and excited by the possibility that this woman could be her mother. "And where is she now?"

"Hailstone is about forty miles west of where we are now. But the hospital has been closed for many years. As for Edith, we don't know where she is."

"You've taken her, too, haven't you?" Rosa said, her voice

suddenly shaky. "Thousands dead, and all you can do is lock people up!"

"Rosa, please, I'm on your side. If I had it my way, you wouldn't be here. You know that. As for Edith Dubois, we have learnt something about her past, but I honestly have no idea where she is now. Especially as Hailstone Hospital has long since closed. Yes, it is possible that she's been interned. But I doubt it."

"Why?"

"Because I don't think the government is that well-organised. Oxford has been all but abandoned now. There have been cases in many other cities. London will be affected soon enough. People everywhere are on edge. There are even rumours that they'll build roadblocks in Northern England. A buffer in case the illness continues to spread. Suffice to say the government is really struggling to control the situation."

"They still managed to get me. They probably have my brother, too."

"Yes, it is possible that Nathan is under surveillance somewhere. But it's all different now. Things are much more chaotic. No wonder other countries have closed their borders."

Rosa glanced across at Lillian, at her greying hair tied neatly in a bun. Though she felt frustrated, she knew Lillian was a friend and their relationship wasn't one-sided. She recalled how Lillian had confided in her about how she had recently lost her partner. Not to the epidemic, but after a long battle against cancer. They had been together for twenty-five years.

"Lillian, I know you're on my side. I trust you, and I can't say that about many people here. But I don't understand why you are working here."

Lillian smiled. "I'm the one who's meant to ask the questions. Though I admit it's a fair one to ask. Do you want the short or long answer?"

"The long one."

"Good," Lillian said. She leaned back in her chair. "I was a professor in clinical psychology. I still am. One of my main research interests has always been mass hysteria. What brings it about, its long history. One afternoon, in the early days of the epidemic, I saw two government scientists sitting outside my office. I had just finished a lecture to undergrad students. They wanted to discuss my early research."

Lillian sipped her coffee. "I suppose flattery might have been a factor. Hearing people talk about my early research so enthusiastically, research I had put so much effort into, but which had never received any real recognition. I admit it felt good. They were desperate for me to work with them."

"What was your research about?"

"Jung. Specifically, one fascinating insight he had: his notion of the *collective unconscious*. He believed that we all have shared memories and ideas inherited from our ancestors. Archetypes, primitive hopes and fears that go beyond what we have directly experienced. When I was much younger, I imagined these hopes and fears were somehow connected to ideas of God and Satan, to good and evil. Back when I still believed in those dichotomies. In my PhD I was arrogant and naive enough to argue that we could gain credible insights into Jung's notions of the collective unconscious by monitoring sleep patterns. I thought I'd found a link between certain peculiar sleep patterns and suicidal tendencies. To me this was huge. Even though I could only publish my findings in an obscure scientific journal – leading journals rejected my work on methodological grounds – I knew I was on to something. Ever since, I have been investigating people's sleep, as well as dream analyses of mental health patients."

Lillian put her cup down and leaned forward. "But EEG machines are blunt tools," she said, "like the ones used to analyse your sleep. And my research has changed significantly since then. Still, Jung's theories continue to fascinate me. I might be seconded to the government for now, but I was and remain an academic at heart. I'm not like John, who has practical experience working in the NHS as a clinical psychologist. Nor like Claire Godley, with her background in neurology."

"If anyone can understand this thing, it's you."

"That's kind of you to say. I still don't know very much, but I do believe I can contribute. I wouldn't be here otherwise."

Rosa nodded. They both leaned back in their chairs. Rosa sipped her coffee, comfortable in the silence, and looked up at the sky. A hawk soared above, searching the land for prey. It came closer, hovered as if in preparation for attack, but then flew up and away.

Lillian was a decent woman, Rosa thought. She didn't seem to be hiding anything from her. It was through Lillian that Rosa learned about the various conspiracy theories. Drug-induced sleep suppression experiments, contaminated water supplies, mutated GM crops. Although Lillian didn't discount them completely, she did not believe they explained the extent of the epidemic today. She also said that everything she knew about the Panic, all her research, pointed to it being predominantly a psychological phenomenon. Throughout history, there has been examples of collective hysteria, she said, though never anything on this scale. Lillian believed the Panic was somehow connected to Jung's theories of the collective unconscious and shared fears.

The government had detailed records of Rosa's background and medical history. But Lillian's request to see Rosa's childhood medical records had been denied. Like other researchers at Cloxham Manor, she did not have sufficient security clearance to dig deeper. Still, she felt she needed to understand exactly how this current epidemic was connected to her patient's past. She believed Rosa's early childhood, the time before she'd had surgery, could help them uncover shared traits with the survivors of the Panic. Lillian hoped information on Rosa's biological mother – the woman in the red scarf, maybe – could help with this, too.

Lillian leaned forward in her chair. "Rosa, I'm not saying you're responsible in any way," she said. "That's very important. It's likely we'll neither understand it fully nor find some miraculous solution. But I do believe you have something important to share with us all."

"Like what?" she asked, noting the deep lines around Lillian's eyes.

"Listen, if I had my way, you and I would be having these sessions within the comfort of a university, where you would be free to come and go. I've been working on that, talking to Shaw about a timeline. He is supportive of the idea, too, though I don't want to give you false hope. It's going to take quite some time before we obtain official approval."

Rosa drank the rest of her now tepid coffee. She tried to focus on the flowers in the garden, but all she could really see were the brick walls topped with broken glass. Her mind wandered to that terrible moment when she'd forced open the bathroom door and found her mother dying in the bathroom. *My real mother*, she thought, *the one who brought me up and made me who I am, not the biological mother who had given me up for adoption.*

"Let's forget about those last photos for now," Lillian said. "It can wait for another time. And Rosa, if there's anything I can do to make your stay here more bearable, please tell me. I know I can't offer you much, but I'd like to help in any way I can."

"I appreciate that. Now, let me see those three women again."

9

A crow flew into the garden, settling on the grass close to where Rosa sat. It cocked its head to one side, as if it were listening, waiting for her to speak.

"January thirty-first," Rosa said aloud. *I've been trapped in this prison for exactly one hundred days*, she thought. Cut off from society because they stupidly believe she could help them understand this epidemic. How long would they keep her here?

Not much longer, the voice whispered inside her head. *They need you. The whole world is waiting. When you are ready to escape, nothing will be able to stop you.*

"Shush," she muttered, pushing Ana away and concentrating instead on the crow. It had hopped up onto the patio and was pecking at a crack between the tiles.

Lillian would be here soon. Despite her respect for the woman, she knew it would be another pointless session. The investigation into her biological mother didn't seem to be going anywhere. Still, it wasn't as bad as Godley's clumsy questions on whether she had ever been sexually abused. Or the sessions with electrodes attached to her head, and John Okoro asking her to describe her dreams.

The crow cawed, then flew away. She watched the bird rise in the sky, recalled sitting with her mother in one of the Oxford parks on the day she killed herself. *What is happening out there in the world*, she wondered. *How many people has the Panic taken? How many more will die?* She looked up at the late afternoon sun, at birds flying in the sky and trees swaying in the breeze, then at the brick walls enclosing her. Not so high, she noted. With a rope, she could climb it easily enough. Even with the barbed wire and broken glass, she could do it.

"Hello, Rosa."

It was Lillian.

"Hi."

"How are you doing today?"

"You know how it is."

Lillian nodded. "Would you prefer to have the session out here or inside?"

"Here is fine."

"Sure. You want a cup of something before we get started?"

"No thanks. But help yourself."

"I'm good."

Lillian sat down next to Rosa, adjusting her seat so that they were facing each other. Something about her manner was different today.

"It's nice to have some fresh air," Lillian said. "In the main building you have to undergo a million security checks just to step out for a cigarette. Despite the fact we're surrounded by countryside. Did you know that right behind the brick wall here are farmers' fields? They lead directly to the nearest town, only a couple of miles away."

"I had no idea," Rosa replied neutrally. She wondered if Lillian was trying to spark a reaction within her, taunting her that freedom was so close. It seemed out of character. But then how well did she really know Lillian?

"Anyway, I digress. So I have a set of questions I've been

instructed to ask you. But before I do that, is there anything you want to ask me?"

"Only what I always ask. When will I be released?"

"I'm sorry, Rosa, I still don't know. Shaw says he is working on it, but I must admit it's not looking good. Government bureaucrats are making all the decisions, they've become increasingly paranoid."

Rosa looked at Lillian. She seemed visibly deflated.

"Things are pretty bad out there," Lillian continued. "The Panic keeps spreading, even though officially it is not contagious."

"Surely it's contagious if it's spreading?"

"Probably, but not necessarily. From a biomedical perspective, no one has identified a mode of transmission. Let me put it this way. We don't know if someone can pass the illness to another. Like, say, the flu. Or if it's more like food poisoning: infectious, yes, but not contagious." Lillian sighed. "Either way the situation is bad. In most towns, the English and Welsh ones at least, streets are deserted. Especially at night," she added, fiddling with something in her coat pocket. "But the lights stay on. People are afraid of sleep. And now the pharmaceutical companies have gone too far. Developing new drugs..."

Lillian stopped, her face slightly flushed.

"What about them?"

"Sorry, Rosa, I went off script. I'm not meant to talk about that. What I can say is it's not relevant to you. The drugs they're developing haven't helped. Listen, I better start with the questions."

"OK."

Rosa watched Lillian open a folder and put on her reading glasses. She was clearly distracted and had none of her usual spontaneity. Rosa wondered what caused it.

"Right. The questions today relate to the military and your

views on them. And the first one is this: do you distrust the military?"

"What type of question is that? I'm hardly going to have a positive view of them, given they've locked me up here."

"True, it is worded clumsily," Lillian replied, taking off her reading glasses. "Let me rephrase. Before this all began, before the Panic, how did you view the military?"

"I don't know."

"Think about it. Maybe about whether you can recall any interactions with military personnel before the start of this epidemic. Take your time."

Rosa glanced at her surroundings. She had never encountered any soldiers, at least not that she could remember. Aside from her dad's murder investigation, she'd had contact with the police just once. It was after a fight outside a shopping mall had left one man badly hurt, and they were interviewing potential witnesses. But she'd never had contact with anyone in the military.

"I don't think so, Lillian."

"You're sure?" Lillian asked, glancing around the garden and the building behind them.

She shrugged.

Suddenly Lillian stood up. "Let's go inside," she said. "It's a bit cold for me."

She ushered Rosa inside. As she slid the veranda door open, she quietly slipped Rosa a key. Rosa felt a surge of adrenaline and her heart beating fast, but she acted as if nothing had happened.

"I'm not feeling so well," Lillian said as she had closed the door. "We'll have to call it a day."

"Is there anything I can do?" Rosa asked, keeping the key hidden in her hand.

"Thanks, I'll be OK after a lie-down. Though it's probably better to wait until later tonight, I suppose," she said, motioning with her eyes to the veranda door. "It never works if I try to sleep too early."

Rosa nodded.

"Enjoy the evening. There won't be any more intrusions today, other than to set up the monitoring equipment. Take care."

Rosa lay in bed, adrenaline coursing through her veins. She pulled the key Lillian had given her from her bra and clutched it tightly. She had been awake for many hours, waiting for the right moment, hoping Ana would tell her what to do. But Ana had remained silent.

Initially she had thought of tying some of her clothes together as a makeshift rope. Her plan being to lasso them around one of the posts to which the barbed wire was attached. But she quickly realised that would be too risky, given she was under surveillance. So her plan now was to simply grab one of the chairs from the porch and make a run for the wall, bringing a blanket with her to place over the glass.

Why is Lillian helping me, she wondered. *Would it even work? Yes, it could.* The wall wasn't very high. Certainly, it was worth a try: what did she have to lose? She glanced at her watch. It was almost two in the morning. *It's time*, she told herself.

Carefully she removed all the various wires that monitored her sleep. She slipped out of bed and put some shoes on. Pressing Lillian's key inside her clenched fist and holding a blanket under her arm, she tiptoed into the main living area of her apartment. Moonlight came through the windows, dimly lighting up the room. Holding her breath, she inserted the key into the veranda door. It went in smoothly. Turning the key clockwise, the door unlocked with a hefty click. She exhaled and slid the door open.

An alarm sounded, a high-pitched *beep-beep-beep-beep*.

"Fuck!" *I can still make it if I'm quick*, she thought. She grabbed a chair and lugged it to the wall. The blanket fell from her hands as she ran.

"Rosa, stop!" a man shouted. Her apartment lights flicked on. Beams of powerful torches wandered the walls. She realised then she had left the key in the door.

"There she is!" someone else yelled.

Standing on tiptoe, she could just about reach the top of the wall. She glanced back and saw them running towards her. Focusing again on the wall, she carefully felt for gaps between the shards of broken glass. Desperately she lifted herself up, struggling for purchase.

"Don't do it!" someone exclaimed, a voice she recognised. John Okoro.

Rosa yelped, feeling a sudden sting in the back of her leg. She must have cut herself on the glass.

Straddling the wall, she quickly assessed her options. To her right was the main building. In front and to the left were farmers' fields, just as Lillian had described. Behind the fields, she thought she spotted woods, but it was difficult to tell in the half-light.

"Rosa, stay still," a woman said. "We'll get you down safely."

She must have been close; Rosa could almost feel the woman's breath on her skin. Not close enough – Rosa was already in the air, hurtling to the ground.

Thud. The ground was soft, breaking her fall. Her leg hurt. Not from the jump, but from a gash on her leg. It felt swollen and wet, as if blood had soaked through the back of her jeans. Ignoring the pain as best she could, she picked herself up and started running towards what looked like woodland. Less than a kilometre away, she estimated, about the distance of two or three football pitches. *I'm quick and I've got a decent head-start*, she thought. *They haven't spotted me yet.*

Be careful, Ana said, emerging from nowhere. Her voice was a quiet whisper yet still perfectly audible. *They shot a sedative into your leg.*

"What?" Rosa mouthed, her breath showing in the cold night air. *No, I cut my leg on the glass. Didn't I?*

Trust your instinct. Don't believe everything you see.

What do you mean?

But Ana didn't respond, and Rosa knew she was gone. *What should I do? Keep running, as fast as I can. Think later.*

Torchlights searched the fields, flashed over her head. The ground was muddy, sometimes her feet sank into the soil. Somehow, she managed to keep her balance as she ran.

"There!" someone exclaimed.

Sharp jolts of pain emanated from her leg, worse than before. The trees weren't far away, their branches seemed to be reaching out for her. "I can do it, I can, I can, I can," she mouthed, over and over again. But her leg felt like it was on fire.

Suddenly the woman in the red scarf appeared in front of her. Her eyes bulging with fear, she seemed to be floating in the air.

"Turn back!" the woman screamed. "You'll never come out alive. Let them take you back."

"No!" Rosa shouted. "You are not my mother."

She shut her eyes, forcing the woman out of her mind. When she opened her eyes again, the apparition was gone. Rosa ran harder now, but her legs felt heavier with each step. It felt like she was hardly moving at all.

"Rosa, come back!" a man called. "We won't hurt you."

The trees were there finally, their gnarled branches promising her concealment. She accepted their embrace.

Her heart was pounding; the pain in her leg had intensified. Burning hot, like someone was prodding her with a molten rod. She touched her trouser leg. It was sodden. Glancing back, she spotted people approaching, their torchlights searching for her among the trees. There were at least ten of them, spread out across the field. Very soon, they would reach the woods.

Got to keep going, she thought, but she felt so weak. She stumbled on in the darkness, the trees' canopy blocking out most of the moonlight. There didn't seem to be a clear path, the woodland becoming more and more dense. And all the while the pain in her leg worsened, searing through her body and into her brain. She slowed down, breathing heavily, lurching from one tree trunk to the next. For the first time she wondered whether she should have given herself up.

An owl screeched. She turned around, couldn't see any torchlights searching for her. The moonlight was much stronger now, lighting up the forest. Looking ahead, she noticed a clearing, an elongated circle with a large rock at its centre.

She walked trance-like into the circle. The rock's surface was smooth. She climbed onto it and lay down. Through the trees she saw the moon, three quarters full. Feverish, she felt herself rising to it, heard waves lapping against a distant shore. She struggled to keep her eyes open, sensed herself drifting towards sleep.

"Rosanna?" a woman's voice said, and then another, echoing through the trees. "Are you Rosanna Day?"

"Who's there?" Rosa replied, sitting up. *And who is Rosanna Day,* she wondered.

Then she saw them, their slender figures outlined in the moonlight. Eleven women, hand in hand, forming a circle around her. Each of them naked, except for a dark blindfold wrapped around their face.

"Our children will never be born," they murmured together.

Only then did Rosa notice that they were all clearly pregnant. Their swollen bellies seemed taut, over-stretched. Their legs did not look strong enough to support them.

Trust your instinct. Ana's words came back to her. *Don't believe everything you see.*

"Why?" she asked the women.

"Because we are filled with the hate of the world," one of them said. "Our children are better off unborn."

"It's OK, Rosanna. I understand," another added, a young woman with thick, wavy hair. Her feet were sinking into the mud. "You think we are diseased, don't you? Let us die."

"No," Rosa said, holding back tears. "You're beautiful."

"Better to start afresh. Cut out the illness before it festers. That's what you think, right? And we are better off dead."

"Please," Rosa whispered, tears streaming down her face. "Listen to me," she said, trying to compose herself. "You are all beautiful," she continued, looking at each of them in turn. "And your children will flourish."

But she knew it was too late. They came towards her, then stood still. They were close enough that she could reach out and touch their faces. Above her she heard wings fluttering. One after another, the women untied their blindfolds, their frail hands ghostly white.

Rosa clamped her eyes shut. She screamed for a long time.

10

R osa woke up, stifling a scream, her heart beating fast. She opened her eyes. The EEG machine used to monitor her sleep was turned off. No wires were attached to her head, and there was no John Okoro waiting there, ready to question her. *What had happened? Hadn't she escaped? Or had it all just been a dream?*

Obscure images flashed through her mind – her running as fast she could, people chasing her, birds hovering in the sky. Then afterwards, an overpowering feeling of guilt, as if she had unleashed something terrible.

She glanced around the room. It seemed too quiet. Nervously, she rose from bed. As she stood up, a sudden jolt of pain surged through her leg. She pulled up her pyjamas. Wrapped around her leg was a thick bandage, just below her knee.

Her failed escape attempt came flooding back to her then. Scaling the wall, cutting her leg on the glass, running over the muddy ground as security guards chased her. But then what? The last thing she could remember with any certainty was entering a forest. She couldn't even remember the moment they'd caught her.

She limped out into the main room and to the veranda door. It was locked. Droplets of rain glittered on the glass. With her index finger, she traced a raindrop as it slid down. *Will they punish me?* Looking out the window, she realised she didn't care. Whatever they did now didn't matter. Sighing, she went to the kitchen, turned on the tap, filled the kettle and placed it on the stove.

"Another day in paradise," she muttered sarcastically. She added a teaspoon of instant coffee granules into a cup and waited for the kettle to boil.

The doorbell rang. She heard someone entering the apartment.

"Rosa," a man called. "Rosa, it's Andrew Shaw. Is it OK to come through?"

"I'm in the kitchen," she said flatly. *I can't exactly say no,* she thought bitterly.

Shaw appeared, holding a tray with coffee and croissants. His hair was cut shorter than on the day he'd brought her to Cloxham Manor. She hadn't seen him in all the time since. She felt like screaming at him.

"They're freshly baked and the coffee is good," he said. "Organic milk, too, warmed lightly. My staff told me you drink your coffee white."

Rosa turned off the kettle. "So, what's my punishment?"

"No punishment. Someone mistakenly left the key in the apartment. I understand why you tried. I'm sorry you got hurt."

Rosa regarded Shaw carefully, trying to read his expression. She couldn't tell if he really believed what he said. She considered asking him how they had caught her, then decided against it. Better for them to think she remembered everything.

"This is a waste of time," she said. "Just tell me when I will be released."

Shaw put the tray down on the table, then brought out some crockery from a kitchen cupboard. "I'm sorry, Rosa, I can't answer that yet," he said. "But I will know soon, I promise."

"How soon?"

"Can we sit? I'll tell you everything I know."

"Fine," she said reluctantly.

"I know this situation seems unfair," he said, pouring coffee for them both. "Still, it will be resolved eventually. As Lillian told you, I have been negotiating with the relevant people on your release. I'll be frank. It is proving more complicated than I thought."

Rosa looked at him without saying a word.

Shaw ate a small piece of croissant and took a few sips of his coffee. "People think it's just Oxford and neighbouring towns that have been affected," he said. "But there have been cases all over, the whole of Southern England and Wales is at risk. The government is ensconced in Edinburgh, and we're left to hold the fort. For now, all I can offer you are two small consolations. First, I will give you your date, the day you can leave, before the end of next month. The government is under pressure, and they have informed us that there will be a policy change soon. Funding for all safe houses like ours will be phased out, with a timetable for closures to be confirmed in the coming weeks."

Shaw broke up the croissant, brushing the flaky crusts to one side.

"The second consolation is this," he continued. "I can arrange for a small break from your daily routine. Every Wednesday, starting today if you wish, we can leave the grounds for lunch. There is a pub not far from here. It's a small token, I know, but hopefully it could help break the monotony."

"The scientists you work with could join us for lunch, too, if you prefer, if their work shifts allow," he continued. "Though not Lillian, unfortunately. She left Cloxham last night."

The short drive to the pub took them through moorland and a one-street village. On the way, no cars or bikes had passed by and they hadn't seen anyone in the village. From what Lillian had told her, Rosa knew Cloxham was located somewhere in Norfolk, but where exactly she wasn't sure. The few road signs they had seen en-route had been blacked out with spray paint.

Checkers Inn was a pretty, thatch-roofed pub set a little way off a minor road. There were no other buildings nearby. Inside were two small dining areas in an L shape, with a bar between. Large watercolours of sun-drenched farmers' fields hung on the walls. Behind the bar there was a signed photograph of a group of hikers smiling at the camera. Folk music was playing. Shaw told Rosa that the pub used to be popular with hikers and bird-watchers before the epidemic.

They sat by one of the back windows in the pub. Shaw had changed his clothes from when they had met in the morning. Now he was wearing a bulky turtleneck jumper and faded corduroy trousers.

There were no other customers inside. Their driver and another of Shaw's staff waited in the carpark. Rosa stared at the menu, then out the window. Behind the garden ran a small stream. Faintly, she could hear the water's flow.

"What can I get you?" a waiter asked.

"I'll have a steak, Kevin," Shaw said. "And a small beer. One of your weaker pale ales."

Rosa read the menu again. Gammon, egg and chips; fisherman's pie; lasagne with new potatoes. It all felt unreal.

"The catch of the day is always good," Shaw advised her.

"OK, I'll have that," she said, returning the menu to the waiter. He took it from her without making any eye contact.

"Anything to drink?" Shaw asked her.

"I'll have a small beer, too. The same as you."

The man nodded and went back to pour their drinks. He returned with two beers, then disappeared behind the bar.

"Kevin is now the owner, waiter and cook," Shaw said. "Meaning the food will take a while. His chef was from Poland, if I recall correctly. He had the foresight to leave the UK in the early days of the epidemic, when it was easier to do so."

"Kevin is not very sure about me, is he?" Rosa said to Shaw.

"No, that's just how he is."

"Does he know about Cloxham?"

"Yes, a little. Probably about as much as you do. I know what we're doing appears secretive, but it is for a good cause. I can tell you more about it all, if you want? How it links to what's happening outside."

Rosa shrugged. She was interested to learn more, but she was still preoccupied with Lillian's sudden disappearance and the failed attempt to help her escape.

"All right, yes, tell me," she said finally.

"Good."

Rosa and Shaw were back at Chequers Inn again, the fourth Wednesday in a row they had lunched there. She enjoyed the outings, even though she was well aware of how artificial the arrangement was. It helped that she had a potential timeline for her release. Over those last three trips, Shaw had told her more and more about the epidemic survivors at the complex. None of them could speak, even under hypnosis. The patients were in a stable condition, bedridden and largely uncommunicative but able to respond to basic stimuli. They had been transferred in from various hospitals around the country soon after the epidemic began. But most of the patients died within a few weeks of their arrival. They succumbed to neurogenic shock, their vital organs failing from a lack of oxygen as their minds finally gave way. The only useful information garnered by Shaw's team was their near-identical sleep patterns, including unusual high-amplitude theta waves that continued throughout the night for every single one of them, the same theta wave patterns demonstrated by Rosa.

Now they were sharing a pot of Earl Grey tea, having finished their meal. It was cold outside, and you could hear the wind through the rickety windows. But the sun shone brightly and the sky was an unblemished blue. Rosa could almost make herself believe she was free.

Once again, none of the scientists could join them, but Rosa didn't really mind. She thought it would perhaps have been nice if John Okoro were there. Their sessions were starting to seem a bit more like a two-way conversation. That wasn't the case with Godley. And certainly she wouldn't want Dr Fersatan, Lillian's replacement, to join. The way he looked at her made her feel uncomfortable, his eyes roving over her body like she was a scantily clad woman in a men's magazine.

If only Lillian still worked at Cloxham Manor. Rosa had pressed Shaw on why she'd left, but all he said was that she had resigned. He wouldn't tell her any more than that. And neither of them ever brought up her failed escape attempt.

"Has Cloxham always been used as a secret jail?" she asked Shaw as she sipped her tea. She felt like she knew him well enough now that she could speak frankly.

"Now Rosa, I know the setup isn't ideal. But I wouldn't call it a jail. Before the SED epidemic, I'm not sure exactly what it was used for. A government research facility, I know that. But I don't know the details."

"You weren't working there before?"

"No. I had been stationed in Afghanistan. My next post was

due to be in the North Waziristan region in Pakistan. But then the epidemic struck."

"How long have you been in the army?"

"Almost thirty years now. I'm a product of the Royal Military Academy at Sandhurst."

"I see," Rosa replied, glancing out the window. Daffodils had sprung up in the garden, close to the water.

"I've told you about Cloxham Manor and other government safe houses," Shaw said, looking at Rosa directly. "I can also tell you about my career, if you like. It's not a secret."

"It would even things up, I suppose. You already know everything there is to know about my past."

"Not everything. But yes, it would even things up," Shaw said, smiling. "Well, let me start by saying that as an adolescent and young man I never planned to join the army. The army found me, if you will.

"My parents were shocked. They assumed I would pursue a career in academia. At secondary school, I had been a diligent student, my grades were good. Then at university I studied philosophy. My parents, friends – everyone – thought I'd excel. But I only scraped through the exams. What they didn't realise was how frustrated I had become with my studies, with academia as a whole."

"This disillusionment came to me gradually," he continued, "a gnawing sense of pointlessness that only grew. When I started university, I genuinely believed that philosophy could provide useful insights. But by the end of my degree I thought philosophy was too abstract, trapped in a recursive discourse of logic and meaning that was of no use to solving real, everyday problems."

Shaw leaned back in his chair. "I didn't talk to anyone about how I felt. Instead I ran obsessively, every morning, as a means of distraction. Became rather obsessed with boxing, too. It helped a little. What would have helped more is if I'd talked to someone. I only learnt much later that many university students view their courses like that. Did you?"

"A little," Rosa said.

"What did you study?"

"PPE. Politics, Philosophy and Economics."

"A good mix. And enough philosophy to empathise."

"Yes. Though I preferred it to politics and economics. But how did all of this lead you to join the army?"

"Good question," Shaw replied. "Back then I recognised my views on philosophy probably reflected a limited understanding of the subject. Yet I also knew that my malaise spread further than my studies. The whole university environment, with its preponderance of bearded and bespectacled men who stuttered through lectures, it seemed out of touch with reality. Near the end of my course, I knew I needed the antithesis of the academic world. Something practical and entirely without ambiguity. When a brochure for Sandhurst was slipped under my door, I had the answer to what I was going to do next."

"I see. And how did that go?" she asked, pouring them both a second cup of tea.

"Well. It made me who I am today. Military life became my passion, I never married or had kids. I liked being in the field. It was difficult, yes, but real. Iraq, Sierra Leone, Afghanistan. I was looking forward to Pakistan. But then this epidemic. Like many of the older officers, I was kept back in the UK to manage safe houses."

Shaw paused, shifting his chair closer to the table. "Rosa, I'll admit this to you. Managing Cloxham is a job I feel wholly unqualified to do. Not that the work is unimportant," he said quietly, leaning forward. "Rather, that placing military people like me in charge feels more like political manoeuvring than what is actually required. For the first time since I joined the army, I've doubted whether I am the right man for the job."

Rosa sat alone by the window, waiting for Shaw to return from settling the bill with Kevin at the bar. She gazed out at the daffodils by the stream, tried to imagine she was somewhere else. The daffodils seemed fragile, as if they had bloomed prematurely.

She thought about Shaw's account. She didn't doubt the veracity of his story. But she suspected an ulterior motive – that he talked about his past only so she might talk more candidly about herself. She also had the sense he was altering subtle nuances of his experience so that she might better relate to him. It was his manner, how he said things, as much as what he actually said.

A door slammed, plates smashed on the floor.

"Hey!" Kevin yelled.

Rosa turned around. Three men had appeared right behind her; from where, she wasn't sure. Their faces were covered by balaclavas. One of them grabbed her arm and pulled her out of her chair, dragging her towards the exit.

Shaw ran to the door, and Kevin hid behind the bar.

"Move! Get out the way or we'll kill you," one of the men shouted at Shaw, pulling out a gun. He was close enough to Rosa for her to see sweat dripping from his chin.

"How did you find us?" Shaw asked calmly, ignoring his request. Rosa glanced at Shaw, noticing how his blue eyes appeared almost transparent in the light.

"That doesn't matter. Move out of the way, now!"

"Listen," Shaw said in a slow, assured voice. "We have trained marksmen surrounding the place. I'm impressed that you've made it this far. Conceivably, someone well trained might be able to sneak past them, but three? That is practically a miracle. The problem is, miracles rarely happen twice in a day. If you step outside, our snipers will kill you within a matter of seconds. I don't want to see that happen."

"Bollocks! There was only your driver, and we took care of him. You're bluffing."

"Try me."

The man with the gun and the other holding Rosa looked at the third man. It was clear he was their leader. He raised his palm as a signal to the armed man, then spoke. "Sir Andrew Shaw," he said condescendingly. "Director of Cloxham Manor and disgraced military official. If there were snipers, wouldn't we be dead?"

Shaw looked back at him. "Who are you? Do you work for FRJ?"

"Do you not recognise my voice?" the man asked.

Shaw shook his head.

The man pulled off his balaclava, revealing a gaunt, pock-marked face. "How about now?"

Rosa noticed Shaw's expression change, to one that couldn't disguise his dismay. "Sergeant Iain Hardy," he said, recognising the man.

"Yes, Shaw, I know all about you. It's sickening what you've done. And to think I once looked up to you."

"Iain," Shaw said, struggling to keep his voice steady, "don't you think that –"

"Shut up! I'm a mercenary now, just like you. Only difference is, my superiors are leading the resistance, not a corrupt government."

"PureForce."

"That's right."

"Iain, listen. I know I can't stop you. But if you step outside, you will be shot. I honestly don't know why they haven't shot you already. So tell your men to release her, to drop the gun. I can then ensure you leave this place alive."

"That is not an option," Iain Hardy replied. He nodded to

his accomplices and the man with the gun shot Shaw and Kevin in quick succession. Rosa watched them crumple to the floor.

"What have you done?!" she screamed, struggling to pull herself free. The man holding her was too strong.

"Don't be frightened," Hardy told her. "We mean you no harm."

She looked at Hardy and the other two men. It was pointless to resist, she knew.

"We're here to rescue you," Hardy continued. "Now it's time to go, Rosanna Day."

That's not my name, she thought, but she didn't say anything. A surreal image flitted in her head – naked women moaning in the moonlight, hands linked, their eyes blindfolded – and then slipped away.

It felt like she was floating. As they stepped outside harsh sunlight greeted them, blinding them momentarily. A howling wind pierced their clothes.

DEAL

March

11

Nick watched the elderly lady struggling to stay awake. Ten minutes ago, she had shut her eyes, finally giving in to the sleep she needed, but almost immediately another passenger had coughed loudly to wake her up.

No sleeping in public! It had started off as an unspoken rule; now it was the law. Not that the officials needed to do much to enforce it. No one wanted to see a stranger asleep. The fear of them waking without really being awake was too much to bear.

The woman popped a tablet in her mouth. A pale blue pill, he noted, thinking back to his first conversation with Harold about LC+ last year. How right he had been: so many people were on LC+ already.

The old lady was too tired to be particularly discreet about it. In less than a minute she was alert, but artificially so. Her eyes bulged open, her hands shook with the adrenaline rush. *Surely that dosage is too much*, he thought. He watched her pull out a magazine from her bag. She flicked through the pages rapidly, pausing now and then to read a headline or glance at a photo. When she finished with the magazine, she reached for her bag again and brought out an iPad. He noticed how hard she was pressing on the screen. Probably she was playing *Alert!* or *Tick-tock-tick!*, two of the most popular games to have come out since the epidemic, designed to chase away sleepiness.

Not that those games stopped the headaches, the forgetfulness and inability to concentrate, Nick thought, tapping a finger against the window. Worse still was the deep-rooted sense that something was fundamentally wrong with the world. No drugs could fix that, let alone some stupid computer game.

He looked out through the train's window. Sunlight reflected harshly on glass-fronted offices. Reading remained a largely functional town, even with all the reported cases there and its proximity to Oxford. Indeed, Reading was prospering. It acted as the de facto gateway into Oxford, shifting supplies in and out via Nuneham Courtenay village.

A dull, throbbing pain reverberated in his head. He popped a painkiller in his mouth, brought out a bottle of water from his bag, unscrewed the cap and swallowed. He had slept fitfully last night, despite it coming at the end of a thirty-six-hour day. He had spent the night at Elmore Facility, a purpose-built government complex on the edge of Nuneham Courtenay. Now everyone arriving from Oxford had to pass through Elmore to be assessed.

The isolation rooms at Elmore Facility were carefully sound-proofed. They were tiny, containing only a single mattress, a toilet and a washbasin. If you were a government official or paid a hefty premium, you could stay in one of the larger isolation huts, complete with en-suite bathroom and a real bed. But whoever you were, the rule was the same: a minimum of twenty-four hours at Elmore Facility before you could move on, and much longer if you didn't have the right paperwork. They called this the 'community observation period' rather than what it really was: quarantine.

On-site there was a large canteen serving overpriced food and drink, and a smaller lounge area with TV screens around the room. It was in the canteen that he would keep abreast of the latest rumours, and yesterday afternoon he had heard that Rosanna Day had escaped. The rumour going around was that members of PureForce had rescued her. A scrawny teenager told him Rosanna had been held in a remote location in the Lake District, where the government was running invasive tests on her. The government wanted to extract the cure before they disposed of her, the kid had said. This rumour was broadly consistent with the usual conspiracy theory, namely that the government was carefully controlling research because they wanted to closely manage the cure once it was found. Key politicians and high-ranking civil servants supposedly had financial ties to the pharmaceutical company FRJ, which was leading the research effort.

Of course it was all hearsay. No one knew what Rosanna Day looked like; it wasn't even certain that she existed. But the boy fervently believed in Rosanna Day, like so many did. He told Nick how PureForce planned to showcase Rosanna up in Edinburgh, opposite the government's new headquarters, any day now. *It's like she's some gilt-edged trophy,* Nick had said tiredly. He had wanted to hear more, but the kid took offence to Nick's comment.

The train stopped at Banbury. Nick watched the elderly lady who had taken the tablet earlier hurry off the train, then the new passengers alighting. They all looked exhausted, every one of them wary of catching another person's eye. *Where are we heading*, he wondered. *Down a blind alley filled with blind idiots. Everyone so caught up in staving off sleep that they have forgotten how to live. And how can Rosanna Day possibly help? Even if it were true that she had suffered from the Panic as a* young child, even if she had been able to fight it off, what difference did it make?

People believed Rosanna Day resisted the Panic based on the way she slept. When Nick had been snarky about this belief, Kiyoko scolded him. "She gives people hope. Is that such a bad thing?" Kiyoko had said.

Looking around the carriage, he knew Kiyoko was right. Too many people had accepted this new reality of artificial sleep deprivation, as if it were the only way. It was one thing taking the weaker drugs like GreenShoots or Outreach Green to help regulate your sleep. But not W&R; and LC+ was a whole other level. You could always tell the people on them, with their bulging eyes and fidgety hands. He should go back to only selling the weaker, first-generation drugs, however hard it would be to scratch a living that way. Better than being a hypocrite.

"Mister? Mister? Hey!" another passenger said, a woman sitting behind him.

"Yes?" Nick said, turning around. The woman looked exhausted, with dark bags under her eyes.

"Your shoulders looked slouched," she said. "I thought you might be, you know."

"I wasn't."

"Sorry. I wondered this and that," she stammered. Her cheeks reddened, her eyes started to blink rapidly, "and I don't know. I thought...Christ, I don't know what I thought."

"It's OK," he said as gently as possible. "No offence taken. Have a good journey."

"Thanks. You too."

He turned back around, gazed out the window. For a moment, he'd been irritated by the woman's supposition. But as soon as he saw her, he'd only felt sympathy. It was clear she was on W&R or LC+.

The train started moving at a slow crawl. Outside the roads were deserted. His eyes felt so heavy, he pinched himself hard to keep awake. The thirty-six-hour routine was taking its toll. He felt tired all the time, sometimes so much so that he couldn't follow a basic conversation. Perhaps it wasn't worth it. Better to risk it and return to a normal twenty-four-hour schedule.

He took out his phone, glanced at a photo he and Kiyoko had taken a month or so ago – a selfie of the two of them at her place, smiling goofily at the camera. They had taken it just after she'd told him about her family's first camping trip in Canada. She had been eleven or twelve years old, was so paranoid about grizzly bears that every night she shook little bells in her tent until she fell asleep.

Whenever Nick stayed overnight in Oxford now, he stayed at her place. The last time, he'd awoken in the early morning, with her asleep next to him, her head on the edge of his pillow. He hadn't noticed her coming in after her shift watching over a father and his son.

Just friends, he reminded himself. She lay down next to me because she needed comfort. Understandable, given that the boy she was watching over may well have killed himself if it wasn't for Kiyoko. Good that I was there for her, as a friend. Whether our relationship stays that way or develops into something more is up to her. She's beautiful and brilliant, and I know I could fall for her in an instant. Still, I would be happy only being friends, if that's what she wants. I'm simply glad to have met her.

12

"Do you want to meet her or not?" Robert asked Nick, fussing with his napkin. He had dark bags under his eyes. "Her house is in the country, about half an hour's drive from town."

They were eating brunch at the Chalkhouse Kitchen, an inexpensive diner near Nottingham University campus. Strips of harsh fluorescent light made sure every spot of the diner was well lit.

"Maybe," Nick replied, looking at his housemate, then around the room. All the waitresses seemed a little jumpy, as if they were monitoring the customers to make sure none of them fell asleep. "Do you really think it's worth it?"

"Professor Reilly is a bit of an oddball, but she's brainy. Supposedly she's well connected, too. I've heard she has links to both PureForce and the government."

"Like a double agent."

"Yeah! PureForce is edgy but kinda cool, too, don't you think?" Robert said excitedly. Nick could tell how tired his friend was by the tone of his voice and his constant fidgeting.

"And if what she said is true, we could have ourselves a nice little earner on the side," Robert continued. "I'm not sure if it's legal and all, what with the government's over-the-top rules, but it sounds harmless to me. I have my contacts here, and you know the broader market for these kinds of things. We'd be the perfect team. And Professor Reilly, she'd already heard about you. She specifically told me that she wanted you in on it. It seems you've built up a reputation as a reliable businessman."

"Fucking hell, Rob, I'm nothing of the sort. I do what I do to make ends meet. You know that."

He had previously described his work to Robert and other close friends as that of a glorified postman. Told them he transported coffee, tea and energy drink powder in and out of Oxford. Still, his friends probably suspected that he also peddled the sleep-suppression drugs, even if they hadn't said so.

Robert was more likely than anyone else to be suspicious, given that they shared a flat. Nick was careful, though. He sold most of his drugs in Oxford or Reading, towns that he knew well and where hardly anyone knew him. He sold them quickly so that he never held too large a quantity, and those he did have were well hidden in their apartment, in a concealed cavity within a wardrobe door in his bedroom.

"All right, no need to get antsy, man. What I meant is that you're brave enough to do business in Oxford. Not many are."

"Lots of people still live there, you know. Normal people like you and me. They need caffeine as much as, more than, the rest of us."

He looked across at his friend shovelling sausage and egg into his mouth, then out of the bay window. Sunlight filtered weakly into the room.

"I suppose. Coffee is expensive enough here; you must be making a killing. I don't understand why they'd stay in Oxford, though. They could get out if they wanted to," he said. "Couldn't they?" he added when Nick didn't respond.

"It's not so simple," Nick said. He'd been thinking about the desperate revellers in Cowley Park, and wondering how much longer he could walk through there without getting himself seriously hurt, or even killed.

"What do you mean?"

"Huh?"

"You said people can't leave Oxford so easily."

"Oh right, yes," Nick said, adding more salt to his food. As he cut into a hash brown he noticed how much his hands were shaking. "The checks at Elmore Facility have become more stringent," he continued, setting down his knife and fork for a moment.

Nick glanced out the window again. It had begun to drizzle. It made everything outside seem to blur together – a hazy, disorienting mix of people, traffic, pigeons and soggy litter.

"Nick?"

"If you don't have the right paperwork, they'll never let you through," he told Robert, trying to keep his mind focused. "And there are reasons why some people would choose to stay."

"Fair enough. You know the situation there much better than I do. So, what do you say? Do you want to meet Professor Reilly tomorrow?"

"Maybe."

"Have a think about it whilst I pop to the gents. I've got to get back to work by one."

Nick nodded as his friend left the table. Glancing around at the other customers in the room, he was both relieved and depressed to note that he wasn't the only one struggling to keep focused. He finished his food, mopping up egg yolk with a slice of bread. His hands were still shaking and now his head was beginning to pound.

Robert came back to the table a few minutes later, humming something under his breath.

"All right, I'll go," Nick said. "The earlier the better. I didn't sleep well last night."

"Go where?"

"To meet Professor Reilly."

"Oh yeah. Cool!" Robert said, tapping his hands against the table as if he were playing the drums. His rhythm was all over the place. "Man, it'll be easy money!"

"Maybe. Let's see," Nick replied, eyeing Robert as he continued to tap the table. He wondered if his housemate had popped a pill in the bathroom.

"You're too pessimistic."

"I'm just tired."

"You still on the thirty-six-hour day?" Robert asked, staring at Nick's hands.

"Yes."

"Cold turkey?"

"Yep."

"Nicholas Parry, you're quite something!"

"Not really, I'm half asleep most the time," Nick said, smiling. "And as you can see, my hands are shaking like I've been on an all-night bender. Sometimes I think it'd be better to go back to a normal sleep schedule."

"Are you out of your mind?" Robert exclaimed, staring at him manically and banging his fists on the table. People glanced nervously in their direction. "You know the risks."

"Don't worry," Nick said, surprised at his friend's reaction. "Just a thought, but I'm not going to do it. OK?"

"Good," Robert replied, exhaling loudly. "You had me worried there for a moment, chief."

"I'm good. Dog-tired but otherwise fine. How about you? How are you finding the thirty-six-hour day? It's quite an adjustment at first, isn't it?"

"It was, but I'm good with it now. In fact, I've recently started the 1-to-3 schedule."

"Really?"

"Yep. I want to minimise risk."

"One sleep in three. That's hard to do cold turkey," he said, looking at Robert but unable to make eye contact. "Rob, what are you taking?"

"Oh, nothing much. Mostly the Outreach Green, you know, to ease me into the new routine. And sometimes the W&R. Only when I really need it, about once a week or so; they're too expensive in any case. And I never buy LC+. That stuff sounds lethal!"

"Good, you're not taking LC+. But you shouldn't take W&R, either. You know what I said about it. I've seen the effects first-hand. So many people in Oxford are dependent. They walk around not knowing where they are, paranoid of everyone and even themselves. Stick with Outreach Green. Better still, nothing at all."

"Yeah, I know. But I can't keep to the schedule otherwise."

"Then go back to the thirty-six-hour day."

"I can't. It's spreading too fast. Supposedly there are hundreds of people dying every day, right here in Nottingham. Soon it'll be like Oxford. They're keeping it quiet, but I've heard the hospitals are filling up. And all the while, people hold on to the dumb hope that this Rosanna Day will magically save us all."

"Is that so bad?"

"You're not a believer now, too, are you?" Robert said, jovially punching him in the arm.

"I'm not sure," Nick answered, trying to read his friend's expression. The punch, though clearly not malicious, had hurt. "I believe she had the illness as a child. Beyond that I'm sitting on the fence."

"Good old Nick, hedging his bets. I don't know either. But in the meantime, I have to minimise risk. The thirty-six-hour day has been shown to work, the government says so. Not just the government, it's all over the papers, too. Plus these new reports I've read say the 1-to-3 schedule is even better. That no one has died who has stuck to it."

Nick clasped his hands together to control the shaking, then glanced around the room. He caught a middle-aged man as he was swallowing a tablet. The man's whole body immediately stiffened up, then he started moving his head back and forth in a strange jerky motion. As if he were a puppet in which only the head was amenable to the puppeteer. The waitresses and other clientele paid him no attention. LC+, it had to be. *Robert could end up just like that soon enough,* he thought.

"Rob, even if that's true, which I doubt, they'll die soon enough," he said. "It's not the way. Trust me; it is better to risk sleeping a bit more than take those drugs. You'll have pounding headaches even worse than on the thirty-six-hour day. You won't be able to think straight. It's worse than paranoia: you'll likely start hallucinating if you keep it up. I've seen it in Oxford."

Nick looked at his friend. Robert seemed irritated. They had known each other since secondary school, used to go to football matches together. On the few occasions Nick had offered him advice over the years, he had taken his suggestions seriously. Yet he wasn't confident Robert would listen to him this time.

"Trust me, please," Nick said, gently. "It's better to stay off the stronger pills."

"Since when have you become so moral?" Robert asked, his voice suddenly rising.

"Huh?"

"You sell drugs, don't you? The whole range of them, W&R,

GreenShoots, LC+, whatever else. All that talk about coffee and energy drinks was just crap. Don't try to deny it."

"OK, yes, it's true," Nick sighed, too tired to say otherwise.

"Yet you tell me not to take them."

"You shouldn't."

"You're a hypocrite."

Nick looked at his friend with sadness. "Maybe I am," he said. "When I first got into this business, I honestly believed the drugs could help. That's the truth. But from dealing the stuff I've learnt that they aren't worth it. Certainly not the stronger ones."

"They're a nice little earner, though, aren't they?"

"Listen, Rob, please. The drugs make it easier to stay awake. But if you stay on them too long, you'll suffer. Pounding headaches, hallucinations, teeth falling out, skin going grey. And it's only going to get worse."

"So why don't you quit dealing?" Robert asked, his voice a little calmer now.

"I'd love to. Unfortunately, it's not that simple. If I quit, they'll come after me. Once you're in the system, there's no way out."

"I get that, I do. But how did you get caught up in it?"

Nick looked away from his friend for a moment. He gazed at the raindrops on the glass, remembering how it all had started.

"I needed the money," he said, looking his friend in the eyes. "There was a dead man on a side street. This was in Oxford. His pockets were lined with W&R drugs. I took them, sold them in Cowley Park. At that point, it felt like I had no choice. I needed money quick to pay for my father and sister's funeral."

They sat in silence for a while, neither of them knowing what to say next.

"Nick, I'm sorry," Robert said. "Really I am. It must've been hard."

"It was."

"I should've been a better housemate."

"You were fine, Rob. It helped when we went out for drinks."

"But I could've come with you to Oxford."

"No. I wanted to be alone then."

Nick glanced at his watch. It was almost one. He knew Rob should return to work: his job wasn't so secure. Many firms were struggling to stay afloat, with workers being laid off all the time.

"You should get back to work."

"It's OK."

"Seriously. You've told me about your boss. I don't want you losing your job because of me."

"My boss is a prick, but he couldn't fire me for being late. Still, I should get back. Only if you're OK, though."

"Honestly, I'm good."

"Are you sure?"

"Rob..."

"All right. Well, then, I'll go."

"Let me know about Professor Reilly."

"Will do. I'll try getting hold of her during a break. I'll let you know once I do."

"Sounds good."

"Sure. Call me if...you know."

"Thanks. I'm fine, but thanks. You better hurry."

He watched Robert leave the diner. They were still good friends, he thought. Even if their lives and their ways of coping with the Panic were very different. Not that either of them was really coping.

A waitress came over and he ordered another coffee. His head was pounding again. He rested his chin on his hands and looked out the window. The sun remained hidden behind thick clouds. He tried to distinguish the people outside from one another. But every one of them was walking alone, with their eyes to the ground, lost in a blur of extreme tiredness that drained all colour from the world.

Kiyoko came into his mind. He could picture her perfectly, how she looked the last time, her hands clasped round a mug of tea. Something had been bothering her; he could tell by the way she kept biting her lower lip. He had assumed it was about them, that she was feeling awkward about how they had lain in bed together. But then she started telling him about the clients she'd watched over that night, a boy called Sumon Chakma and his father.

"Could the boy be right?" she'd asked Nick. "And if so, what does it mean?"

"Sir! Excuse me, sir!" the waitress said loudly. "Your coffee."

"Thanks," Nick said, wondering if he had momentarily shut his eyes. He lifted the cup, spilt most of it over the tablecloth.

"Shit," he muttered, setting the cup down then mopping up the hot liquid with a paper towel. His hands were shaking badly again. He felt the stares of strangers on him, judging his every move.

The waitress helped clean up the spillage. He thanked her but she didn't say anything.

"Do you want to order another cup?" she asked, pointedly avoiding eye contact.

"Sure."

"We can do it for only ten pounds, given the accident."

"Ah I see. I'll leave it, then. Just the bill."

The waitress nodded and walked quickly away.

Fuck it, he thought, holding his shaking hands. *This schedule is killing me*. So what I'm going to do is step out of this depressing place, breathe in the fresh air outside and marvel at the raindrops falling on my skin. Once I'm home I'll dry off, put on my pyjamas and brush my teeth. Then I'm going to sleep like a newborn. And in a few days' time, as soon as it's feasible, I'll go to Oxford again and see Kiyoko. Tell her exactly how I feel.

13

"Both his parents are dead, early victims of the Panic," Professor Reilly told them.

"Professor Reilly, I..."

"Lillian, please."

"Sorry, Lillian. It's, well, I just still don't get it."

The three of them were sat in a modest house. It was like many other British homes that hadn't changed ownership in years. Fading wallpaper, scuffed carpets, a few photos and ornaments dotted around.

"That's OK. The point is, Nathan has been barely conscious since February. Before then, he was doing well. Reasonably alert, able to feed himself, responsive to questions with a nod or a shaking of the head. I know that doesn't sound like much, but believe me, he was in a far better state than any other SED survivor we have taken in. Being able to communicate, even in this basic way, is rare amongst survivors. And he's never tried to claw out his own eyes since. However, in the last few weeks his condition has been rapidly deteriorating. Colleagues are looking after him as best they can, not far from here."

Lillian had told Nick and Robert a little about her group

Alliance and its search for a cure. She had also talked about the government safe houses and Alliance's connections with key members of the PureForce movement. What she hadn't told them was that Nathan Newton had a sister named Rosa who was locked up in Cloxham Manor. Nor that she used to work there.

"And the Oxford hospitals are the only option?" Nick asked.

"As far as we know. The drugs that could help him are still at the experimental stage. Meaning they'll only have them in Oxford. By the time the government approves them, if they ever do, it will be too late."

"I see." Nick took a sip of the herbal tea. He felt much better, having slept for fifteen hours straight. For the first time in months, he could follow a conversation without his mind drifting away.

"Nick has contacts there," Robert interjected, his voice scratchy and uneven.

"I do?"

"Yes, you do," he said, frowning at Nick. His hands were visibly twitching. Earlier that morning, Robert had pulled his car to the side of the road after they'd almost crashed into a stationary vehicle. He had taken a W&R tablet then, and had been fidgety ever since.

"I do have a contact, at Mantle Hospital. The problem is, I'm not sure he'll be open to a deal."

"Dr Harold Stone."

"Yes! How did you know?"

"That's why I wanted to work with you," she said, smiling. "We have our contacts, too."

Lillian's mobile phone rang. "Excuse me," she said, answering it. Nick could make out a man's voice on the end of the line.

"One minute, Andrew," she responded. Then to Nick and Robert: "Sorry, I have to take this. I won't be a moment."

"What do you think?" Nick asked Robert after Lillian had stepped out of the room.

"I had no idea until now that this Nathan Newton was so important to her group. It's totally different from what she told me before."

"I know. Specialised water filters and all that. But this is more interesting, isn't it? Worthier too."

Already Nick was thinking of how he could persuade Harold to procure the drugs. Harold would be suspicious. He wouldn't mention Nathan or Lillian and their links with Pure-Force. Harold disliked that organisation even more than the generics manufacturers competing with FRJ. Instead, he would tell him that the drugs were for a charity supporting SED survivors. No, better still, a desperate and wealthy single mother whose only child was unconscious. A perfect narrative to convince Harold, combining an ethical imperative with the chance to make a substantial profit.

"Don't get on your moral high horse," Rob said lightly. "But more to the point. Where is the money in it?"

"I'm sure she'll make it worth our while."

"You think?"

"Yes. Anyway, it's not just about the money. Look, I'm no angel, and I need the money, too. But this is a chance for us to be part of something bigger. If what she says about Nathan is true, then we might be close to finding a cure. He has some kind of immunity, isn't that what she said?"

"Maybe, something like that. Either way, I don't see how I fit into this. With the water filters, I could talk to people, make things happen so that the councillors and the police wouldn't cause us any problems. But with this…"

"My apologies," Lillian said, returning to the room. "Nottingham University is an old-fashioned place. Harking on about Freud, and that I'm meant to be teaching psychoanalysis to the final year students this term. They're living in a bubble, oblivious, or wanting to be oblivious, to what is ripping our country apart."

"I'm not exaggerating," she continued. "Everyone knows this terrible illness will keep on spreading. I shouldn't complain too loudly, though. The University allows me to pursue my own research, gives me a certain legitimacy," she said with a wry smile. "But we should focus on the task at hand. We'd just started discussing Dr Harold Stone, hadn't we?"

"That's right," Nick said.

"What about the water filters?" Robert asked.

"Yes. I haven't forgotten. The problem is, it's still too early. It's just one of many competing hypotheses at this point. The fact is we still don't have any concrete evidence that the Panic spreads through drinking water. Maybe it does, maybe it doesn't. What we do know is that the prototype filters my colleagues developed haven't reduced the risk of SED. So there's no point distributing them more widely, at least for now."

"People would still buy them," Robert replied. "With the right marketing, that is."

"I'd be lying if I said resources aren't important. All the same, we have our principles."

"But..."

"Don't worry. If my colleagues' theories are proved right, I will tell you straightaway. You have my word. But Nathan is the priority for now, and, Robert, your role is just as important here. While Nick goes about procuring the drugs, I need you to obtain a fake ID and the necessary paperwork for me to visit Oxford. I don't know when exactly I'll have to go there, but I imagine it will be soon enough.

"I've lost good friends to this illness," Lillian continued. "I don't want to lose Nathan, too. Not only because of how he might be able to help. Nathan is a brave young man suffering for a good cause. So you see, I cannot let him die without trying. And I can't do that without you both."

"What about PureForce?" Robert blurted out, his voice jumpy and erratic. "What's its role in all of this?"

"Security, if we need it."

"How do you know that PureForce can be trusted?" Nick asked. "I mean, I'm no fan of the government or FRJ, but I'm not sure if PureForce is much better."

"Yeah," Robert pipped in. "I've heard they're a terrorist organisation."

"Government propaganda," Lillian replied. "Though there is always some truth in rumours. PureForce is far from perfect. Still, what is certain is that people from PureForce helped my group rescue Nathan. We couldn't have done it without them."

"They killed innocent people. The government said they were responsible for the bomb that went off near Parliament a few weeks ago. I heard it on the news."

"The government says a lot of things that aren't true. It is just as likely others were responsible. PureForce has its faults, but I wouldn't call it a terrorist group."

Lillian leaned back in her chair. Patiently she outlined what she knew about PureForce. How they had, according to various sources, tried and failed to free the woman they call Rosanna Day. That they had radical views on big pharma, believing FRJ and other companies to be complicit in the cause and spread of SED. They were also against GM crops, the use of pesticides, even the adding of fluoride to the water supply. But at their core they had the same goal as her group Alliance: to fight the illness.

"What about Rosanna Day, what do you think about her?" Nick asked. "Some people place so much hope in her. If she even exists, that is."

"The government has her locked up, I'm quite sure of that.

And what I definitely know is that those government safe houses are...well, as I said earlier, they are misguided. There are better, more transparent ways of dealing with the situation. We have all these great universities in our country. World-leading institutions and researchers, and yet the government doesn't want to utilise their scientific expertise."

"People believe Rosanna Day had the Panic as a child and learnt to fight it off. Do you think it's true? And if so, can she help us?"

"Maybe, I don't know," Lillian replied.

"What about your group?" Robert interjected. "I mean, how can we know for sure that you're not on the wrong side? Whatever side that is."

Nick glanced anxiously at Lillian, then across at his housemate. He saw his friend tapping his fingers rapidly on the table, noticed how one of his legs was twitching up and down. Robert was going to ruin their chances of working with Lillian's group. He wanted to tell him to keep his mouth shut and to never again take any of those damn tablets.

"Our only aim is to stop the Panic," Lillian said, "this cruel epidemic of madness. It's as simple as that."

Lillian sipped her drink. None of them spoke for several minutes.

"Look," Lillian said eventually, "I can't promise you much. There is, I admit, a lot of uncertainty. Our relationship with PureForce isn't straightforward. We need each other, but we don't see things the same way. And though I'm hopeful, the truth is I don't know if Nathan's case can help us find a cure. But what I can offer you is this. First, three thousand pounds each. Second, and more important, being able to say you helped keep a young man alive."

Nick searched out Robert's eyes, but his friend was staring at the floor. He looked at his own hands, which were shaking slightly.

"So, what will it be?" Lillian asked, looking directly at Nick.

He met her gaze, seeing in her eyes what was lacking in his. A calling, a belief in doing the right thing. For a moment his heart felt lighter, elevated.

"I'm in," he said. "I'd be honoured to be part of it."

"Me too," Robert added, after a pause.

"Thank you. I'm really, really relieved to hear that," she said, smiling. "Now come, let me show you something. It's in the basement. It can probably help explain what we're trying to do."

Lillian led them down the stairs, holding a torch. The room was pitch-black other than the dim torchlight. After some scrambling around, she flicked a light switch, revealing a couple of covered cages on a long table, and a pile of books stacked on a chair.

"Sorry about that, the switch at the top of the stairs is broken, and I've no idea how to fix it. Anyhow, welcome to one of our makeshift laboratories! This type of research is normally the preserve of my chemist and microbiologist colleagues, but I wanted to show you what they've been doing."

She pulled off the covers from the two cages. There was a black rat in each. Nick peered at the creatures. They were lying on their sides, seemingly unconscious, though their bodies twitched occasionally.

"The government is always nosing around at the University, and they'll get a search warrant for this place soon enough. That's not such a big problem, though, as we'll hear of it before they can find anything. This lab is portable, and besides there are many more. But let me get to the point and show you what we have learnt. Two lab rats. On the outside they look the same, don't they?"

Nick and Robert nodded.

"We can't replicate the Panic, but the rats are in a state that's as close as we can get to that of SED survivors when they are asleep. Not very nice, I know, but it helps us understand. Now watch this," she said, picking up a syringe from a tray on the table.

She plunged the syringe into the stomach of one of the sleeping rats. Its body twitched noticeably for a few moments, but it remained unconscious.

"That syringe was filled with amantadine solution. A drug that has been used to treat Parkinson sufferers and that has shown some early hints of success in treating patients in a persistent vegetative state. Now compare it with this," she said, picking up a second syringe and injecting the second lab rat. There was no response.

"So the first one, amantadine, that's the cure?" Robert asked.

"Wait for it," she said. They stood there, peering through the wire cage at the second rat. After a minute or so its body twitched. Then it started to shake more violently, its tail moving from side to side. Finally, it regained consciousness, emitting a high-pitched squeal before running haphazardly around the cage.

"That's amazing!" Robert said.

"So this could help Nathan?" Nick asked.

"Maybe, even if it doesn't address the root causes of the Panic. And what we have here is in an unrefined form. Amantadine, mixed with zolpidem, methadone and amphetamine. Unfortunately, our chemists haven't been able to work out the right proportions of each drug," she said, pointing at the rat.

The second rodent had collapsed on its back with its feet in the air.

"We keep trying different ratios. We have some very good chemists and lab technicians in other locations. But as you can see, we're not there yet. What I do know is that the hospitals in

Oxford have found a more effective blend. Thanks to FRJ they have incredible resources and multiple SED survivors on whom they can experiment. The problem is, they're deliberately not taking the opportunity."

"Why not?"

She sighed as she covered up the cages. Glancing at the two men, she wondered if she were right to involve them in such a risky project. "Let me put it this way," she said. "When there is money, serious money, to be made, priorities change. Finding a cure or a vaccine is less profitable. Better instead to produce a drug that is only partially effective. The Panic is making some people very rich."

14

A desperate scream resonated through the walls. It sounded like the gurgle of someone drowning. Nick bolted upright in his bed, turned on a light. Quickly he jumped out of bed and went to his housemate's room, expecting the worst.

Robert wasn't there. Nick checked the bathroom, then the lounge and kitchen. Nothing.

Maybe it came from another flat in the building, he thought. He stood by the window, listening. Silence. *Or perhaps I imagined it.* Taking out his mobile phone from his pocket, he called Robert. It was almost four in the morning.

"Rob?" He could hear jazz music playing in the background.

"Yes. Is that Nick?"

Nick sighed, relieved.

"Nick, is everything OK?"

"Yeah I'm fine. Just checking in. Where are you?"

"The Harlington Arms. The music is cheesy but the coffee is as cheap as the booze and it stays open all night. Come join me if you want."

"Nah, I'm good. Have a whiskey for me."

"Sure."

Nick hung up. He tapped on his phone and opened the photos app, started to look at old snaps of his father and sister. But he couldn't bear seeing their faces smiling back at him right now in the middle of the night. So he quickly flicked through to the few more recent photos he had, mainly of him and Kiyoko. *If only I could talk to her now*, he thought. The scream must have come from one of the adjoining flats, it sounded so close. But there was no point checking or calling the police. They wouldn't answer the door at this time, and the police would never come. Nick sighed, realising he didn't even know any of the neighbours.

He went to the window and stared out at the night sky. A thin sliver of the moon was visible through the clouds. He thought again about Kiyoko and her last clients, hoped and prayed that she was doing OK.

"It must have been about one in the morning when it happened," Kiyoko had told him. "A full moon lit up the room. The father was fast asleep when the boy woke up. He couldn't have been more than ten or eleven years old. Sumon Chakma – that was his full name. Sumon sat up in his bed and stared straight at me. No, more like through me. His eyes were open yet completely vacant. He brought his hands to his face and I remember thinking, *Oh shit, what should I do, please god don't make this happen, don't let him die. He's just a kid.*

"At that point the boy let his hands drop and rose from the bed. He walked over right to where I was sitting. 'I forgot to feed the goldfish,' he murmured. It was then I realised he was sleep-walking. 'Sumon, go back to sleep, right now,' I told him, trying to sound both authoritative and calm. He nodded but walked instead to the window, where he opened the curtains a crack.

"'Nobody knows,' he whispered, staring out the window.

His voice was mature beyond his years. 'Not a single person realises,' he continued. 'Not you, not even Rosanna Day. So much needless suffering. The world is irreparably damaged: mankind has lost its way. A rottenness gnawing through our insides, greed and selfishness destroying what once was good. Our hearts are hollow, we have forgotten how to live. Kindness, respect, love. The well is dry.'

"Then his voice changed, a convincing impression of a woman's voice. 'Help me!' he cried. 'I shouldn't be here!' I asked him who this was. I thought he would say Rosanna Day. Not that I believe in those things, but, you know. Anyway, the boy said his – no – her name was Rosa Newton. Told me she was trapped, that she couldn't escape. They were experimenting on her. 'Don't let them remove it', she moaned. 'What are they trying to remove,' I asked.

"The boy turned away from the moon and looked straight at me with his blind eyes. 'My soul,' he said, still in the woman's voice. I told myself that he was asleep and didn't know what he was saying. The boy walked away from me then and crept back into bed."

Kiyoko went on to describe how she woke the boy's father a couple of hours later, and then the two of them had struggled to wake the boy. They shook him, turned the lights on, played music. When they finally succeeded in waking the boy, the three of them shared a light breakfast. The boy didn't say a word throughout.

The father told Kiyoko that they were leaving Oxford. His wife had died from the Panic, and they were quickly running out of money. He was nervous the authorities wouldn't let them leave, despite their papers being in order. They were from Bangladesh, unfortunate enough to have recently gained UK residence visas.

HYPNOSIS

April

15

Rosa stared at the streaks of amber and red colouring the sky. She stood up from her chair on the veranda, wiping tears away from her cheeks.

The marksmen had shot them dead, just like Shaw had warned they would. Three muffled shots rippling through the air, each meeting its target with perfect precision. Rosa stood there, frozen, her would-be kidnappers or rescuers lying lifeless on the ground. A woman wearing a khaki army outfit appeared from behind Shaw's car. She placed her rifle carefully on the tarmac, held up her hands in a passive gesture, then started walking slowly towards Rosa.

"Rosa, it's OK. We won't hurt you," she said.

"Why, why, why!" Rosa screamed, over and over.

"We'll explain everything, I promise. It's all over now."

Rosa saw two other snipers appearing in the car park. For a moment she thought of running, but she quickly realised it would be futile. So she stood there and waited, starting to shake as adrenaline gave way to shock.

Shaw survived, or at least that is what they told Rosa. Beneath his bulky jumper he had supposedly been wearing a bullet-proof vest. John Okoro said that Shaw had undergone successful surgery, though he was still confined to a wheelchair. Rosa even received a handwritten letter, purporting to be from Shaw, in which he confirmed he was well on the way to a successful recovery.

In the letter, Shaw apologised to Rosa for still not having a release date. He regretted promising her something that, in hindsight, was based on hope rather than certainty. *SED is like a tsunami flowing over flat land*, he wrote. *Retreat is the sensible option, at least for now. However, it is imperative that we also create a stronger barrier. This barrier resides in you, Rosa. Help us find it, so we can share it with the world.* Shaw ended the letter by saying how he looked forward to meeting her again once he had recovered, when, together, they could continue to make progress to stop this terrible illness.

There was no such attempt of friendship by Godley, promoted from chief scientist to replace Shaw as director. Sessions with her became even more formal than they had been before her promotion. They met once a week, on Wednesdays, as Rosa had done with Shaw, but the meetings were always in her office in the main building. She told Rosa that it was too risky to leave the Cloxham Manor grounds. Until recently, the meetings had seemed entirely banal to Rosa. Godley would, after some half-hearted pleasantries, pepper her with questions and demands. How was she sleeping? Was her appetite OK? How was she finding the extended sessions with John? What about her diary, was she really putting enough effort into that? Did she realise how important it was for her entries to be sincere reflections of her experiences, thoughts and dreams? They were always the same kind of questions, and not once did Godley reveal anything personal about herself.

However, that all changed yesterday. Rosa was unenthusiastically reciting one of her standard answers to a standard question when Godley interrupted her.

"Rosa, you are not trying hard enough. You need to fucking grow up now, or else I'll..." she said, letting the words hang in the air between them.

Rosa involuntarily flinched, for a moment expecting Godley to stride over and hit her.

"Listen to me," Godley said, visibly struggling to contain her anger. "You have to understand how important it is that you fully cooperate. There are now hundreds of new SED cases every day. And you are the only person who has made a complete recovery."

"I'm not sick," Rosa protested, "and I've never had SED. Yes, I had a serious heart condition as a child. But that has nothing to do with all this."

Godley was not listening, though. "It is my duty to find out why," she said, "and I will."

Godley stood up abruptly from behind her desk. "Come with me. Now," she said tersely. "I have something to show you that will help you understand."

She led Rosa out of her office. They walked past the main reception area – Rosa was aware of people consciously averting their eyes – then through a door beneath the staircase. The door was easy to miss, painted the same creamy white as the wall. Beyond the door stretched a long, narrow corridor, and at the end, a glass-fronted lift.

Up to that point, Rosa had assumed the main building was like the few National Trust stately homes her parents had taken her round as a teenager: grand, slightly dilapidated rooms, oil paintings of barely notable dignitaries, never anything particularly unusual. But as the lift door closed behind her, she knew Cloxham Manor was different. It took a long time before they reached the lower level, and when they arrived, Rosa was shocked at what she saw.

"This is why I need you to cooperate, Rosa," Godley told her as she pressed a passkey against a steel door.

Rosa glanced back at the lift, wondering for a moment if she should make a run for it before discounting the idea. Even if she could outrun Godley, there would be people waiting for her.

The steel door opened into a long, windowless corridor. It smelt musty.

"Don't worry, they can't see or hear you unless we want them to," Godley said loudly, stopping outside the first cell. Inside was a boy around fourteen years old, lying motionless on a bed. "The glass is one-way and the units are soundproofed."

Rosa peered through the glass. Wires were attached to his head in much the same way they were to her when she slept. However, his arms and legs were shackled.

"Why are you doing this?" she asked, trying to keep calm.

"Watch," she said, leading Rosa to the next unit. In it was a girl of similar age to the boy or slightly older. She was trudging up and down within the tiny confines of her cell, pulling at her straggly, unwashed hair.

Godley pressed a button on the wall.

"Helen," she said. The girl stopped, looked up at the ceiling then around her cell. She pulled at her hair.

"Helen, tell me. What did you dream just now?"

"I don't know," the girl said, hugging herself. "I never know," she wailed.

"Thank you," Godley said, pressing again the button outside the girl's cell.

"What does that prove?" Rosa asked.

"You remember your dreams, don't you?"

"Some of them, yes. So what?"

"My colleagues will explain," Godley said, leading her farther down the corridor. There were twelve cells in all, within each of which an emaciated teenager wandered back and forth like a caged animal, their eyes dulled and forlorn. Lillian and others had previously described the fragile condition of SED survivors kept at Cloxham Manor and elsewhere. Still, it was different seeing them herself, especially as no one had told her they were kept like this.

After the last isolation unit, there was a padded barrier. Godley pressed her identity card against a card reader. The barrier opened and she ushered Rosa into a small hallway.

In front of them was another door. Godley pressed a button and spoke into a microphone next to the door. "Five seven three zero two nine," she said, apparently unconcerned that Rosa heard. There was a high-pitched beep, after which the door swung open.

They entered a brightly lit office. Two armed men saluted Godley as she entered whilst a third man with thick spectacles sat watching a row of screens streaming live video of the inmates.

"Gentlemen, you know who Rosa is," Godley said. "She's here to better understand how dire the situation is. Dr Lee, can you tell her about our SED survivors living here."

"Yes," the man with the thick spectacles replied. Rosa thought she noticed a hint of discomfort in his eyes, but she couldn't tell if it was because of her or Godley. "These twelve patients are rare cases. All of them have survived for over a month after the initial bout of hysteria, though none of them would have remained alive unaided."

His voice sounded detached, as if he were relaying scientific findings at a conference.

"Each of them is listless," he continued. "They are not interested in reading, music or television. Most of the time they just stare silently at the walls."

"That's not quite accurate, Joo-Young," Godley said. "They do react to certain videos, don't they?"

"Yes, that's right. It is also true that they seem to be fully self-aware and cognisant of their surroundings. Like many SED survivors, all twelve are teenagers."

"Indeed. Now, can you explain to Rosa what these graphs show?" she asked, pointing to an A3-sized printout pinned to the wall.

"Certainly. This graph shows the results of an EEG machine used to monitor sleep. And this," he said, tracing a red-coloured line on the graph, "is a theta wave, characteristic of the early stages of sleep. As you can see, the peaks and troughs of this line are much less marked than the others. A healthy individual would subsequently enter a deeper stage of sleep characterised by larger delta waves. However, those afflicted by SED never leave the early stages of sleep."

"What Dr Lee hasn't told you," Godley interjected, "is that you have near-identical sleep patterns."

"I knew that already."

"*Near*-identical is the important distinction. Our EEG results indicate that you have the same shallow theta waves lasting much longer than they should. The interesting difference is that REM, rapid eye movement, the period of sleep in which dreams are most lucid, punctuates your sleep regularly. SED survivors do not exhibit REM. They don't dream. Except, that is, just before and after the hysteria strikes."

"I don't believe it."

"Self-enucleation is the scientific term," Godley continued, ignoring Rosa. "Usually done with the index finger and thumb pressing backwards into the eye. Some scientists believe it to be a deep-rooted survival mechanism. One that takes over when the brain malfunctions, that point when life just seems completely unbearable. A crude way of shutting everything out, you could say."

Joo-Young coughed. "Dr Godley," he said, pushing up his glasses on his nose, "shouldn't we be adhering to the guidelines?"

"Now, Rosa, there's one more thing," Godley said, ignoring Joo-Young. "I want you to see this directly. Then you will better understand why it is so important to me that you try harder, that you really cooperate. See that girl in unit nine, on the screen there?"

Rosa nodded. It was Helen, the girl Godley had briefly spoken to earlier.

"I want you to watch how she reacts to something. Joo-Young, please turn on the video in unit nine."

"Are you sure? We're making progress, however slow. Andrew Shaw required us…"

"I don't care what Shaw did or didn't say," Godley snapped. "I am the director now. When I ask you to play the video that is what you will do. We have the keys. It's easy to unlock her cell if we need to."

"But, and I say this with all due respect, it is against the regulations."

"With due respect, Dr Lee, I have the ultimate authority in such matters. Now, if you don't play it, you will be relieved of your duties, and others will be tasked to clean up your mess."

Joo-Young nodded without looking at Godley. "You will find this uncomfortable," he warned Rosa. "But remember this – none of it is your fault."

"What if I don't want to see it, whatever it is?" Rosa asked. "You may have me locked up here, Godley, but you can't force me to watch it."

"I'm sorry, but I can," she said, with what seemed to be the slightest hint of a smile. "It would be much more comfortable for you, though, if you watched it without any physical pain."

Rosa hated her then, even before they played the video.

On Godley's command, Joo-Young transmitted the video to unit nine.

The girl stood transfixed. Her mouth dropped open and she stared at the screen with a crazed intensity. "No, no, no," she started to say, her voice a faint whisper. All colour had drained from her face.

Rosa shut her eyes. But immediately a sharp electric shock administered by Godley forced her eyes back open. She wished she had been brave enough to keep her eyes closed, but the pain was too much.

"Stop it," Rosa pleaded. "Whatever you are showing her, stop it."

Godley ignored her. The video continued to play and they all watched it happen.

The girl had already ripped out clumps of her flaxen-blond hair. It was as if she was in a nightmare but couldn't wake up. The girl looked at the hair in her hands, then directly at the video screen. Rosa recognised the anguish in her eyes.

"Stop it," Rosa shouted. "Stop it now!"

"Not yet," Godley said. "Every case has its trigger. For this teenager, it is your lady with the red scarf, who you saw at the train station. That is what's on the video. Must be more than a coincidence, don't you think?"

"I don't care; just stop it!"

"Joo-Young, wait until the end of stage one. The medics are on call, right by her cell. She'll be OK."

"You heartless bitch! Stop now!"

"Shush. She's going to speak any moment now."

They waited. Then, finally, the girl spoke. "Deep down, it festers," she muttered, "and there is nothing else."

The teenage girl backed away from the screen and sat down

on the edge of her bed. "If your right eye causes you to sin," she said calmly, raising her hands, "gouge it out and throw it away."

Joo-Young quickly tapped on the keyboard then, and the video stopped. But not before the girl had started to tear at her face.

16

The sun sank beneath the brick wall that surrounded the garden. The recently planted primroses seemed fragile, their petals limp and dull. Her failed escape seemed like a lifetime ago.

Rosa walked to the end of her enclosure, pulling her jacket close around her waist. The broken glass on the wall caught the sun's fading light. *Godley may have forced me to watch the girl, but I am resilient*, she reminded herself. *They cannot reach my heart and soul. They will never break me.*

When this epidemic is over, a judge will sentence Claire Godley. And if there is no judge and jury, I will seek her out. She will face justice one way or the other. The others, too, most of them are complicit. Joo-Young and Fersatan. Maybe even Shaw. He was the director before, after all. It doesn't matter that he treated me well in the short period I knew him. Perhaps not all Nazi concentration camp guards were evil, but that didn't excuse their actions. For if Shaw were truly a principled man, he would have helped me leave this place. Like Lillian had tried. At least that is how I want to remember her.

She pictured the teenage girl again, ripping at her own eyes.

The medics would have reached her in time, she told herself, so don't think about it. But what about the video? Was it possible that the girl saw Edith Dubois, the woman who might also be her biological mother? No, it didn't make any sense. Godley had lied to her. Like she herself had done this morning to John Okoro, when she told him that she'd dreamt about the woman with the red scarf. The truth was that she had dreamt about a young boy talking in his sleep. She lied because she didn't want to introduce a new set of questions about some kid she didn't even know.

And what about John, she wondered. She still couldn't decide whether he was on her side. She wasn't even sure if he was privy to what Godley had shown her in the cells yesterday. Their meetings were, on the whole, formal and structured. John would explain to her the results from the EEG machine, then ask her a series of questions about her dreams and memories. Yet it didn't feel entirely one way. She had also learnt a little about his personal life. Certainly, the sessions felt less contrived than those with Godley and Fersatan.

John once told her how despite being relieved his family was safe in Nigeria, he was sad that he rarely spoke with them. It wasn't simply the internet and phone restrictions the British government had put up, for there were ways around that. John had been separated from his wife for a couple of years, and not long before the start of the epidemic, she had asked for a divorce. They had simply lost touch, he admitted to Rosa. He still loved and respected her, and he adored their sons, yet still they had grown apart. For the longest time, his research had consumed him, and now it was too late.

Rosa thought about her own brief marriage then, something she rarely dwelt on. In hindsight, they had both been too young. She was twenty-one years old at the time, Patrick a year older. They had eloped to Paris, and the whole time it seemed like they were in love. Yet less than a month after their arrival, he disappeared. In a hastily written note, he apologised for leaving her so suddenly and promised that one day he would explain. When she returned to London, the divorce papers had already come through, and in all the years since she had never heard from him.

———

"Evening, Rosa; it's time. Are you ready?"

It was John Okoro. Rosa looked at him without responding, turned away.

"We can start the session out here on the veranda, if you prefer," John continued. "It's surprisingly mild for April, isn't it? The days are getting longer, thankfully."

"Inside is fine," she said without making eye contact.

They went back inside. John made a pot of tea, and they sat by the window with their hot drinks.

"So, Rosa, how have you been today?"

"Absolutely wonderful."

"Fair enough," John replied, putting down his cup. "It was a stupid question."

Rosa sighed. "Look, I know you're not allowed to say much about... about anything really. But please, before we start the session, tell me at least something about what's happening outside. It doesn't have to be anything particularly important. I know this country is falling apart, but just tell me something real, however trivial. Like the latest films, music, books, celebrity gossip, anything."

"I think I can do that," John said, a hint of a smile visible. "Now let me see. Something interesting but that will not get me into deep water. Yes, I've got one. Did Lillian or anyone else ever tell you about the Red Hysterics?"

"No."

"Good! They're a controversial punk band from New York.

Their debut album and accompanying video caused quite an uproar. All screeching guitar riffs and crazy drumbeats. At the end of "Night Freak" the lead singer screams for a full ten seconds."

"Wow."

"Officially their music's been banned in the UK, but it's easy enough to bypass the internet controls and download their songs. There's a rumour that they'll come perform in the UK, even with the strict travel ban."

"Are they popular?"

"Yes, though a lot of people hate them, too. They are either ground-breaking or disrespectful, depending which side of the fence you sit on. Their lyrics are all about conspiracy theories."

John stopped. "Hmm, I'm getting carried away. Now you'll ask me whether I like them and I'll land myself in trouble."

"Do you?"

John smiled. "I think they're original, and some of their songs are actually pretty catchy. Still, I do think their lyrics go a bit too far sometimes."

"Sounds like a government employee's answer," Rosa said, and they both laughed.

"Right you are. Right, we had better get on with the session now. And I should tell you straightaway that it won't be an easy session. What I've been instructed to show you might be... confusing."

"Right. Is this the new programme Godley mentioned?"

"No. That will start tomorrow. Now can you have a look at this photo?"

He brought out an iPad from his briefcase and handed it to Rosa. On the screen was a photo of Edith Dubois, the woman with the red scarf. The same photo Lillian had shown her early on.

"You guys have shown this to me before," Rosa said.

"Yes. But here, swipe to the next photo."

Rosa did so and saw what looked like the same woman standing on a train platform. It was hard to be sure, as the image was grainy. But she was wearing a red scarf.

"Does she look like you remember her?"

"Maybe. It's hard to tell from CCTV footage. What's the point of this, John?"

"It'll be clearer soon, I promise. And these images aren't from CCTV. They're restricted files recently acquired from the military. Only with Shaw gone have we been able to access them."

"What? Why?"

"Bear with me. Now, please look at this next set of photos."

First John showed her two figures standing beyond the woman, standing near the platform edge. Then he swiped to another photo of the same two figures, zoomed in but slightly blurred. It looked like an adult and a young child.

"What is this?" Rosa asked nervously.

"Quite possibly they are the individuals the woman is looking at. We've had this part of the photo digitally enhanced using some clever software. Here," he said, taking the iPad back for a moment. With Rosa watching, he tapped the screen. An orange square was overlaid over the child's face. After a few seconds, the image became much clearer.

"That can't be!" Rosa exclaimed, recognising the child as her five- or six-year-old self. "And anyhow, I was much older than that when I first saw the woman at the train station."

"It can be hard to remember back to such a young age. Yet I can assure you that image is of you as a young child."

"Maybe it is," she replied, trying to stay calm. "But so what? Why does it matter?"

"Because of who you are with," John said. He manipulated the iPad's screen so that it focused on the adult next to the young Rosa. The device took a few moments to refocus.

A young man in military uniform. Not her father, that

much she knew. The man did look familiar, though. She tried to place his features. It couldn't be her biological father either, could it? She had been adopted when she was only a few months old. He wouldn't have come back for her, would he?

"Who is that man?" she asked, aware she didn't know what her biological father looked like.

"He had a moustache back then. Still, his features are the same: the high forehead, narrow face, and those light blue eyes – almost transparent in colour – that don't seem to fit with his dark hair. I recognise him. Don't you?"

"No, I don't. John, are you going to tell me who he is or not?"

"It's Andrew Shaw."

Lying in bed, ignoring the wires and tubes as best she could, she considered the facts again. A twenty-five-year-old photo of her and Shaw. Was it possible? They could have easily manipulated the image, combined two photos into one. But why? What would be the point?

To find out about me, the voice murmured inside her head. An ageless voice from another time, coming back to her again. *About our past and future lives.*

"Shut up," Rosa muttered under her breath. "Whoever or whatever you are, shut up."

You know who I am, Rosa. I'm Ana, your guardian angel. You called me that.

"Not any more I won't."

Ana is pretty, better than those other names some give me.

"You are nothing; nameless."

Don't fear me. Remember how I saved you once.

"Yes, but you also knew these terrible things were going to happen, didn't you? I still remember your hysterical cries days before my father's death, shrieking in my head. I didn't understand it at the time."

My dear Rosa, I am nothing more than what you make of me. The Panic resides in all of us. You understand that as well as I do.

Rosa shut her eyes, concentrating on her breathing. In her mind she evoked her family in their old living room, the three of them watching intently as she was about to perform her magic trick. She conjured images of the sea, waves gently lapping against the shore. Yet still Ana remained there.

I mean you no harm. I can only speak the truth, however painful it is. The Panic has always been. Across time and civilisations. A collective fear, long dormant, now emerging from a shared dream. Like a cold chill in your heart, a nagging sense that you have lost touch with what it means to be human. Yet it doesn't have to be that way.

"What do you mean?"

But there was no response. Opening her eyes again, staring at the feeble moonlight behind the curtains, she wondered if the scientists knew about this voice she called Ana. Maybe she had talked in her sleep, unwittingly revealing her hidden madness, the presence she had concealed so well all these years. Or maybe they had hypnotised her – not that she remembered any hypnosis sessions – and she had told them then.

No, Ana was too clever for that. She knew how to stay hidden. An ethereal presence waiting in the shadows, carefully observing Rosa and the world about her.

Rosa closed her eyes. *If I were braver,* she thought, *I would have tried to escape again. I* could have used the gym weights as a weapon. Thrown a dumbbell at one of the scientists, knocked them unconscious and stolen their keys. Then quickly slipped through the courtyard and into the larger complex, and somehow found a way out.

But would I really have been able to hit one of them? Not

John Okoro; he's a good man, I think. I couldn't even take out Dr Fersatan, despite the way he looks at me and his suggestive comments, and despite the likelihood he probably watches footage of me undressing. Even if I had been able to hit one of them, Claire Godley would be out there waiting for me. She would have me handcuffed, then lecture me yet again for not trying hard enough. This time, though, she would tell her minions to tie me down and dig in with their scalpels. Dissect my brain and leave me a gibbering wreck.

17

"Can you hear me? Rosa, can you hear me?"

The voice floated to her in the darkness. She was vaguely aware of the profusion of tubes and wires attached to her. Her body twitched involuntarily.

"This is Claire Godley. I know you can hear me now. Listen carefully. I am going to start with some simple yes or no questions. When we are done, I will say the trigger phrase, 'LC plus is the one', and then you will wake up. OK?"

"Yes."

"Good. Let's start with what you can last remember dreaming. Was it about the lady with the red scarf?"

"No."

"Your adoptive parents?"

"No."

"Andrew Shaw? Lillian?"

"No."

"The teenage girl in unit nine?"

"No."

"Do you remember anyone from your dreams last night?"

"No."

"Think harder, really try to picture it. Beyond the half-formed shapes and sounds there should be someone or something more specific. Can you picture it now?"

"No."

"Think back to when you were fourteen years old. You'd had your first lucid nightmare. The one where you are standing alone in the middle of a great emptiness. Is this what you were dreaming?"

"No."

"Or when you were a young infant. Waiting in a derelict farmhouse in rural Norfolk, surrounded by fields of wheat. The men in uniform approaching. Is that it?"

"No."

"All right. I want you to go back to sleep, and then we shall try once more. This will be the last time today. Right. Now, I just need to do this, a tiny pinprick on your arm. There we go. I will come back in a couple of hours and we'll have another chat then. Do your best to remember."

The medicine quickly registered, and Rosa felt herself falling back into unwanted sleep.

Her eyelids fluttered. She couldn't see anything. She didn't quite know if she was awake or asleep. Then she felt a jolt as a needle was plunged deep into her thigh. The pain extended quickly up her body. A sharp, clamping pressure, like every muscle was being forcibly contracted. From far away she heard whimpering. It sounded like a caged animal. Desperate, she implored Ana to come, but Ana and everything else seemed far away.

"Don't worry about a thing," she heard someone say. "I'm

doing this to help you understand." A man's voice, with a slight lisp. It was Dr Fersatan, Lillian's replacement. She heard the whimpering again and realised it was herself, trapped in some semiconscious state.

"It's like hypnosis, only stronger," he said. "Better not to fight it."

Gradually she became aware that someone or something was moving on top of her. It was an obscure, blunted sensation, yet she knew it was happening. Her heart beat hard and fast, the rush of adrenaline telling her that something was wrong and she should run. But her body was paralysed; there was nothing she could do.

"Don't fret, sweet darling. That was just an alternative introduction into Lillian's theory of the Panic. Delusions and suicide, a mass hysteria born from primal fears. From my understanding, she meant to explain this to you. Of course, she never had the chance, thrown out for her controversial views. Though I for one think her views are more credible than hypotheses based purely on as yet undiscovered bacteria or viruses."

Rosa couldn't move or see, but she could hear him clearly enough. She desperately wanted to scream, but even her voice was frozen. Just as she felt herself losing control, a presence came into her head, silently calming her. Ana.

"It's all under control," Fersatan continued. "The medication will wear off eventually. Right, how should I continue? By telling you about the origins of the term *hysteria*. A classical introduction, Lillian would approve. Hysteria comes from the Greek word *hystera*, which translates as "uterus." Hippocrates, one of our historical giants of modern medicine, believed *hystera* to be unique to women, caused by disturbances to the uterus. So severe it could lead to temporary blindness, or worse. What I did to you just now was not so different from the treatment typical in the eighteenth century, treatment that I like to believe can be highly effective.

His words passed by like leaves floating in water. She heard and didn't hear, was aware then unaware, each moment fleeting and possessed by the dark confines of sleep.

Forgive, Ana's voice murmured.

I can't, she thought.

You must. Even in evil, an innocent soul is hidden.

"But thanks to Freud," he continued, oblivious to Rosa's struggles, "we learnt that hysteria is not uniquely a disorder of women. Building on the work of Charcot, Freud taught us that hysteria relates to our subconscious. It is a way of dealing with our worst nightmares, the ones that haunt us when we least expect them. Hysteria, then, is a by-product of something that protects us from the intolerable. A way of temporarily shutting down the mind.

"For SED patients, though, this something that protects us is absent. Indeed, our research suggests that the afflicted suffer from a nightmare so profound, so central to their very being, that they simply cannot cope with life. Crucially, they are deluded into believing that in this nightmare lies a fundamental truth. Lillian might have speculated that it relates to the classic philosophical problem of evil. Or worse still, the recognition that this evil resides within us. I believe that, and I can live with it. For the afflicted, though, the only solution is to tear out the evil. If your right eye causes you to sin, gouge it out and throw it away, as the Bible taught us.

"That constitutes a large part of Lillian's theory. From hysteria to delusion to suicide. But what it doesn't explain is the collective nature of the Panic. For this, Lillian drew on historical cases to provide us with some important lessons. I don't mean the mass religious suicides that have plagued our societies. What Lillian was referring to were the cases of mass hysteria. The Salem Witch Trials, the Dancing Plague, the Hollinwell Incident, to name but a few. However, none of these examples was truly catastrophic. Innocent people died, yes, but nothing like on the scale of today's disaster.

"This is the big unknown. If the Panic is simply mass hysteria, why then are so many people dying? Perhaps these historical incidents are all linked. A manifestation of a collective delusion that is growing over time. Lillian's speculations, not mine. If that is the case, then why are you so important, Rosa? This is what I struggle to understand. Yes, your early childhood is shrouded in mystery, but that doesn't make you special. At best, you are fortunate enough to have immunity. Ultimately, though, you're no different. You are as rotten inside as the rest of us."

"Three, two, one, your eyes stay closed," Godley said. "Good, let your body relax. You are in complete control. I will ask you questions. Answer them if you can. Do you understand?"

"Yes."

"Good. Now, where are you?"

"I am standing on the train platform. I'm four or five years old. We are waiting to board a train that will take me away. I look up at the man holding my hand. Something is wrong."

"Is it Andrew Shaw? Tell me everything you see."

"I don't know. A young Shaw, perhaps. I'm not sure. The man looks no older than mid-twenties. Slim, tall, closely shaved hair, a thin moustache. Light blue eyes. He is dressed in a starched military uniform, carrying a canvas bag over his shoulder. He doesn't notice me glancing up at him, as his eyes are fixed on the fast-approaching train. I want to tell him that I don't want to leave, but I'm unable to speak. I try to let go of his hand, to move my feet, but they are stuck to the ground. With a great effort I turn around. Everything is frozen: the people milling about in the station are statues, the train a life-size replica of the real thing.

"Except, that is, for one person. The woman wearing the red scarf. Her scarf is a brilliant, scarlet-red. It stands out from the drab browns and greys of the station."

"What happens next?"

"She moves towards us in slow motion. It's as if she is struggling against time. She is far away yet I can smell her perfume. Lilac blossom, I think. Then I see her face properly. Her cheeks are puffy, the make-up around her eyes is smudged from crying. She doesn't look that much like me, but I know she is my biological mother.

"I can hear her now. 'Ana be safe, Ana be safe,' she says, over and over again. She stretches out her hand, desperately trying to reach me. But time has re-started and the man I am with has already lifted me onto the train. I look at her from the carriage door. Her eyes are downcast, her shoulders are slumped."

The scarlet-red brilliance of the scarf fades and merges into the browns and greys, all shapes become indistinct. In the darkness, a barn owl hoots then screams. A young boy approaches, raising his hands in front of him. He is blind.

"Rosa, can you hear me? Rosa, this is Dr Godley. Can you hear me?"

A multitude of bird wings flutter. Something is there, waiting. *Don't tell her. Don't say a thing.*

"I'm standing in the middle of a huge empty space," Rosa said. "The sky darkens. Light slips away fast as the sun is eclipsed. Silence, not even the birds make a sound. I'm petrified because I know it is there, a presence just out of reach.

"I know what will happen and it terrifies me. It's like seeing an enormous hive lying broken on the ground, wasps buzzing around and ready to swarm. Can you picture it, Godley?"

"What? Rosa, are you awake?" Godley asked, startled.

Rosa's eyes were half-open, but only the whites were showing.

"You asked me to tell you whatever I see, so that is what I'm doing. But I am scared for you. If Edith Dubois is locked up, how can I save you? And the blind boy is only a messenger. They will kill him, Lillian too, and many more innocents will die. Are you sure you want to continue?"

"Yes," Godley replied, trying to sound more assured. "I will tell you when to stop."

"Very well. The truth is simple. We are living in a time filled with great unhappiness. Love is consumed by hatred, compassion for others is lost to petty deceits. Desperate to appear successful, we trample over ourselves, break up what is good. Us versus them. They are the others, not one of us. They want to take our livelihoods, our wealth, our sense of who we are. Divide and hate. This mentality explains so much of our suffering. Godley, there is too much unnecessary conflict, we are overwhelmed by it. Subconscious, repressed emotions are transformed into physical illness, and we suffer an epidemic of horrific and lonely deaths.

Rosa felt herself rising then falling, falling, falling. Deep into a dark, impenetrable space.

"Now, Godley, it is coming for you," Rosa continued, the words tumbling out of her mouth. "I can hear it. It's there in the background, approaching. You can hear it, too, if you listen hard enough. No, it's not wasps buzzing. It is moaning, thousands of wretched moans in unison. They're clawing at your back, Godley. Whatever you do, don't go to sleep! Arms are flailing about, grabbing at your skin. You are sixteen years old and your father is there. This never happened but that doesn't matter. You can imagine it, like we all can if we think deep enough. It's one of our primal fears.

"You see the madness in his eyes, the moment before he strikes your mother, and yet you do nothing even though he will hit you next. Your fear is mixed with a shameful feeling. And all the time they are there in the background, moaning as one, arms flailing. They are distorted reflections of yourself, blindly clawing at your eyes."

"Stop! LC plus. LC plus is the one. Snap out of it, Rosa, right now!"

"It's too late. Your mother is lying on the floor. The right side of her face is badly bruised. She is crying. He hits her again and again until she is silent. Then your father sees you, as if for the first time. He raises his index finger to his lips, and then lowers it back and forth across his neck. It's your secret, yet everybody knows."

His voice came to her in the darkness. "You are sick inside," he said. "Hypnosis can only do much; I know my methods are superior. Because it's your fault Godley is dead. Your real parents also died thanks to you, all those years ago. And even though we carefully selected your foster parents, now they are dead, too. Your sickly virtue is a rottenness that infects and spreads like the plague. I feel sick from my desire for you, my craving to pull away your sheen of respectability. But that's what keeps me going. My superiors tolerate my perversions because I'm the best at reaching inside."

Rosa tried to move but every muscle seemed frozen. With a great effort she let out a tiny moan.

"Don't fret, my dear. There will be no more lessons about hysteria today. They politely asked me to refrain from such exercises this time. I do see the value, their arguments for keeping you alive. Population control, survival of the fittest and all that. Yet I still have my doubts. Andrew Shaw supposedly had concluded that killing you was the only solution. Yes, my darling, even with your long history together. That's why they let him be shot the time PureForce came for you.

"But let me come to the point. The purpose of this brief session is to inform you about the initial cause of SED. These are hypotheses rather than facts, I'll admit that, but they are evidence-based. SED's origins can help us better understand it, even if we still don't know how it morphed into today's hell hole.

Rosa listened without wanting to listen, her body completely inert.

"It goes without saying that what I'll tell you is strictly classified," Fersatan continued. "Not that I expect you to recall any of this when you wake. Even if you do, they'll never let you out. So are you ready? Groan if you are."

She heard herself involuntarily make a low, croaking sound. *Don't fight it*, Ana told her. *You are strong inside; nothing can harm you.*

"Well done. Now listen. We are confident the SED illness started in the military. Experimental research gone wrong. Only two years ago, a special training camp was set up in a secluded military base. They called it 'advanced combat preparedness,' with the specified aim of 'preparing soldiers for operations in every circumstance.' Or less euphemistically, to research effective means of sleep suppression. The objective was to create the ultimate soldier, true fighting machines who could operate effectively without sleep for extended periods.

"Twelve promising young officers were enrolled, each with combat experience. Of course, they weren't told of the real purposes of the training camp. For the first week the soldiers completed IQ tests, broken up by intense physical workouts. Then every night, before they went to bed, they were shown a video. A series of disturbing images, designed to test how well they could cope with the most traumatic of situations.

"Each morning the training started an hour earlier, until by the end of the first week, the soldiers were down to only two hours of sleep. From the beginning, additives were put into their food and drink. The problem was that although the additives stopped the soldiers from falling asleep, neither did they keep them fully awake. They became listless, unable to concentrate. They could not complete the physical workouts, their IQ test scores plummeted. But most of all, the soldiers struggled to cope with the video. Some started to hallucinate, shouting that they could see dismembered limbs, dead babies and other atrocities from the video. Others would try to comfort them, but soon enough they were all hallucinating the same horrific images.

"In the third week, two soldiers started fighting. It was soon after the video had been played for them. By this point, they were all down to thirty minutes of sleep a day. The two wrestled fiercely while the others formed a circle around them, chanting, "Fight, fight, fight," as if they were in a school playground. The researchers, safe in their viewing rooms, did not intervene. But then one of the soldiers slipped, giving the other the advantage. In an instant, he grabbed the prone man's head and violently twisted it to the side, breaking his neck.

"When he realised what he had done to his fellow soldier, he crumpled to the ground. Moments later, he started tearing at it his own eyes with his bare hands. The other soldiers stood there, transfixed. They didn't stop him. Within a few hours they were all dead."

Dr Fersatan fell silent. She could sense his innate humanity trapped deep inside, struggling to show itself. *It started much earlier,* she told him in her mind. *This illness has been with us for thousands of years.* For all this time it has been lying dormant in our hearts, but it is awake now, once again.

She saw her mother scratching at her eyes, the countless victims cutting and screaming, felt their pain coursing through her. *I am a deep well*, she told them all. *Thousands of years deep.* Let me take the pain from you; there is no need to suffer anymore. Life is filled with pain and suffering, but I can help you through.

18

"Rosa? Rosa, are you awake now? It's John Okoro."

"Yes," she rasped. She thought her eyes were open but she couldn't see anything.

"Let me help you with that," he said gently. "Keep your eyes closed for a little while, let them adjust," he told her, bending over her bed. Carefully he removed an eye mask, the EEG cap attached to her head, and several further wires taped to her wrists. She kept her eyes closed as he suggested, sensing bright lights on her eyelids.

"That's better. I must leave the needle in for now. It's for the IV fluid, nothing else. We can remove it once you've recovered your strength. How are you feeling?"

"Awful."

"Here, have some apple juice. It will help."

She opened her eyes, expecting the room to be filled with light. But it was dimly lit, one small night light in the corner of the room. John sat in a chair next to her bed, unshaven, his clothes crinkled. He looked worried. She felt conflicting emotions of anger at what they were doing to her and pity for this man who had always treated her with respect.

"I dreamt horrible things, John. Godley, Fersatan. Soldiers killing themselves. It seemed so real. Was it?"

John didn't answer, but she thought she could sense a deep sorrow inside him.

"How long have I been out?" she asked, sipping the juice through a straw.

"Three days, on and off. You've been drifting in and out of consciousness."

"What?! Why, John, why? Why are they, you, doing this to me? I don't understand. Can't you tell them to stop?"

"I'm sorry," he said, turning away, unable to meet her gaze. "It's complicated. What I can say is that I'll be conducting all the sessions from now on."

He sounded distant and aloof. She sensed something was wrong.

"It will be a little different from how Godley did it," he continued. "So I'd like you to answer one more set of questions."

"Really? Now?"

"Yes. Then I'll leave you."

She looked at him, but he didn't meet her gaze.

"John, I thought... I thought you were different. But you're not, are you? You're just as bad as the rest of them."

"I have some sketches here," he said, ignoring what she'd said. "I want you to have a look at them and the accompanying text. I want you to tell me how it makes you feel."

"What is the point? I'm done with all this bullshit."

"Rosa, please have a look. Then I'll explain as best I can. OK?"

"Fine. Not that it matters."

He handed her the folder. There was one of her pencil sketches of the woman with the red scarf that she had drawn for Lillian.

"Look at the second sheet of paper. Take your time."

She did as he said. The drawing this time was of a young girl lying in bed, wearing an EEG cap. Her eyes were half-open so that only the whites were showing. It looked very much like one of her sketches but she couldn't remember drawing it. Beneath the sketch was some handwritten text:

First of all: be careful. They are watching us. There are cameras hidden under the spotlights. So act like everything is the same. Now, the crux – I will help you escape. It is risky but we must try. You'll be drugged once more and this time for an extended period: days or even weeks. When you come to, you will be weak. Wait for me or Joo-Young Lee, and one of us will get you out. Don't trust anybody else.

One thing I must tell you: Godley is dead. Better you hear it from me than anyone else. She succumbed to the Panic. Her superiors think you were somehow responsible, but they are wrong. Godley's death had nothing to do with you.

Now, immediate practicalities. The sketch. After my prompting, tell me that you think the sketch is you, as a young child. Which in fact it is. They've been monitoring you for a long time. I'm truly sorry, Rosa. I believed it was better to be on the inside, but I was wrong. I never knew it would come to this. When we are safely out of here, I will tell you everything I know. I promise.

Rosa looked up at John Okoro, glanced around the room. She felt powerless. *I must stay whole*, she told herself, fighting back the tears. She shut her eyes, pictured herself on a makeshift raft, floating in a becalmed sea.

A nauseating stench filled the room. It smelt like something was rotting. She ignored it as best she could. *How long have I been unconscious*, she wondered. *Days, weeks even?* Once again, she tried to raise her arms so that she could remove the eye mask from her face, but she was too weak.

"Help," she croaked.

There was no response. A large fly or some other insect settled for a moment on her face. Then she heard it properly for the first time. Scores of insects buzzing incessantly. Another one landed on her, crawled over her lips. She tried to move her hands to brush it away, but they were frozen.

"Help me," she tried to shout, but the words barely left her mouth. She felt a panic rising. Desperate, she called to Ana in her mind. But Ana didn't respond.

Keep calm and concentrate, she told herself. Don't be weak; you can do this without Ana. So what if there are a few flies in the room. They didn't shackle you and you're not paralysed. Better to free yourself than wait for someone to appear. Move one arm and then the other. It will come. You've probably been out cold for a long time, like John had warned. You just have to relearn how to move. It's not really any different from when you broke your leg as a teenager. The physiotherapist taught you to stare at your toes until they moved, and it worked. Do the same now. It doesn't matter that you can't see, and forget that awful smell. Just visualise one of your arms, and it will be OK.

She centred her attention on her right arm, willing it to respond, and finally she was able to move her fingers. Concentrating hard, focusing directly on her arm, she managed to lift it to her face. Wires attached to her forearm strained as she removed the eye mask and the EEG cap.

The room seemed unbearably bright even though the shutters were closed. But worse was the smell, like putrid meat. Somehow, it was even more overpowering now that she could see. She noticed the window ledge was covered with flies, most of them dead.

"Is there anyone there?" she said, her voice a hoarse whisper.

Parts of a dream came back to her then. She was standing in an enormous hospital ward. There were hundreds of beds there, two long rows of them. As she walked along, she would peer at a bed now and then. Each time, the patient would be shaking violently, his or her arms and legs shackled, eyes covered by a mask. *They can't handle the truth*, someone said. *But you can help them, show them the way.* It was the same young boy who had appeared in her dreams before. *No. They don't deserve to be helped*, she had replied. *Let them suffer like I did.*

She removed the wires from each of her arms and the IV tube attached to the back of her left hand. Carefully she shifted her body until she was in a sitting position, her feet touching the carpeted floor. She wriggled her toes and moved her legs in small circles, unsure if they would be able to bear her weight.

Finally, she had the courage to stand up. Immediately, though, her legs gave way.

Lying on the floor she discovered the source of the rotting smell. It was Joo-Young Lee, or at least what was left of him. Stifling a scream, she crawled out of the room and into what had been her main living space. The veranda door was ajar. She listened intently, in case somebody was there. But the place was silent, other than the sound of birds calling out to each other.

She crawled towards the veranda. She could see the birds clearly now. A group of magpies hopping about on the back lawn, cawing excitedly. They were pecking at something lying motionless on the ground. She didn't need to move any closer to know what it was. Breathing in deeply, she tried to stay calm.

How long have I been unconscious? she wondered. *And what has happened to the world in all this time?*

CONSPIRACY

May

19

I t was almost midnight. Nick paced around in Kiyoko's living room, waiting for her to return. She wasn't due back for an hour, but he didn't know what to do with himself in the meantime. His mind kept turning over the different permutations of tomorrow's meet, the different ways it could go wrong. If Kiyoko were here, he knew she'd be able to help him think it through.

Lillian was due to arrive in Oxford the following day. It would be the first time she and Harold would meet, despite their dealings over the past months. Initially, Harold had told Nick he was willing to risk pilfering more of the medicine for a higher charge. Then at the last minute, Harold had added in a new condition – he would only sell if Lillian was there in person.

Nick sensed that Harold wanted something more than money from Lillian, and he'd try to extort it out of her one way or the other. He wanted inroads into Alliance, perhaps, or into PureForce. He had warned Lillian of his concerns, but she still insisted on coming. Given Nathan's relapse, she said there was no other choice.

At first, the limited amounts of medication Nick procured from Harold had been incredibly effective. On the third injection of MAZA (unimaginatively named after the active ingredients methadone, amantadine, zolpidem and amphetamine), Nathan awoke from his coma. Although he remained bedridden, he was able to communicate in short bursts. Nick had seen it with his own eyes.

What Nathan said wasn't always comprehensible, but the fact that he could speak at all was a significant breakthrough, as was the fact that unlike most other SED survivors he'd never tried to claw out his own eyes. However, a fortnight ago the medication ran out, and Nathan's condition had steadily worsened since. Now he was barely conscious and unable to string together more than a few nonsensical words at a time.

From her daily sessions with Nathan, Lillian learnt what had been done to him by the government. He had been locked up in a tiny underground cell. Chained to his bed whilst he slept, he was monitored twenty-four hours a day. Worst of all, he said, was a video that they played at regular intervals. They'd hold him down, inject something into his arm, then leave. Soon after, the video would start and he'd find himself standing in front of the screen, transfixed. He could only vaguely recall the content of the video – a series of disturbing images spliced together, each flashing on the screen just long enough that he could picture the blood or dismembered limbs or whatever atrocity they chose to show. But what he clearly remembered was the unbearable panic rising as the video rolled on.

Nick looked out the window. The streetlights shone dimly on the deserted street. He felt the craving, the first time he'd felt it in years. A quickening of the heart, a sudden rush of adrenaline, and with it an overpowering tunnel-vision focus on finding the next hit.

"When it comes, the itch, don't fight it," the counsellor had advised him at Narcotics Anonymous. "Instead, observe. As if you're outside of yourself. That surge, stronger than desire, it's there but it's not yours. Disown it. Then think about someone you respect, concentrate on him or her so that's all you can see and feel."

He shut his eyes, detaching himself from the sensation. He brought his sister back in his mind. Fourteen years old, sitting on the edge of his bed. She was listening to Van Morrison's *Astral Weeks* for the first time, her eyes shut so she could follow the ebb and flow of the music, unaware of how tightly she was holding the CD sleeve.

Nick thought he heard a knock on the door. He opened his eyes and glanced at his watch. It was only a quarter past midnight. He must have imagined the knock. Kiyoko said she'd be back no earlier than one. Still, it made him worried. Of course she's OK, he told himself. She knows how to look after herself.

Over the past couple of months, they had grown steadily closer. He'd even finally told her about his previous drug addiction and how his sister helped him overcome it. Kiyoko talked more about her studies and how she'd planned to apply to the International Red Cross after university. At least that had been her plan before the Panic.

If circumstances weren't so crazy, things may have moved faster between them. But the Panic – it made him more cautious, probably her, too. Lying together in bed was as far as it had gone. And he valued their friendship. It was good to have someone he could completely trust. Robert and his few other close friends were all hooked on the harder medications now, becoming more insular and paranoid by the day.

He pictured Kiyoko now, no more than a few streets away, watching over one of her clients sleep in the dead of night. She'd be humming softly, filling her head with positive images to keep a client's fears at bay. It seemed to work. Kiyoko had talked about setting up self-help groups where people could come together. She saw it as a way to channel positivity, to stop people spiralling into doubt and suicidal thoughts.He started worrying again. Perhaps one of her clients tonight had succumbed to the Panic. That would be awful to witness. The odds were not on Kiyoko's side. Although no one had died yet on her watch (and her reputation had grown accordingly), surely it was only a matter of time.

The epidemic had worsened considerably in the last month. Hundreds of thousands were now dead from the Panic, all across the south of the country. On the streets, everyone avoided eye contact, yet at the same time monitored others to make sure their eyes weren't closed. Those on the medication were the worst, flitting between a trundling daze and unpredictable mania. Whilst passers-by were always on the lookout for public sleepers, no one paid attention to people with odd tics or those arguing with themselves. Not even to those dying from exhaustion. The number of strokes and heart attacks had skyrocketed since the start of the epidemic. As long as people didn't kill themselves in public, that's what mattered most, it seemed.

Before too long, London would be like Oxford, isolated and unruly. The capital was already heading that way, with people fleeing and roadblocks rumoured. But the city was too large and porous to be managed. Whole London neighbourhoods were rumoured to have become like the anarchic Cowley Park in Oxford. The government was losing control.

And how about me, he wondered. *Am I still in control? I'm sleeping slightly better, only sell the weaker drugs now, and I don't take any myself. But is it enough? I'm still stressed out, wary of strangers, scared of what I might dream at night.*

He glanced around the room, noticing a new photo hanging on the wall. Kiyoko's parents, he presumed, smiling at the camera, the John Radcliffe library in the background. Her mother shared the same light brown eyes and delicate nose. Kiyoko had told him about their visit last summer. How different the world had been back then.

Knock, knock – someone was definitely rapping on the door now. As he approached the front door, it dawned on him that it probably wasn't Kiyoko. She had taken her key, so she could have just let herself in. Unless she was badly injured. But, then, would she have made it this far? He grabbed the hammer they kept on the sideboard and went to the door. Squinting through the peephole, he saw a young woman standing there.

"Who's that?"

"It's Teresa. Is Kiyoko there? I'm her old housemate. I used to live here."

"She's not in."

Teresa. Kiyoko had mentioned her a few times, though he thought she'd said Teresa was Scottish. Certainly, she'd never commented on her having such a posh accent.

Keeping the latch on, he opened the door a crack.

Slam! Suddenly the latch had smashed and the door was open. She kicked him hard in the groin. He doubled over and she kicked him again. Before he could respond, someone else was forcing his arms behind his back. His hammer fell uselessly to the floor.

"Help!" he shouted, as two men held him down. One of them had kicked the front door shut.

"Quiet," she hissed, quickly wrapping duct tape around his mouth. "Now get up," she said. As the men pulled him to his feet, she brought over a kitchen chair. He noticed one of the men carried a briefcase. "Sit down there, and don't you dare move a muscle."

After his hands and legs were tied, she sat down in the sofa opposite him. The two men stayed standing.

"Nicholas, do you have any idea why we are here?" she asked. "I'm not Teresa, if you haven't worked that out already."

Nick shook his head, wondering how she knew his name. One of the men was talking quietly into a phone.

"I thought not."

Nick tried to speak but the duct tape muffled his response. He was scared and angry. Most of all, though, he was worried about Kiyoko coming back while they were here.

"I can remove the tape, but if you shout or make any fuss, one of my men will kill you and Kiyoko, too. Understand? Good."

She motioned to one of her goons, and he pulled off the duct tape. It stung.

"What do you want? Drugs? Money?"

She stood up from the sofa. Without looking him in the eye, she came and sat on his lap, letting her breasts rub against him. He tried not to feel aroused. She touched his lips softly with her finger, and then spat in his face.

"The difference between you and us," she said, settling back in the sofa, "is that we are part of the struggle. PureForce. Whereas you make money from other people's suffering."

"I do it to make ends meet," he replied, feeling her spit drip down his cheek.

"Like your chinky girlfriend? Her watching over people is a pathetic business."

He looked at her with contempt. "I never knew PureForce was run by racist Nazis."

She nodded to one of her accomplices who was standing behind him. He came around to face Nick, punched him hard in the stomach.

"Don't be an idiot. PureForce is pure, unsullied, whereas you are part of a corrupt machine that wants the Panic to spread. FRJ, the government and middlemen like you. You've turned desperate people into addicts. They consume those unnatural concoctions and the machine keeps turning. How many customers do you have now?"

"I do it to make ends meet," he repeated. *I don't have wealthy parents to support me like you probably do, you spoilt, haughty brat,* he wanted to add.

One of the men came over and passed her his phone.

"Yes, this is Samantha. Tell him to inform Shaw what we have done," she said to the person on the other end of the line, then handed the phone back to her accomplice.

"Listen, how can I help you? I'll do whatever you want, as long as you leave."

"Who says we want anything from you?" Samantha asked. "We might be waiting for Kiyoko."

"Then you'll be waiting a very long time," he said as coolly as he could. He glanced up at the clock on the wall. It was twelve forty. If and when he heard Kiyoko approach, he would shout as loud as he could to warn her. It didn't matter what they did to him.

"Don't worry. We're not interested in her. We're more concerned by what you can deliver to us. Now, we know you meet regularly with a certain Harold Stone. And Harold has something we want: a video. It's very simple. He'll give the video to you if you can tell him where Nathan Newton is being hidden."

"Why? I thought PureForce helped rescue Nathan."

"We did. It's complicated."

"Fine, I'll do it. Now will you let me go?"

"Funny. Do you think I'm that stupid?" she said, standing up. "We need a guarantee that you'll fulfil your task. So we will wait for Kiyoko. When you have provided us with the video, we'll release her."

Nick looked at the woman and the two men, tried to stay calm.

"Don't worry. We won't hurt her, as long as you get that video. Now, I've got something else to help you see it through. Stuart, keep him still."

One of the men came over and held his shoulders down. He watched as the other man opened his briefcase and took out a bottle and syringe.

"Kiyoko," he yelled desperately, "if you're out there, run!"

Samantha quickly gagged him.

"Don't make it harder than it has to be," she said quietly, holding the syringe. It was filled with a cloudy white liquid. "What I'm going to inject into your thigh is not so different from the LC+ tablets. It's the same principle, just much stronger and with no downer. It'll keep you awake for longer than a week. When you bring us the video, we'll administer a neutral-ising agent."

She let her hand brush against his leg. "Without the neutraliser, you won't be able to sleep. Tomorrow you'll be mostly fine. Perhaps even the next couple of days you won't feel too awful. After that, though, you'll have thumping headaches, and then the hallucinations will come. Soon enough you won't know what is real and what is imagined. Though, of course, you should know all this already, given your drug peddling expertise. So make sure you get us that video."

She nodded to Stuart. He lifted Nick up whilst the other man pulled down his jeans, then sat him down in the chair again.

"Now, here it comes," she said, caressing his leg for a moment before jamming the needle deep into his thigh.

A huge rush of adrenaline surged through him. His muscles felt tense to the point of cramping, his senses were suddenly heightened. He heard the floorboards creak as Samantha's accomplices stood laughing at him, he smelt Stuart's stale body odour. Samantha herself stood a few feet away, observing him closely. He could see every detail on her face: the heavy, dark blue eye shadow, the mascara, the way her eyebrows had been neatly plucked, the unwavering certainty in her cold blue eyes, her thin nose and the way her nostrils quivered slightly every few breaths, the deep red lipstick that exaggerated her unsmiling expression.

He looked away from her, and around the room. Somehow, he could sense that Kiyoko was approaching the front door. He tried to shout out and warn her, but the duct tape muffled his voice. He heard a key turning, and Kiyoko was there, standing in the doorway and staring at him and then the others. Tears slipped down his cheeks as he saw Stuart walk towards her. What chance did she have?

20

"I can't do this," Nick told Lillian. His hands were shaking. Cowley Park had been worse than usual: he'd had to fight off more than one of the drugged-up revellers there, and that was in broad daylight. Now he and Lillian were resting in Bury Knowles gardens, a rare safe haven within Oxford. They had obtained the necessary forged documentation for Headington and were waiting for Harold's phone call. It was a bright, sunny day, and he knew they weren't in any immediate danger, yet still he felt on edge.

"Listen to me," Lillian said, turning to face him on the park bench. "The drugs are making you feel agitated. You have to consciously push yourself to relax. Breathe in and out, slowly. That's it. Now, try not to worry. It's all going to work out fine, I promise. Your bravery and skill brought us through that horrific place. The rest is easy in comparison. It's a straightforward transaction. On top of that, I have a contact working at the hospital who'll be looking out for us. Brian Bradley. He knows the situation and is a canny operator. He even has an apartment in the same block as Harold."

"What about Kiyoko? What's going to happen to her?"

Awful, depraved images filled his head, of the woman, the two men and Kiyoko. He felt himself shaking.

"Kiyoko will be fine. You must trust me on that. One thing I do know about PureForce is that they are ultra-logical. By that I mean they understand perfectly well that they'd be foolish to harm her."

"Why?"

"Because only you can obtain the video for them. And because they need to maintain a good relationship with my group. Not that I can trust them anymore."

"Maybe. Still, how do I know Harold will give me the correct video?"

"He will. He doesn't care about official government policy; he's above that now. Getting hold of Nathan is very important to him and FRJ, more important than this money he's earning on the side from our dealings. So I'm sure he'll be open to a deal. A way of safeguarding their investments, if you like. And if you're still not sure, you could ask Harold to play the video. You'll know whether it's genuine quickly enough."

"How?"

"It's the same one that Nathan described. You remember?"

"Yes." He recalled how Nathan had nervously recounted the blur of disturbing images, each flashing by before he could unscramble them in his head. That and the unbearable moaning.

"Don't watch too much of it. As soon as you feel... as soon as you feel nauseated, stop watching. OK?"

"Right."

Nick looked away from Lillian. His heart beat rapidly, as if he had just been sprinting. He stared out at the expanse of manicured grass, trying to slow his pulse. A middle-aged man was walking his dog, seemingly oblivious to the troubles, but otherwise the park was empty. Lillian had tried to hide her concern when he told her that he'd been drugged, yet it was obvious she was worried for him.

"Have you seen the whole video?" he asked her.

"Once. The government produced it, that much we know. Said it would help them understand the Panic. Rubbish if you ask me. It is horrific, but if you haven't been medicated, it is bearable."

Nick glanced around, clearly anxious. Their plans seemed so fragile. It was all going to unravel, he was sure of it.

"Don't worry, Nick. The medication I'm referring to is very different from whatever PureForce injected in you. You'd know by now if they'd drugged you with that."

"I guess that should make me feel better," he said, trying to make a joke of it. "Yes, it should."

Nick placed his hand to his chest. His heart was still beating hard and fast, his hands continued to shake. He wondered how long it would be before he started to hallucinate. Already Kiyoko's face kept appearing in his mind, looking at him as Stuart handcuffed her. Her expression seemed to tell him to remain calm, that somehow everything would be fine. He wanted to believe it but couldn't.

"Nick, you really have to try to relax," Lillian said. "Don't fight the medication. Your pulse rate will come down eventually. OK? Nick, do you hear me?"

"Yes."

"Listen, let me tell you something to take your mind off Kiyoko, our meeting with Harold, and anything else that might be worrying you. We have the time and this feels like an appropriate spot: a peaceful, open space not so far from where it all began. Will you listen?"

Nick nodded.

"Good. It's something I've wanted to share with you for a while, yet I've held back – it's hard to know whom to trust these days. I am certain, though, that I can trust you now. I want to tell you about my research and how it links not only to Nathan but also to Rosanna Day. We've talked about her before, but I never told you that I once knew her well. I'm telling you this because you are stronger than the drugs, and because I trust you."

"Rosanna Day is as remarkable and important as many of the rumours suggest," Lillian said, confirming what Nick had heard elsewhere. Lillian went on to describe how Rosanna was being held at Cloxham Manor, the short period during which she had worked there, and how she and others had tried but failed to help Rosanna escape. She also said it was true that Rosanna Day had suffered from something akin to SED as a child, long before the epidemic began. The only details she concealed were that Rosanna's real name was Rosa Newton and that Nathan was her brother.

"Do you think people could learn from her?" Nick asked. "Would they then be protected from the Panic?"

Lillian sighed. "Maybe, I don't know. This was one of the hypotheses I was trying to explore. I'd wanted to take Rosanna out, to share her sleeping experience with a wider audience. Unfortunately, though, other researchers held more influence than me at Cloxham Manor. Said she was a security risk, and that was that."

Windmill Road was quiet. There were no cars and only a few soldiers patrolling the streets. Many of the shops had been boarded up. Still, it felt more functional than other parts of Oxford. The cafes had regular customers; there were even a couple of open restaurants on the street, popular with the wealthier hospital workers.

"Is there never any unrest in Headington?" Lillian asked.

"Rarely. Their policing is very effective."

"Even with all the forged permits?"

"Yes. It's a regulated black market. You can only acquire acceptable forged permits from the Tonge building, where we got ours. A permit from anywhere else and you'll quickly be kicked out."

"I see."

"The Headington councillors make good money out of it. It's a low-risk arrangement for them. Acceptable forged permits are never valid for more than a day, and their price is set high enough to deter casual visitors."

A cafe door opened, and a couple of hospital workers came out. They walked past Lillian and Nick without making eye contact.

"Now, let's run through it one more time," Lillian said. "Whilst I'm waiting in the lobby downstairs, you'll tell Harold where Nathan is being hidden. Harold will probably call his contact to confirm. The same Brian Bradley who works with us. And although I doubt Harold will ask me about Nathan, if he does I'll feign surprise and indignation, before confirming Nathan is indeed being kept in Farmborough village."

"This Brian can definitely be relied upon?"

"Yes. He's proved his worth as a double agent before, more than once. I know it sounds complicated, but our group is sufficiently fragmented for it to work."

"I hope so."

They walked on. *When this is over*, Nick thought, *I'm going to head north and make a fresh start. Perhaps I can persuade Kiyoko to come with me. A picturesque village in the Lake District, up where the Panic has not taken hold. I have a little money saved, enough to keep me going. And maybe, when the situation has calmed down, I'll leave the country. Go to Canada, somewhere with wide-open spaces. I just hope and pray that Kiyoko will be OK. If only she could have heard me yell out last night.*

"Lillian," he said, stopping by a broken traffic light. "Are you sure it's all going to work out?"

"Yes. Look, I'm no hero. I'm just an academic with some theories about how we might combat this illness. But it will be OK. Believe me, it will. Brian is highly skilled in these more practical matters. He's done the groundwork for us already, assured me that contingencies are in place. He makes the Pure-Force people seem like amateurs. So please, try not to worry."

21

Harold looked terrible. There were dark bags under his eyes and his skin seemed ashen. He sat across from Nick, smoking a cigarette. When Nick told him about PureForce's request and what he could offer in return, Harold seemed uninterested. He went over to his study table in the far corner of the room. There he picked out a USB stick from beneath a pile of notes. "If that is what you need to rescue your Kiyoko," he said, "then take it. PureForce doesn't know what it's doing. And there's no need to tell me about Nathan," he continued. "I already know where he is. Let me show you what PureForce is wasting its time on."

Harold plugged the USB drive into his laptop. Together they watched the first few minutes. The video was just as Nathan had described. Indefinite images flickering by, hundreds of people moaning in unison. Nick's heart beat quickly, he felt nauseated, and yet he remained transfixed to the screen.

The camera panned out so you could gradually make out the source of the moans: men and women pulling their naked torsos – yes, just the torsos – across a dusty, parched expanse.

Every one of them had been chopped in half, entrails spread in a horrifying mess as they dragged their bleeding midriffs closer and closer, towards the camera. Their eyes were wild and desperate, pleading. It wasn't a movie, it was real, he was suddenly sure of it.

Harold stopped the video and handed the USB stick to Nick.

"What is this shit? Some cheap horror crap?" Nick said, nervous adrenaline flowing through him.

"I agree. It's disgusting the length to which the bureaucrats will go. Disgusting and pathetically misguided. They think they can understand SED through this? Stupid. Unless, that is, it's some clever ploy to lead PureForce down a blind alley. I highly doubt it, though. That would be giving the politicians far too much credit."

"I don't get it. Why does PureForce even want this?"

"Beats me. Anyway, we'll have to save that discussion for another time. Because before Professor Reilly joins us, I want you to hear my side of the story. I don't know exactly what she told you, or how you became one of their dealers, but you need to be careful. Seriously. OK?"

Harold tapped his cigarette on the edge of the ashtray. Nick watched him but didn't say anything in reply.

"Nick, I say that because I'm worried. You may see me solely as a business partner, but I like to believe we are...well, if not friends, at least that we're on the same wavelength. I've always valued your honesty in our transactions. I want to keep it that way."

Nick grunted equivocally.

"Let me keep it short," Harold continued. "I'll be the first to admit that Alliance has done some great work. Moreover, it was Professor Reilly who first identified the peculiar sleep patterns of those struck by SED. That was an important break-through. She is a talented if eccentric academic whose ideas have always interested me, despite our very different specialities."

He paused, absently touching his thinning hair.

"Now then," he continued, "I've learnt that her group may have recently made potentially vital inroads into a vaccine. That's good news, too, of course. However, in the process they are going to make some frankly outlandish allegations. The problem is, these claims will do more harm than good. My employers have asked me to ensure this doesn't happen."

Nick waited for him to continue, but Harold said nothing. Instead, he lit another cigarette and took a long, deep drag.

"What are these allegations?" Nick asked eventually.

"That the government is in cahoots with FRJ; and they want SED to spread."

"Lillian never mentioned this to me."

"If she hasn't told you yet, she will soon enough."

"Maybe. It sounds more like a PureForce conspiracy."

"Yes, but PureForce has no credibility, whereas Alliance has some respected and rather persuasive individuals. Such as Professor Reilly and Colonel Shaw," Harold said, looking at Nick.

"So?"

"They think they have sound, scientific evidence, but they're mistaken. The problem is, people may actually listen to what they have to say. That would cause a real panic, worse than the 'Panic' moniker used for SED. SED is controllable: sleep suppression works. Whereas if people thought the government and FRJ were involved, it would be a catastrophe. There'd be rioting in the streets. Worse, people might stop taking the tablets, and then the SED outbreak would really spread. The country would quickly descend into anarchy."

"Isn't it going that way already?" Nick asked. "Most of London will soon be like Oxford; there are cases all over the south now. Have you not seen how paranoid and fearful people are?"

"The situation is difficult, yes, but it's under control. People are doing OK. They're learning how to cope. I wish we could discuss more, but there's not enough time. Hopefully it's enough to help you understand my point of view."

Harold stood up. He patted his greased hair carefully, so that it partially covered his bald patch, then went over to the intercom. "Bring her up now," he spoke into the device.

"Wait. What are you going to do to her?"

"Why, Nicholas, who do you think I am?! First and foremost, I'm here to do business. I have secured sufficient MAZA, which I want to sell for the right price. And don't worry, you'll receive your fair share. As for her group's claims about the government wanting SED to spread, it can be resolved amicably enough. A simple phone call from her and the situation won't get out of hand."

"Really?"

"Yes. I don't want my colleagues to become involved if I can help it. There are so many risks and pitfalls, things that she and her group don't know about. All I want is for Professor Reilly to listen to reason."

"Fifty thousand pounds for twenty doses."

"But that's over twice what you charged before."

"Professor Reilly, you have to understand how difficult it has become for me to obtain MAZA. With the quantities you require, I need to bring others on board, and they won't collaborate for free."

"Call me Lillian, please. Now I understand your constraints. Still, you need to come up with a more realistic price than that if we're going to make a deal."

"It will be cheaper once the government officially approves it. However, that's a good six months away, maybe longer."

Lillian didn't say anything.

"Fine. Forty thousand."

Nick looked at Harold and then at Lillian. He felt like a spectator waiting for the main event. He was nervous but didn't know what to do. If only he could speak to Lillian in private. Earlier, he'd tried to signal to her that something was wrong, but she hadn't read his expression.

"Nicholas. Tell Professor... tell Lillian that forty thousand is a good price, given the situation."

"I don't know. It still seems a little steep to me."

"All right, all right. Thirty-five thousand pounds. That's my final offer."

"Fine," Lillian replied. "It's a deal."

"Smart girl." Harold smiled, leaning across the coffee table to shake Lillian's hand. "And here I was thinking academics couldn't do business. I'll be back shortly."

"Did he give you the video?" Lillian asked as soon as Harold had left the room.

"Yes, but listen. Harold already knows where Nathan is. He was more concerned about some allegations your group might make. Said it can all be resolved by a phone call, but I'm worried."

"How did they find out?" she said under her breath. "Damn, could it be Brian? He's always been reliable. But it's the only explanation that makes sense. If so, we're in trouble."

"What about your other contacts in the building? They know you're here, right?"

"Brian is our only contact. I should have picked it up in his voice when I spoke to him earlier. He didn't sound the same. Maybe I've made a mistake."

"Then we need to get out of here. Right now."

"It's too late for that. Security guards are outside Harold's front door. We'd never make it out. Our only chance is to convince Harold of the truth."

What's the point of that? he wanted to say. Wouldn't it be better to just make the phone call? But Harold was already at the doorway, holding a transparent plastic bag with the medicines inside. He brought the bag over to Lillian.

"Thank you," she said, counting the vials and inspecting the packaging. Nick could tell that she was distracted. After she had completed her checks, she handed over a wad of crisp fifty-pound notes, half of the agreed amount. The rest would follow after Lillian's pharmacists had checked the product, as they had done in previous transactions between Nick and Harold.

"We'd better go," Nick said, standing up. Lillian didn't move from her seat.

"You can leave if you want," Harold replied. "Lillian and I, though, have some unfinished business."

"Yes, you should leave," Lillian said. Her voice sounded tired.

Nick looked at Lillian. Her expression was blank. "No. Lillian, you don't know Oxford well, and you've already paid me to accompany you."

"I don't want him here," Lillian said to Harold. "He's one of your cronies, I know that."

"I'm staying put," Nick said. He knew Lillian was trying to protect him, but he couldn't leave her now.

"Well, that's settled, then," Harvey said. "So, Lillian. Perhaps Nicholas already mentioned this to you when I was out of the room. I need you to make a short phone call."

"What is this about?"

"I think you know. It's about the allegations your group plans to make. I want you to stop it."

"It's not me making those claims. It's the chemists in our group who have come to that conclusion."

"Maybe, but you can stop them."

Lillian paused. She looked down at her hands, turning her wedding band. "Harold, I don't know you very well," she said. "In fact, I hardly know you at all. But you came into this business with good intentions, didn't you? To find a cure, not a profit. You understand as well as I do that the drugs are, at best, a temporary reprieve."

"Maybe. But a reprieve is better than nothing."

"You're missing the point. In fact, so are our chemists. Your drugs, even our attempts at a vaccine, they suppress rather than cure. They don't address the psychological root of the problem. It's like a pressure cooker without a release valve. If everyone ends up on GreenShoots, W&R, LC+, or whatever else we concoct... at some point it'll be too much. Today's situation will seem like nothing in comparison."

"Lillian, I have read your ground-breaking research. I respect the science. As for what you've just said – interesting but it's not relevant right now. One phone call and we are done. It would be much better if we could sort this out without my colleagues intervening."

"Can I share with you one more thing? And if you're still not convinced, then I will do whatever is required."

"It won't change anything. But fine, if you insist. My colleagues will be here soon." Harold lit a cigarette, then looked at his watch. "You have five minutes, no more."

"Listen, you've already heard the main allegation: that the government wilfully wants the Panic to spread, in partnership with your employer, FRJ. I'm sure you also know about the rumoured military experiments, and how they may have resulted in the first known cases of SED, right?"

"Go on."

Lillian shifted in her chair. "What you might not know is this. Years earlier, psychiatrists at Hailstone Hospital in Norfolk had been trying to do something similar to the military, though not with the same drugs. The psychiatrists there believed sleep suppression, particularly of REM sleep, might cure or at least alleviate the suffering of their troubled patients. One of these patients was a woman called Edith Dubois. Most nights she would wake up, screaming hysterically. Her recurring nightmare was a remarkably accurate premonition of the coming Panic: she dreamt of an epidemic of suicides. The psychiatrists there tried to deprive her of REM sleep, but it made it worse. Her nightmares started intruding into her waking life."

"That's an interesting story, but I don't see how it's relevant."

Nick glanced at Harold. His expression seemed troubled, as if he believed some of what Lillian had said.

"The simple point is this," Lillian continued. "In the end, the drugs will only make it worse. Nightmares, hysteria, delusions, madness, suicide – these have been with us since the birth of mankind. Sleep, healthy sleep, it's a way of dealing with our worst fears in a safe environment. Look, I don't pretend to fully understand SED, no one does. But I know using drugs to suppress sleep is not the solution."

"Lillian, with all due respect, what matters is that we manage the situation. That means keeping the population calm. We don't want everyone to stop taking the medication because of some unproved allegations. They'd be more at risk of SED. Our country would descend into anarchy."

"I don't take the medication. Do you?" She paused. "That's OK. It's probably hard for you to answer that question honestly."

"We're out of time," Harold said, looking at his watch. He lit another cigarette and inhaled deeply. Nick thought he noticed a change in Harold's demeanour.

"Your hypotheses do interest me," he continued, "and if the situation were different, I would like to discuss it more. That is the truth. Sadly, though, our time is up."

As if on cue, four men entered the room. Each was armed. Nick noticed that the guns had been fitted with silencers.

"Don't worry about them. FRJ can be heavy-handed sometimes in its protocols. There isn't really any choice in the matter. Now, you must make the phone call. Our deal will then be concluded. It will be a short call, straight to the point. We know that Andrew Shaw will listen to you. So after you have identified yourself to him, what you will say is this."

Harold took out a sheet of paper from his jacket pocket, unfolded it then read it aloud.

"'Just a quick update. I met with PureForce. The plan is off for now. We still need more evidence before we can go public. One more thing. Bad news, but I know you'd want to be informed immediately. Rosanna Day is dead. I will tell you more when it is safe to do so. Goodbye.'"

He passed the note to Lillian. "Nothing more than that, and nothing less."

"What are these lies about Rosanna Day? This is all a farce and you know it."

"Have you not heard what happened at Cloxham?"

"No. Whatever it is, I won't believe it. Neither will Shaw."

"Maybe, maybe not, but I'm telling you it's true. I've seen the CCTV footage there. It was a massacre. You need to make the phone call now. My colleagues standing at the door there aren't the most patient people."

"OK. Then you'll let us go?" she said, taking out her mobile.

Harold leaned across the table and grabbed the phone. "Sorry about that. But I must be sure you're calling the right number. Here," he said, handing the phone back to her, then standing up. "It's ringing now," he said before walking over to the window.

Nick watched as she held the phone to her ear. There was nothing to do but wait.

"Hello, Andrew, it's Lillian. Yes. No. Yes. Now, just a quick update. I met with PureForce. The plan is off for now. One more thing."

Lillian paused, glancing across at Nick. He saw it in her expression before she spoke: a mixture of apology and defiance.

"Bad news," she said, "FRJ are with me now. They know where Nathan is. Throw away this phone, get Nathan safe if it's not too late. And go public. Tell people the truth about the government. Goodbye, Andrew."

She carefully placed the phone down on the table and put her hands together. Nick looked at her, then over at Harold, who had stubbed out his cigarette and was slowly shaking his head. He heard metal clicking and what sounded like heavy books being dropped to the floor. The next moment Lillian was slumped on the sofa, one bullet hole piercing her forehead and three more cutting through her chest. He waited for the next round of bullets to kill him, but they didn't come.

"What have you done?" Nick shouted, tears blinding his eyes. "What the fuck have you done?!"

"I'm sorry, Nick," Harold said. "Really I am. But she had a choice. I didn't want this outcome."

"That's bullshit. She was a middle-aged woman, an academic, not a terrorist, for Christ's sake! You're a coward. You're a feeble, dirty coward. Why don't you get your lapdogs to kill me, too?"

"Don't say that."

"Do it, you son of a bitch. Just *do* it!"

Nick saw how Harold's colleagues were waiting for his order. He looked across at Harold, who was staring out the window. Nothing happened.

"Why won't you kill me?"

Harold turned around to face Nick. "Because we were once friends," he said, his voice wavering.

"That's a goddamn lie."

Harold tapped out another cigarette from the pack, but didn't light it. His hands were shaking. "If that's what you think," he finally said. "Then, if you prefer, because no one will believe anything you say. Now take Nathan's medication, for what it's worth. And go rescue your pretty Kiyoko. I am not going to kill you. But never ever come back here. If you do, well... And if it wasn't already obvious, our dealings are over."

ORION

May

22

Rosa had been running for less than five minutes but already she was exhausted. Her legs were unsteady and she felt nauseated. She glanced back to see if anyone was coming after her. No one was there. Up ahead she saw a wire fence stretching for yards, maybe miles, in each direction. It marked the perimeter of Cloxham Manor grounds and appeared taller now that she was closer to it. As she ran, she scanned the fence, searching for an opening but unable to locate one. Her heart sank. It had been difficult enough to scale the brick wall enclosing her apartment, and this fence was perhaps twice the height. There was no way she could climb it in her current condition.

She couldn't go on. Squatting down in the long grass, breathing hard, she knew she was feverish. Disturbing recollections from her semiconscious state came into her mind, images that didn't, couldn't, make sense. She pushed them away, focused on assessing her surroundings. The grass had grown to knee height in places. To her left she could make out the remnants of what must have been a major fire: blackened tree stumps for as far as she could see.

It made her wonder how long she had been unconscious. Initially she had thought it had been, at most, a couple of days. But now she feared it had been much longer. Certainly long enough for human bodies to look bruised and brittle, and emit a foul odour. She had come across three dead Cloxham Manor employees so far. Joo-Young Lee and two men she didn't recognise. In each case the eyes were missing, whether pecked at by birds or clawed out before death by their own hands.

If only she had brought some water with her. In hindsight, she knew she should have stocked up on supplies. They had always left her food and drink in her apartment. She could have walked back around to the main complex after she had scaled the wall at the foot of her garden. But she'd been too panicked to do anything but run.

She forced herself up, looked left and right. The fence stretched out as far as her eyes could see. To her right, the fence curved inwards, towards what she thought might be the front gates and drive where she had first entered the grounds. Too tired to run, she walked in the direction of the main entrance. In the distance, rye grass gave way to cornfields, rising high in the setting sun.

She could hear her heart beating in the silence. She shivered, brushing her arms to try to keep warm. The temperature had dropped markedly since she had first run out, and she was only wearing a t-shirt and shorts. As she walked, her mind wandered back to a childhood memory. She was happy for it to stay there.

They were walking in the Landimore marshes in southern Wales. Rosa was fourteen, her brother eight. Their family always went to the Gower peninsula during the school half term in October, renting the same pretty thatched cottage in Reynoldsten, a few miles inland. It was a beautiful day. Sunlight had burnt away the morning dew, its rays catching the green and yellow hues of the marshes. The blue sky seemed to stretch forever, like a boundless ocean up above.

Their parents were far ahead with the family dog. She and Nathan had been distracted by an object shining in a puddle. "What is it?" Nathan had asked, his voice filled with awe. "Is it a magical dagger?"

Rosa picked up the rusty knife. At the top of its handle was what looked like a red jewel. She wondered if it was valuable.

The two of them ran over to their parents, excited by their discovery. But when they showed the knife to their parents, they were severely reprimanded. Their mother warned them that such sharp, rusty items were dangerous. It could easily cause infection, she said, before handing the knife to their father.

Later that day, after Nathan was already asleep, Rosa's father knocked on her bedroom door. They talked about the heart surgery she'd had as a child. For the first time, he told her how, after they had adopted her, she suffered almost daily seizures and bouts of high fever, how every night she would talk in her sleep.

Rosa stumbled on something hard and almost lost her balance, distracted by these recollections. Looking down, she saw it was a decomposing body, lying face down on the path. Flies were buzzing around. The stench quickly attacked her senses. She lurched to the side and retched. *I can't take this*, she thought, tasting the bile on her tongue, wanting to cry but forcing herself not to.

Something around the dead man's waist caught the light. Holding her nose, she peered down. On his belt was a pair of handcuffs and next to it, a holster holding a gun. His back seemed bloated; the navy-blue cloth of his uniform had been largely eaten away. Holding her breath, she carefully removed the holster. "You poor man," she whispered, shaking her head. "What were you all doing here? And what went wrong?"

———

Going back inside seemed like the best of a bad set of options, but it had been a difficult decision to make. An hour or so ago, when she had finally reached the main entrance to the grounds, it was almost dark. Along the pathway running by the fence, she had come across three corpses. At the main entrance two more security guards lay dead on the ground. The gate was wide open, so she could have easily walked out. But her fever had worsened, so much so that she had almost fainted a couple of times. She realised, reluctantly, that if she left then, she would struggle to find shelter for the night.

Inside the building, she was relieved not to come across anyone, alive or dead. She hypothesised that they had died at night, when presumably there were fewer Cloxham Manor employees on-site. Especially as most of the dead seemed to be security guards, other than Joo-Young Lee.

Now she was sitting in what had once been John Okoro's room. She had turned the lights off and left the door ajar. The room was adjacent to Claire Godley's old office. She wondered if John had ever overheard her sessions with Godley, and if so what he made of them. He had in that hastily scribbled note promised to tell her everything he knew. She had so many questions. If she did find him – assuming he wasn't dead – the first thing she'd ask is whether Godley was still alive, and, if so, where she was. She wanted the woman to suffer.

Don't think like that, she told herself. *Concentrate on the here and now.* She looked around, moonlight illuminating the room. Although she felt reasonably prepared for the night ahead, she was nervous. She was wrapped up in a blanket, sitting on the carpet behind John's desk so that anyone entering the room wouldn't immediately spot her. It felt safer there than on his couch, less exposed. Every time she heard a noise, she found herself reaching for the gun. It had only three bullets in the chamber. Not that she was even sure she'd know how to use it.

To calm herself, she once again went through the meagre food supplies and medicines she had cobbled together. They were laid out neatly on the floor, next to a battered leather briefcase she had found in John's office. Cereal bars, salted crisps, tinned tuna, tea bags, some soup sachets. A mostly empty medical kit containing nothing more than one strip of painkillers and a few plasters. Earlier she had boiled some water and mixed it with the powdered soup she'd found, but she hadn't managed to keep much of it in her stomach. Still, she felt a little better for it, and her fever had gone down slightly since she'd taken some painkillers.

She picked up the photo frame that she had placed next to the gun, and stared at the four happy faces in the fading light. It was a holiday snap of John Okoro with his family. She had never seen him like that, dressed in traditional Nigerian clothes. He looked much younger then, in his early thirties perhaps, not much older than her. He appeared to be so content, sitting there with his beautiful wife on one side and his adorable kids on the other. *He must have been in one hell of a rush if he hadn't taken this photo with him,* she thought. If he were still alive. Of course he was alive; he had to be.

For a moment, she considered returning to her old apartment, even though her only personal belonging there was the diary Godley had asked her to write. She had Godley's passkey, which would probably unlock the door. She could hold her breath before going in, and not even go into the room with Joo-Young Lee's decomposing corpse. She could grab her diary, some more practical clothes, too. But she knew she couldn't do it.

As with all the rooms she had entered, John Okoro's office

seemed bare. Bookcases and filing cabinets were empty. There was a monitor, keyboard and mouse, but no computer. It was as if they had intentionally cleared the offices of any documentation related to the research they were doing at Cloxham.

Somewhere nearby a door slammed shut. Her heart raced. *What should I do, Ana? Tell me what to do!* But the voice inside her head remained silent, as it had since she'd awoken. She grabbed the gun, listening intently for footsteps.

Nothing. *Must have been the wind*, she told herself, her heart beating fast. *I thoroughly checked all the rooms in the main building before I came here.* But then she remembered she hadn't checked the door beneath the staircase, and the basement concealed behind it. What if SED survivors were still trapped down there? Could any of them have survived?

23

The sun shone weakly through the windows. Rosa glanced up at the clock on the wall. It was a little after five in the morning. She put the painkillers and few other supplies into the battered briefcase and stood up, but immediately felt dizzy. *I can do this*, she told herself. *It's light outside and I have everything I need.* Gingerly she walked to the door and left the room.

Outside, the air was fresh. A light layer of dew made the grass seem more alive. She wrapped the blanket around her and stepped forward.

Go back.

"Ana, is that you?" she mouthed.

To the basement.

"No, I can't do it. It's too much."

She waited for Ana to reply. Nothing. "Fuck it," she muttered, knowing she had to do it. She turned around, opened the door and went back inside. Keeping her mind blank as she walked, she came to the door beneath the staircase and stepped into the glass-fronted lift.

The air was stale. Rosa flipped a row of switches, turning the lights on. She passed by the first isolation unit, the next, the one after that. In each of the twelve cells a child lay completely motionless on a bed. She was pretty sure they were different children to the ones Godley had shown her weeks or months ago. *Maybe they are just asleep,* she thought, even though she knew it was unlikely.

She came to the barrier after the last isolation unit, pressed Godley's passkey against it, came to the steel door where she had last seen Joo-Young Lee alive.

"Five seven three zero two nine," she said, repeating the code Godley had previously used. The door opened.

The office was empty, the screens that had once shown the cells were all blank. Rosa scanned the room, looking for keys, saw them hanging by the entrance.

She went back to the row of cells and opened the cell door nearest the office. As she did so a terrible stench hit her. Plugging her nose, she went up to the child lying on the bed. A girl, perhaps thirteen or fourteen years old. Her eyes were closed. She had an EEG cap on her head, various wires and tubes were attached to her body. Gently Rosa checked her pulse. Nothing. The flat line of the electrocardiogram monitor by her bed confirmed she was dead.

It was the same in the next unit and the ones after that. The same sickening stench as she opened the cell door and a young boy or girl lying there on their backs. Each time she tried to imagine the child had passed away peacefully.

She came to the last cell. There was a distinct smell of excrement and urine that wasn't fully masked by the strong disinfectant. But not the rotting stench that pervaded the other cells.

The boy looked a little younger than the others, ten or eleven perhaps. He was of South Asian origin. He looked familiar, though she couldn't recall having seen him before, back when Godley had taken her down here.

She checked his pulse, as she had done with all the others, couldn't feel anything. But then she glanced up at the monitor. The line wasn't flat.

"Hello, can you hear me?" she said, gently shaking the boy's arm.

No response. She looked at the monitor again. There were long gaps between the peaks and troughs, but the line indicated a heartbeat. An IV tube was inserted in the inner crook of his left elbow, the skin around it discoloured and swollen. She bent down closer to him, thought about trying to remove the tube. But there was still some fluid in the IV bag hanging above his bed. *Maybe better to leave it,* she thought, *just in case it was keeping him hydrated.*

She stood staring at him, unsure of what to do. She didn't want to leave him but she felt weak and nauseated, barely able to stand. So she momentarily left the room and brought back a chair from the office. Sitting by his side, she started singing a lullaby from her childhood. Closing her eyes, the words came to her easily:

> *I see the moon*
> *The moon sees me*
> *God bless the moon*
> *and God bless me*
>
> *I see the stars*
> *The stars see me*
> *God bless the stars*
> *and God bless me*

I see the world
The world sees me
God bless the world
And God bless me.

I know an angel
Watches over me
God bless the angels
And God bless me.

If only I hadn't lost my faith, she thought, as she repeated the lullaby. *God would bless this unconscious boy, and God might even bless me.*

Finally, she opened her eyes. The boy was awake and staring right at her. His eyes were wet from crying.

"Hello there. It's OK; you are safe now," she said, crying herself. "I'm here to help you. I'm on your side."

She placed his hand in hers and he smiled.

"Their tests are over now," she told him. "So now we can leave. Do you think you're able to stand?"

The boy shook his head.

"I understand. Let me find some food and water, OK? I'll be right back."

"Wait," the boy said, his voice a weak croak. "Stay with me, Rosanna Day."

That name again.

"I'm Rosa, not Rosanna," she said, leaning closer to him. "Rosa Newton. What's your name?"

"Sumon Chakma," the boy whispered. "I dreamt about you many times. You were my guardian angel. Protecting me from all those moaning people crawling along the ground, grabbing at my feet. My mum was there, too, moaning with the rest of them. She went for me with a knife, but you protected me.

The boy started sobbing. "It was like she didn't recognise me," he said, his voice a little stronger now.

Rosa squeezed his hand.

"It's OK," she said. "Everything will be OK."

"I know it was a dream," he said, wiping his tears away. "My mum is on the other side of the world."

Rosa looked at the boy. She wanted them to leave Cloxham Manor as soon as possible, but she didn't want to push him too hard.

"Until today, before you came for me, I was so scared," he said, his voice sounding more assured. "But now it's fine. You are my saviour. Like my mum once said, I am blessed. I'm so lucky to have seen my guardian angel before I die."

"What? Don't say that," Rosa said, glancing at the various tubes and wires still attached to his arms. "You won't die, Sumon. I'm here. I'll help you. Once you're strong enough, we'll leave this place together. We will find your mother."

The boy shook his head, looked down at his wrists. There were scars across each of them. "I got a knife. I cut myself. I don't remember why. It looked like paint. An ambulance came, and they took me to a hospital. Later they told me my dad was dead. Then they brought me here."

"If only Kiyoko had been there, watching over us," the boy continued, "maybe then I wouldn't have done it. And maybe my dad would still be alive."

"Sumon, I'm sorry, I'm so sorry. What happened to you is terrible. But I'm here with you now, and you are safe. I'm going to take you out of this place. We'll find your mother, I promise. And this Kiyoko, too."

"Please don't be sad," he said, his voice both young and ancient. "I'm very happy, I promise. I will be born again, into a better time. By then you will have saved us all, as you are Rosanna Day."

The boy smiled at Rosa before shutting his eyes. He gently squeezed her hand, holding it tight for a moment. Then his muscles relaxed, becoming limp. Soon he was far away.

24

Rosa forced herself to keep moving, despite the fever. The gravel road snaked left and right, flanked by a dense canopy of trees on either side. She glanced back. She could still just see the gates by the main entrance, but Cloxham Manor was no longer visible.

At the gates, she had undertaken the practical but unpleasant task of going through the dead security guards' pockets. She knew she needed money; a mobile phone and more bullets would be useful, too. From their moist, decaying pockets she'd picked out sixty pounds. More than enough for a train ticket to Nottingham or wherever else she decided to go. Their gun holsters were empty, though, and neither of them had a phone.

She stopped for a moment, adjusted the holster around her waist, made sure the gun remained easily accessible. Her meagre food and medical supplies were safely stowed in the briefcase. She was sweating profusely; her arms and legs ached.

Once again, the boy Sumon came into her mind. Though she'd hardly known him, his death had hit her hard. It was less than an hour ago when she had kissed him goodbye. Afterwards, she had returned to the ground level of Cloxham. In the office opposite Godley's, she'd found a set of golf clubs. She picked one out and proceeded to destroy everything she could. She smashed windows, lights and computer monitors, tore down the empty bookshelves, hacked through art canvases hanging on the walls, clubbed tables until the wood splintered.

Now she was exhausted. She was disappointed with herself for having lost control. Maybe she should have stayed inside longer, rested a while. Maybe she should just rest here, by the side of the road.

"No," she said aloud. "Got to keep moving."

She trudged onward. After perhaps a mile, the gravel road gave way to tarmac and soon she was at a junction. She struggled along the tarmac road, stopping regularly to catch her breath. Her fever had worsened; she felt dizzy and constantly nauseated. She fought it as best she could, determined to keep walking until she encountered someone.

To motivate herself, she thought of her brother, Nathan, pictured their joyful reunion. She would surprise him at his room on Nottingham University's campus. He would be sitting at his desk or lying on his bed, reading a magazine and listening to music. When she knocked on his open door, he'd absently say come in, and she would speak his name. Oh, the look on his face! Picturing his smile sustained her as she walked along the road.

There were no buildings in sight. No car passed by on the narrow road. Hedges lined either side of the tarmac, broken up now and then by dirt tracks that led to farmers' fields. The scenery seemed so familiar, though she couldn't remember ever having visited Norfolk before her incarceration at Cloxham. Each time she came to a bend in the road, she expected to see Checkers Inn, the pub she used to visit with Shaw all those months ago. But every time she was disappointed.

· · ·

Her fever had reached a point where she could hardly stand up straight. Still she carried on, each step forwards an effort. Soon enough it became too much. The last thing she remembered before fainting was the banal thought that her job in London just might have been kept open for her. She was wondering how she could politely inform her boss that she had no intention of going back.

Eric Howell found Rosa lying in the middle of the road. He had almost run her over in his rickety pickup truck. Rosa came to after he poured a few drops of water on her face. She remembered him asking if she was all right, then saying he could drive her to the hospital. She had planned to say she was fine, that if she could just get a lift to the next town that would be great. But it suddenly hit her that she had no idea of anything. She wasn't sure what day of the week it was, or even what month. Perhaps the epidemic had become so severe that the whole country had fallen into anarchy. Maybe the Panic had even spread to other countries.

Before she could speak, she found herself sobbing. It wasn't simply the uncertainty of the situation that made her cry. As much or more, it was the kind and sincere way the old man looked at her, his genuine concern for a stranger. Eric suggested that she stop at his house. It was lunchtime and his wife always had extra food. On a full stomach, she could better decide what she wanted to do, and their home was only a couple of miles away.

That was three days ago. In all the time since, she hadn't left their home. She was thankful the old man had found her when he did. Sally, Eric's wife, made her soup, salads and other simple meals she could digest. They told her she should stay as long as she needed, and neither of them asked any questions about how she had ended up unconscious on the road.

The old couple were unaware that Cloxham Manor was now being used to experiment on SED survivors. But they both knew its history. Up until a few years ago, a wealthy family had owned Cloxham, though it had a different name. The estate had been with the same family for centuries. However, the current generation had squandered their inheritance and so had been forced to sell the property. Eric and Sally had never seen the new owners, nor had any of the other locals, though the rumour was that a religious sect had bought the place. Rosa didn't tell them that Cloxham was run by the government. She wondered how long it would be before someone discovered the corpses there.

The old couple's home was part of a tiny hamlet a few miles from Cloxham. It was one of a dozen or so houses; there were no shops. The nearest town was Wells-Next-The-Sea. From there, regular buses went to Kings Lynn, which in turn connected to London and the Midlands. Each morning Rosa planned to make the trip to Nottingham, but she hadn't yet felt physically strong enough to leave. She had also held off from trying to contact her brother. She didn't want the old couple to get caught up in any of this.

The three of them would often talk about the Panic, though never at night. Like more and more people across the country, Eric and Sally no longer had access to the internet. However, they read the papers, watched the news and listened to the latest rumours floating about. They told Rosa that almost half a million had now died from the Panic. Most deaths were still in Oxford and London, but cases had started to appear all over England. The local news channel had recently reported on a sudden flurry of deaths near Kings Lynn that bore the hallmarks of the illness.

It was also the first time Rosa learnt about the popularity of sleep-suppressants. The old couple hadn't taken them yet, but were seriously considering it. One of their neighbours had started on the GreenShoots tablets, soon after his niece had fallen ill. A government-approved outlet had recently opened on the outskirts of Wells-Next-The-Sea. It seemed to be making a healthy turnover already, with queues outside the building every day of the week.

Rosa woke up suddenly. It was three in the morning. She rushed out of bed, making it to the bathroom just in time. Afterwards, she turned on the taps and poured cold water on her face. The fever was still there. She looked at herself in the mirror. Her face looked drawn and pale, her eyes dulled of light.

I am getting better, she thought, in hope more than expectation. *By the morning, I'll be strong enough to move on.* The old couple had been so good to her ever since they had taken her in. Still, she knew she couldn't stay with them for much longer.

She crept quietly back into her room, careful not to wake them. She walked over to the bedroom window and gazed out at the sky. Hundreds of stars were visible. She searched for and found the Orion constellation. For a moment, she imagined a twin, her mirror image, gazing back at her from a distant planet. Maybe her name was Rosanna Day. Her 'Earth' would be orbiting one of Orion's stars, and our sun would be part of a constellation named the Hunted.

INSOMNIA

June

25

Nick dragged himself forward, ignoring the shifting, edgy glances of office workers and students pretending to enjoy the sun. All of them pretending that everything was normal, that the Panic had been contained to Oxford. Don't let the anarchy in London trouble you, or the cases that have sprung up all over England. The riots, the roadblocks, the dead bodies on the streets – these are just part of everyday life now. Better to keep on, to leave others to worry. Yet Nick knew they all were as nervous as he was. He could see the fear in their drug-addled eyes.

He wasn't far from the Lace Market, which meant he was about fifteen minutes from where he needed to be. Ten days straight he had been awake. Wiping away spittle from his chin, he lurched on. "On the seventh day, why didst thou not rest," he muttered glibly, laughing at himself.

If only Samantha and her goons from PureForce were still alive. He and Kiyoko could then plot their revenge. That is what he wanted, even if Kiyoko did not. But they were dead. He had seen the carnage with his own eyes.

His mind slowly churned through all the terrible possibilities now facing them. None of it quite made sense, yet it was obvious he and Kiyoko were in danger. PureForce would be coming for them. It was only a matter of time before they tracked them down. That is, if FRJ or the government didn't get there first.

Whoever caught them would first dispatch of him. It would be done quietly and without much fuss. They wouldn't even bother to hide his body, now that there were people dying all over the place. No one would question it. The poorly paid government workers would shovel him up and add his corpse to one of the mass graves assigned to SED victims. After that inconvenience was resolved, their kidnappers would take Kiyoko somewhere remote. First, they would barrage her with pointless questions. Naturally, they would demand to know who had helped her do it. They'd also ask who her clients were, what were her sleeping patterns, why she hadn't tried to return to Canada earlier.

Kiyoko would tell them the truth, but they wouldn't believe her. Depending on which organisation caught them, she'd be expected to point the finger at one or more of FRJ, the government, PureForce or Alliance. Finally, they would give up with the questions and resort to physical methods. They wouldn't stop until they had their explanation. Eventually Kiyoko would break and tell them something that matched what they wanted to hear.

He glanced around, conscious of the barely concealed weariness of people on the street. The atmosphere in Nottingham already reminded him of Oxford in the early days. People stealing glances at one other, checking for some sign of illness. Never any eye contact, though. Never more words with strangers than were absolutely necessary.

It must be the same in cities across England and Wales. The government had closed down its offices in Birmingham; there were even rumours of a wall being built across the north of England.

As for him and Kiyoko, what would be the plan exactly? To drive north until they reached Scotland? No, that wouldn't work; they'd never be allowed in. A better strategy would be to find passage on one of the illegal ferries that dotted the coast. They could then head over to France or Holland. They couldn't tell anyone where they were going, no one at all. It was a risky plan, as the French and Dutch coastguards would be vigilant. Still, it was a better alternative than trying to leave the country through official means. Visas to most countries were almost impossible to obtain now, requiring extensive medical records, and even foreign citizens like Kiyoko couldn't easily repatriate. Given that they had both lived in Oxford, the officials would never allow them to leave the country.

Kiyoko should have stayed on the waiting list, he thought. If she had, maybe she would have been back in Canada by now. She would be safe.

"Spare tablets, mister?" a man asked. His clothes were torn, his shoes falling apart.

Nick ignored the tramp and struggled on as fast as he could. His appointment with Shaw was at two o'clock, and he didn't want to be late. Initially, Kiyoko had tried to dissuade him from going.

It's far too risky, she had said. Not only does he have links with PureForce, he will also think you're culpable for Lillian's death because of your business arrangements with Harold.

But Nick didn't believe that. He hoped Shaw's chemists might have a cure for his insomnia, the antidote that Samantha had mentioned. He also had the medication Nathan needed, for which Lillian had lost her life. One of Shaw's staff had confirmed that Nathan was unconscious but still alive. He felt duty bound at least to deliver the vials.

From an office block ahead, he heard a piercing scream. Suddenly he felt wide awake. His heart was again pounding hard. He wanted to bolt as fast as he could, but he forced himself to keep walking at a steady pace. It was happening everywhere now. When was it going to kill him? Surely it was only a matter of time. Worse still, what if it struck down Kiyoko?

He started muttering under his breath. Another made-up limerick. A stupid habit, but it was the most effective way he knew of blocking out the fear. "I once had a dog called Clown; he walked behind me with a frown. One day I said stay, but he trotted away, and left me alone in this town."

The fear was still there. He repeated his idiotic limerick, over and over. *If only I could sleep*, he thought. *Surely my body can't take much more, let alone my mind.*

Most of the time he felt drowsy, his body leaden and slow to respond. But every so often a sudden surge of adrenaline would strike him, particularly when he was sure he was finally going to fall asleep. His hands and legs would twitch, his heartbeat would soar. Recently he had started to hallucinate. Worse than that, though, was what he heard inside his head. Those terrible moans of despair that he had first heard in the video Harold had shown him.

Turning down a narrow passageway, he thought he could hear it again. He listened intently, and there it was, a single moan, muffled but clearly audible. Someone struggling alone in the shadows. It seemed even more harrowing to him than the screams of those struck by the Panic. He recalled the horrific images in the video, of men and women crawling on their bellies, their bodies ripped apart. Their moans had haunted him every day and night since the failed deal in Oxford. To him it seemed like a stark reminder of all the suffering and evil in this world.

He peered at the huge heap of overflowing bin bags piled in front of him, looking for movement. He heard the moaning again, much closer now. Maybe he wasn't imagining it this time. It sounded so real.

"I won't hurt you," he said, staring at the litter spilling out of the bags, then up at the artless graffiti on the walls. "Let me help you. I have painkillers, I can bring you food and drink. Please, let me help."

A rustling sound came from within the rubbish heap. He stepped into the middle of the refuse, ignoring the stench of rotting food and stale urine as best he could. Someone was in there, he was sure of it. He told himself it was simply a matter of sifting through the rubbish in an efficient manner. He started tossing the bin bags to one side. Each time he expected a nervous face or twitching limb to be revealed. The moaning was deep inside his head now, but that didn't deter him from his foraging.

Initially, Kiyoko didn't want to talk about the night she was held hostage. She just wanted to be outside, to keep moving and never stay still. They spent the next few days walking the streets of Nottingham or the deserted Wollaton Park by the university campus. Walking arm in arm, Nick waited patiently for her to talk. At night, unable to sleep, he would sit by her bedside and watch over her, conjuring up positive images, as Kiyoko had done for her clients.

On their third day in Nottingham, Kiyoko finally told Nick what had happened that night. Sitting on a bench in Wollaton Park, they were watching a deer that had ventured to the lakeside.

"They let me lie down on the sofa," Kiyoko said, "but they kept my arms and legs tied."

She went on to describe what had happened. It had been about four in the morning when events started to really spiral out of control. Samantha and Stuart were asleep upstairs, with the other man – Jason – on guard duties. Kiyoko was exhausted. She shut her eyes and tried to sleep, but she was too frightened to do so. Giving up, she opened her eyes and saw Jason standing over her.

"Shush," he said before gagging her. Then he was running his rough hands under her top. She tried to yell out but the gag was bound tight. With one hand he grasped at her panties, with his other he undid his own trousers until they fell to his ankles. Then he was groaning as his hands did their work.

She shut her eyes and tried to block out what was happening. It didn't help. Horrific images came into her head, a film reel of women being raped over and over. She didn't try to push the images away. Instead, she focused on the women's suffering, trying to comfort them as best she could, as tears ran down her cheeks. It didn't work. In her mind she kept seeing their assailants, and then Stuart's bland, emotionless face as he masturbated. All she could feel was disgust. She opened her eyes and stared directly at Stuart, hating him with all her being.

At that very moment, she heard a loud scream coming from upstairs, quickly followed by gunshots. Stuart abruptly let go of her. He was trying to pull up his trousers but his gun holster had caught on something. Swearing, he finally succeeded in removing his holster just as the next bullet was shot. It pierced his left buttock. He fell to the ground, howling in agony. Kiyoko glanced up, spotting Samantha coming down the stairway. Moments later Stuart was dead, another bullet ripping through the back of his head.

Samantha pulled up one of the kitchen chairs and sat down next to Kiyoko. Her eyes were red from crying. She stared at Stuart's body on the floor, then at the gun in her hands. She hardly seemed to be aware of Kiyoko's presence. "I killed them both, and they deserved to die. Rotten to the core, like me," she murmured. "We have lost our way, forgetting what it means to live. Because deep inside us, it festers. Gnawing away at everything that is wholesome and good. It must be carved out."

Kiyoko wanted to tell her that it didn't have to be that way. But she was gagged and tied up, unable to speak or move. Looking at Samantha, with her hunched shoulders and reddened eyes, Kiyoko knew there was nothing she could do for her. She sensed how close the Panic was. Moments later, Samantha was dead.

26

The beat-up Land Rover chugged along, passing through gentle hills as they approached Sherwood Forest. Every few minutes Nick felt himself twitch. An involuntary jerk of the head, sudden rapid blinking that he couldn't stop. He pinched his wrist hard enough to register in his dulled mind.

Nick glanced across at the driver, a man in his forties with a large unruly beard. He seemed calm and steady, his eyes focused on the road ahead. *Probably used to freaks like me*, he thought. They had hardly spoken throughout the journey; Nick didn't even know his name.

He stared out the window. They couldn't be far away now. He wanted to shut his eyes and relax, but he knew if he tried, the adrenaline would kick in. Sheep and cattle grazed in lush green fields, the sun appeared from behind puffy cumulus clouds and shone its rays on the land. For a moment, he pictured strolling through the countryside with Kiyoko, hand in hand. Her beautiful eyes, confident and gentle, a soothing balm for all the world's ills. They would lie on the earth and gaze up at the blue sky. Beside her, at peace, his eyes would grow heavy and he would fall willingly into a deep, restful sleep.

If only life were so simple, he thought as the idyllic image faded away. Instead our days are filled with suffering and fear. Unnecessary conflicts, selfishness rewarded, communities crumbling in on themselves. We live in a time of loneliness. Separated from one another, we have become broken pieces of what was once whole.

"You walk from here," the driver said matter-of-factly, stopping the vehicle. They were in the middle of dense woodland. A young woman stood on the edge of the narrow road, waiting for them. "Ruth will take you to see Colonel Shaw. Once you are done, I will come back to this spot and drive you back to Nottingham."

Ruth led Nick through the woods without saying a word. She was armed. There wasn't an obvious path to follow, as they went deeper and deeper into the forest. The sunlight struggled to penetrate the canopy. They came to a point where the vegetation seemed weaker, more brittle. The soil was parched; many trees had fallen or had been chopped up for firewood. Even the trees that were still standing seemed to have lost their solidity, swaying uncertainly in the wind. Images from the video came into Nick's head: the broken men and women were crawling towards him. Their moans echoed all around.

"Holding up?" Ruth asked. "Here, have some water."

"Thanks. How much farther is it?"

"Not far."

They walked on. He blocked out the moaning as best he could. He tried to picture Kiyoko as she was this morning, smiling as he brought her a cup of tea in bed. But quickly the memory shifted to a week and a half earlier. He could picture it so clearly. Opening the door to her apartment in Oxford. Immediately seeing in her eyes that mix of relief and despair. Removing the gag and untying her. Kiyoko trying to stand up but her legs giving way. Then they were sitting on the floor together, turned away from Samantha's body. He held her carefully as she sobbed in his arms.

"We're here," Ruth said.

Nick had lost track of time. They seemed to have been walking for hours. He glanced around. They were in a small clearing, though there were no obvious footpaths leading to it. The surrounding trees seemed sturdier here, with thickset trunks, and roots extending across the forest floor.

"Hello, Nick," Andrew Shaw said, appearing from behind a large oak tree. A man pushed his wheelchair closer. "Thank you for coming all this way," Shaw continued, proffering his hand. "I appreciate it, though I can't say I'm surprised. Lillian told me you were principled."

"It's the least I could do. She was a good woman."

"Indeed she was. Please, have a seat," he said, indicating a thick tree trunk a few feet away. Its wood had been sanded down. "You've met Ruth, and this is Vincent."

Vincent nodded a hello. He was a stocky five foot six, looked about Nick's age.

"I'm sure it seems like a strange spot to meet," Shaw said after Nick had sat down. "But believe me, it's one of the safest places. FRJ and the government would never think I'd be in such a place, what with my disability," he said, pointing to his paralysed legs.

"Colonel Shaw, I have the vials here in my rucksack. For Nathan. Do you want them now?"

"Thank you. And, please, call me Andrew. Nathan isn't doing very well, though. He's been unconscious now for a long time. At least we were able to move him in time, thanks to Lillian."

"The MAZA drug can help him. Can't it?"

"I sincerely hope so."

"Why is he so important? I mean, saving anyone's life is important. But... you know what I mean."

"I do. It's like Lillian had said. Nathan has some kind of immunity, so he can help us find a cure. Like his sister."

Nick looked at Shaw, his mind slowly piecing together strands of information. "Are you saying he is Rosanna Day's brother?"

"No," Shaw said without shifting his gaze. "I don't know whether Rosanna Day exists. But Nathan's sister is in a government safe house. She may well already be dead."

They sat there for a while without saying anything, Nick doing his best to keep the moaning and hallucinations at bay. But horrific images kept reappearing in his mind, a distorted slow-motion reel. Earlier, back in Nottingham city centre, he must have been delirious. Yet it had seemed so real. A pair of brown eyes staring at him as he approached. They seemed to follow his every movement as he clumsily waded through the pile of bin bags. But once he was within touching distance, the eyes disappeared. Pushing aside some sodden cardboard boxes, he saw a dead woman. Her body was at an unnatural angle; her eyes had been gouged out.

"You must be wondering what happens next," Shaw said, turning his wheelchair slightly.

"Huh? Yes, I suppose."

"It is entirely up to you. I'd understand if you wanted nothing more to do with us. We'd respect that."

"Right," Nick responded. "The group Alliance. Are you in charge of it?"

"We don't have such a formalised structure. But yes, if you like. I help keep things organised."

"My insomnia, whatever PureForce drugged me with. Is there anything your chemists can do?"

Shaw gazed out into the distance. "I want to say yes," he said, "but the honest answer is: I don't know. There isn't an obvious antidote, despite what PureForce told you. Some of our medics are hopeful that – under the right regimen – your body will be able to heal itself. If you'd taken a strong dose of LC+, that's what would happen. The problem is we don't know what else PureForce added. We can take blood samples, if you're comfortable with that, but it will be a long process."

"Maybe, I don't know. I don't know what I want. Just to get out of this messed up country. Can you help me do that?"

Shaw shook his head. "I understand why you'd want to leave, but it's practically impossible. Especially for Kiyoko."

"Why? What about her?" he asked, immediately aware of his defensive tone.

"After what happened to those PureForce members, she no longer has a low profile. Kiyoko would never have been allowed to leave Oxford via Elmore Facility without my contacts. I used to work there, back when I was still with the government. Not that I'm proud of it."

"Is she safe?"

"Not really. Since you got in touch with us, we've had people watching out for you both. But they can only do so much."

Nick glanced across at Ruth and the young man by Andrew Shaw. Their expressions were inscrutable. "That video of mutilated men and women moaning as they crawled across the ground," he said. "Was it real? Do you know anything about it?"

"What I know is that it was a mistake. A twisted attempt to try to understand the Panic. All it succeeded in doing was causing a relapse amongst SED survivors."

"I don't get it."

"Nor does anyone, really. Suffice to say the government did many things wrong, and I was part of that for far too long. Millions of pounds spent on research that should have never been attempted, then millions more trying to undo whatever it was we had accidentally unleashed. There are conspiracy theories involving the water supply, GM crops and pesticides. There might just be some truth in them. And FRJ is certainly profiteering from it all, as are some politicians and senior civil servants."

"Have you gone public yet about that, like Lillian had wanted?"

"Not yet, but we will very soon. Our evidence implicating the government in this shameful proliferation of drugs, drugs that do more harm than good, is compelling. That being said, the fact remains that we don't really understand what really caused the Panic."

Shaw paused for a moment. "I thought we were close, that we'd made a breakthrough," he continued. "Some of the microbiologists in my group were convinced that they had found the root cause: a newly identified parasite in water and soil samples from around Oxford. We used this to help develop an experimental vaccine."

Ruth looked at Shaw. "Don't worry, Ruth," he said. "We can trust Nick. So, the vaccine. We put volunteers on it and they seemed to be protected. However, in the last few weeks, most of these volunteers have suddenly succumbed to the Panic. From the numbers of dead and dying, it was evident that the vaccine had, if anything, increased the risk of acquiring SED. It was as if the illness was adapting."

Nick glanced down at his shaking hands. "Why are you telling me this?" he asked.

"Attempts to develop effective treatment have proved to be equally unsuccessful," Shaw continued, ignoring Nick's question. "And I admit we're at a loss of what to try next. Some of our group will continue down the traditional biomedical route of vaccines and medical treatments. Others, building on Lillian's insights, continue to explore psychotherapy-driven approaches. I'm not that hopeful, though. Society is breaking down. Levels of cortisol – a hormone indicating chronic stress – have increased exponentially across the country in the last year. As have the number of deaths, of course. And what I know with any certainty is that FRJ's latest drugs will only make the situation worse."

Shaw wheeled his chair a little closer. Nick noticed the weariness in his eyes as he leaned forward.

"Look at the trees around us, Nick. Oak, yew, beech. They used to be strong, but now they seem frail, don't they?"

Nick nodded.

"Some of these trees must be hundreds of years old," Shaw continued. "The whole forest here used to be like this. And the UK was mostly woodlands long ago. Lillian once pondered if the Panic has been growing within us for centuries or more. Ever since we lost touch with nature, she said, we have lost touch with ourselves. For years we have shared a nagging, subconscious fear that humanity is slowly rotting. The Panic, then, is simply a profound cognisance of that fear."

Shaw paused. His eyes seemed moist.

"It's more than that," he continued. "Perhaps only those struck by the Panic understand the full extent of our rottenness. That we are contagious, infecting and destroying everything. We're in the midst of the sixth mass extinction. Species are dying out at unprecedented rates because of us. This mass epidemic of suicides might be nothing more than an extreme acceptance of the truth: that the Earth is better off without us."

***

"I'll do it," Nick said. They had been discussing a plan to infiltrate Mantle Hospital, which would involve him and Vincent.

The sky had darkened. Vincent and Ruth were setting up a makeshift shelter, planting branches in the soil and covering them with some tarp.

"Are you sure?" Shaw replied. "It won't be easy."

"Yes."

"Good. Then let's talk practicalities. Vincent, pass me a stick, would you?"

Shaw took the stick and sketched out a square on the ground with three lines inside. "These are the main voluntary wards of Mantle Hospital," he said, pointing to the top third of the square. "They're on the first floor. Emergencies, labs and miscellaneous on the ground floor; SED survivors in the basement. That's the basic lay of the land."

"Yep. I have a general sense of the layout from when I'd previously enrolled, and from conversations with Harold."

It started to rain hard. Vincent came over and pushed Shaw's wheelchair. The four of them huddled under the sagging canvas. Nick felt calm and clear-headed, at least compared with how he normally was.

"The biggest risk is that you'll encounter Harold on the wards," Shaw continued. "Our intelligence tells us he stays mainly in the labs, but still. As well as the fake ID card, safer to change how you look. Wear glasses, grow a beard, cut your hair short. Hopefully that'll be enough from Harold taking a second look, if he ever passes through the voluntary wards."

"And basically my job is to create a diversion for Vincent. Befriend the volunteers who are most on edge, the ones addicted to the 'uppers'."

"That's right. From your previous experience, we're hoping you'll be able to identify and befriend them quickly."

"Should take about a week, I'd say. Got to build some trust even if they are desperate for a hit."

Nick stared out at the pounding rain. Puddles were forming in the mud. "So at the right moment – between twelve and two pm on a Tuesday or Thursday – I'll create a diversion. Tell these addicts where the medicines are stored and convince them I know a way in."

"Yes. And Vincent, you'll need twenty minutes?" Shaw asked.

"Max," Vincent replied. "More likely ten to fifteen."

"That's not a lot of time to wreck their data systems," Nick said.

"It's enough. I just need access to their control room. The rest is easy. Since working undercover there, I've gathered the info I need."

"So logistically it's doable. But, Andrew, how are you sure you can trust me?" Nick asked. "Or Vincent or Ruth, for that matter. No offence meant, but you know what I'm getting at."

"None taken," Ruth replied. Vincent just shrugged his shoulders.

"Vincent and Ruth have been with me long enough. And we've run our checks on you," Shaw said. "But you're right, there are no guarantees. Indeed, I thought we could trust Brian Bradley. I was wrong."

Nick heard something, a faint whispering in the woods, then flashes of movement. *Calm, calm*, they seemed to be saying, their voices a dulled monotone. He clenched his fists. *Shut up! Get out of my fucking head.*

"Nick, everything OK?"

"Yeah, all good. This new drug that FRJ is working on, Calm. It's even more effective than LC+ at keeping people wake, right?"

"It is. The real innovation, though, is that it regulates the heart rate so there are no adrenaline jumps. Keeps users in a placid state. Makes them docile and obedient."

"Calm is also highly addictive," Ruth added.

"It would be a disaster if the drug went to market," Shaw continued. "FRJ and the government would have a captive, pliant market. Trapped by a blockade stretching across the north of England."

"A huge conspiracy," Nick said. He felt himself losing focus, his own voice sounded far away. He dug his nails into his wrist until they drew blood.

"Yes and no," Shaw said, eyeing Nick. "It's rumoured that FRJ was on the verge of financial ruin before all this began. A hedge fund stepped in, FRJ's board members changed, the requirement for shareholder returns probably increased substantially. So on that side, maybe a conspiracy. For the government, though, I think it's much simpler. The bureaucrats and politicians, now safe in Scotland, have conceded defeat. They're just intent on protecting themselves, whatever the cost."

"Right. If I do all this, you'll protect Kiyoko?"

"Yes. Protecting Kiyoko is also in our interests. It would be a disaster if PureForce or the government got hold of her."

"Right."

"Nick, the reality is we're not any closer to finding a vaccine or a cure. But our group is certain about one thing: the need to stop FRJ from getting this drug to market."

27

"I think it's a bad idea on so many levels," Kiyoko said. They were sitting in Nick's living room, eating stale bread and tinned tuna for dinner. Nick had just outlined Andrew Shaw's proposal. "Do you really think it will be so easy to sabotage a multi-million-pound operation?"

"There's a chance; I wouldn't have agreed to it otherwise."

"Maybe. But you're not in any shape to attempt this."

"I'm OK. Some days are worse than others. But I can do it. More important, don't you want to go back home?"

"Yes. I do and I don't," she replied, placing her hand on top of his. "Really, I want to be back in Oxford, helping my clients. I shouldn't have left."

"We had to. It was too risky."

"And this isn't?"

Nick nodded. He sipped some water to help the stale bread down. She was right, he knew that. Yet he also felt it was the only thing he could do.

"How do you even know you can trust Shaw?" she asked, moving her hand away.

"I don't. But I trusted Lillian, who was part of Alliance, too. She was on to something, I'm sure of that."

"You mean with the lab rats?"

"No. The psychological side of the illness. It's more important."

"Could be."

He looked at Kiyoko, at her intense but delicate eyes looking back at him. He pictured that first time they'd met, on a dilapidated side street in Oxford. She had been wearing the same pale blue dress.

"All these drugs suppressing sleep," he said, "they're only going to make it worse. It's like, it's like a dam built in the wrong location. A poorly constructed one at that. The pressure is mounting to unsustainable levels. Sooner or later, the whole situation is going to explode. When it does, everything will break apart. My god, it'll be terrible. It will be like that video. I hear them all the time, Kiyoko, moaning, despairing at this world. What can we do?"

"Nick, please," she said, bringing her hand back to his for a moment. "You have to try to stay calm."

"Yes, you're right, I know you are. Still, probably almost everyone is on some kind of meds today. Maybe the drugs kept the Panic at bay for a while, but look at where it's brought us. There are cases all over the country now. The drugs are making it worse."

"How do you know that?"

"I don't, but it's what Andrew Shaw said. He could be lying, but Lillian had hinted at such things before."

Nick shifted in his chair. *If only I could sleep,* he thought.

"Even if it's true, what can we do?" Kiyoko asked.

"Stop FRJ from producing new drugs."

"It's as simple as that?"

"Yes. Maybe. God, I don't know," Nick said, looking down at his hands. The concoction he had been drugged with was making them shake again. "I haven't slept properly for weeks now," he mumbled. "I can't always think straight. Sometimes I think I'm drifting off, but then whatever they injected forces me awake. I'm scared. Because I know when I finally manage to sleep, it'll be too late. The Panic will take me."

"Don't say that. I'm with you, I'll watch over you."

He glanced at Kiyoko. "I'm glad," he said, looking again at her gentle eyes. Gateways to the pure compassion within her. "Really, I am. Kiyoko, I know we've become close these last few months. But do you think if things were less crazy, you and me, we could have…"

"Shush," she replied, moving closer to him.

She placed her hands on his until they were steady. Then she brought one of her hands to his face, gently closing his eyes. "Shush," she murmured again, shutting her eyes before bringing her lips to his. He felt her hands running down his back, drawing him closer, her unsteady breath as he unbuttoned her top, her lips kissing him harder.

ACCEPTANCE

June

28

Miles of sand stretched along the coast, backed by dense pine forest. The beach used to be a popular spot for young families and retirees alike, but now it was deserted. A harsh wind blew, carrying the sand up so it stung Rosa's arms and legs. Her fever had gone but she still felt weak. Taking shelter in a sand dune, she stared out to sea. The water was opaque; seagulls squealed as they dove in and out of the churn of the waves. Gazing beyond them, to the far horizon, she felt tears welling up in her eyes.

The wind had weakened. Rays of sun started to show through the clouds. She picked up a pebble, feeling its smooth edges before tossing it out to sea. It skimmed across the surface, jumping up once then sinking.

Was I wrong to have abandoned Eric and Sally? But what else could I have done? If I had waited for the ambulance, they would have asked questions. How long had I been staying with the old couple? Was I related to them? A niece perhaps (they didn't have any children of their own). Soon enough they would have become suspicious. The police, if they weren't there already, would be called in. They'd make sure I couldn't leave. Someone there would have surely known about the horrific scenes at Cloxham Manor, and maybe even about her. Calls would be made; government officials would come and I'd be locked up again.

Anyway, hadn't Sally told me to run? With her husband already dead and her own life slipping away in her bloodied hands, she had screamed: "Run! Get out now! Do it! Do it now, I beg of you. Don't let me infect you."

That had been less than three hours ago, not long before daybreak. Rosa had hurriedly packed John Okoro's battered briefcase, stuffing in a few belongings. Then she'd walked to the beach by Holkham. On the way, she'd made an anonymous call from a telephone box, disguising her voice as she told the emergency services where they would find the old couple. Even though she knew the ambulance would be unlikely to reach Sally in time.

I was a coward, she thought. When I heard them scream, first Eric and then Sally, I should have gone straight to their room. I might have been able to help them. Not maybe. I could have saved them. All I'd needed to do was reach inside, find that connection before the Panic took them over the edge. Together we could have identified the fear that gnawed at them, seen it for what it was and accepted it. Then they would have lived. It could have been as simple as that, I'm sure of it, but I was too much of a coward to try.

And how well they had looked after her. Three weeks she had stayed with them, relying on their kindness to nurse her back to health whilst the world outside grew sicker with each passing day. During those weeks, the three of them had pored over the newspapers. The pages were filled with terrible accounts of mass suicides, whole communities found dead, graphs illustrating the exponential rise in SED cases. Oxford was all but abandoned, and many of the major road links in and out of London had ground to a halt. The government, safe in Edinburgh, had just announced new emergency measures that granted the military extra powers. And although other cities around the country were still more or less functional, journalists suspected that martial law wasn't far off.

Rosa stared at the sea, noticing how much clearer the water was with the sun's rays shining on it. The seagulls had flown farther down the beach, leaving the waves to lap peacefully against the shore.

Before anything else, she would find her brother. She had tried telephoning him, but someone else had picked up his old number and she'd quickly hung up. Still, she was hopeful he would still be in Nottingham.

Perhaps she would also try to contact John Okoro. However, she had no idea where he might be. That was assuming he hadn't died at Cloxham Manor with all the others. The grounds there were extensive. She pictured his decaying body lying there somewhere in the mud, birds pecking at his eyes, then pushed the image away.

A dog barked, making her jump. For a moment, she expected to see an Alsatian bounding towards her, teeth bared, and police officers not far behind. But it was a Jack Russell terrier chasing after a stick its elderly owner had thrown. She exhaled, calm again.

It's good that people are still carrying on with their lives, she thought as she watched the terrier retrieve the stick from the waves. At least some people: the beach was otherwise deserted. She stood up, wiping sand off her skirt and the battered briefcase, and walked towards the old man and his dog.

"He won't bite yer," the man said in a thick Norfolk accent. The terrier came up to her, danced around her legs.

"What's his name?"

"Pebbles. He's a kind old soul, the same age as me in dog years. Fine day, isn't it?"

"It is," she said, stroking the dog. "And no one is enjoying it but us. Is the beach always this quiet?"

"Only these last few weeks. People are right nervous and jumpy, what with more and more cases right here in Norfolk. Can't blame them. But I keep telling myself I'm too old to let these things worry me. And I don't take any of them medicines they're selling."

"I think we should all try to be like you."

"Maybe. But it ain't easy, is it?"

Rosa nodded.

"Well, I better be off. Enjoy the good weather," he said, picking up the stick. Pebbles barked, wagging his tail.

"Wait. Sorry. Before you go, I was hoping you could help me with something."

"At your service."

"Cloxham Manor. Do you know anything about it?"

The old man fiddled with his collar. "You're not from around here, are you?"

"No. But…"

"How do you know about that God-forsaken place?"

"I… it's just rumours I've heard, that's all."

"Them rumours are probably true. Look, I don't mean to be rude and all, but I'd rather not talk about it. What with all the troubles."

"Of course. I'm sorry."

"Nothing to apologise about. Just be careful, missus. Every place has its secrets, even my calm, peaceful Norfolk."

Wells town was almost as quiet as the beach. All the shops in the centre were closed. The few people Rosa passed on the street seemed to be at pains to avoid eye contact. Everyone seemed to be heading in the opposite direction, perhaps towards the government outlet selling FRJ drugs on the edge of town. As she walked away from the quay and up the narrow streets to the bus stop, she sensed that people were watching her from inside the rows of terraced houses. Nervous sets of eyes peeking through curtains, following her every movement.

A portly woman in her forties was sitting at the bus stop off Station Road, a rucksack by her side. She was tapping her feet but her head was drooped, as if she were on the verge of sleep and fighting it. Rosa noted the dark bags around her eyes and her pale, blotchy skin. When she spoke to her, asking if she were waiting for the bus to Kings Lynn, the woman didn't respond. It was as if she were in a reverie, staring blankly at the concrete road by her feet. Only when Rosa touched her jacket sleeve did she react.

"What do you want?" she muttered, glancing up, her eyes vacant, her voice a defeated monotone.

It was like talking to someone coming out of a deep sleep. After much effort Rosa learnt from the woman that a bus should be due at eleven or soon after. She wasn't sure of the exact time, as the service had been reduced to twice per day, and she'd been sitting there an hour already. Rosa tried to continue a conversation, but the woman shook her head and slumped forward, her eyes just about open but her mind already closed.

Rosa stood up and paced around. Once again, she pictured the scene at Eric and Sally's home. Maybe the police had already contacted the government. Soon enough sirens would be whirring, disturbing the silence of this deserted town. Then a car with blacked-out windows would appear. Men would jump out and bundle her into a car, where a smug Claire Godley would be waiting. "My dear Rosa," she would say, her voice dripping with hate and condescension, "don't you realise that you're responsible for all those deaths at Cloxham? Now we're going to fix you, once and for all."

. . .

The woman's mobile phone had been buzzing for a while, ringing out in the silence. Rosa walked back to the bus stop and tapped her gently on the shoulder.

"What is it?" she muttered, looking faintly irritated with Rosa.

"Your phone's ringing."

She stared at Rosa, then down at her pocket. She slowly pulled the phone out of her pocket, turning off the ringer, then proceeded to take a tablet from her other pocket. Rosa noticed its pale blue colour. She popped it into her mouth, swallowed it down dry.

"My god my god my god!" she stammered quickly, her voice higher pitched than before. "What time is it? What time is it, my sweet Jesus?" Her whole body seemed to be shaking.

"Eleven o'clock."

"Huh? Then that means, that means it's too damned late. The bus has gone, flown away! Do you understand what I'm saying? It's a fucking shambles!"

"It's OK. I've been waiting for the bus, too," she said, quietly moving a safe distance away from the woman. "It will be here soon."

"Do you know what I was gonna do?" the woman said, her eyes darting back and forth between Rosa and the road. "Do you? It's not fair," she said, her voice wavering. "It's not fair at all."

"Do you want to tell me what you were going to do?" Rosa asked, trying to calm her.

She looked at her suspiciously.

"Only if you want to," Rosa added.

"We'd been saving up," the woman said finally, her voice a little calmer. "Neither of us earned a lot, but every week we'd both been putting money away. Enough to get my husband, me and my girls out of the country. There's this boat you see, a new service not far from Norwich. For a thousand pounds per head, they'll ferry you across to Holland. No need for exit visas, no questions asked. We almost had enough. But then the Panic got them all. That was a week ago. I haven't slept since."

Suddenly the woman started crying, big heaving sobs.

Rosa handed her a tissue. She wanted to comfort her but she didn't know how.

"Thank you," the woman said, blowing her nose, then looking at Rosa as if for the first time. "It's a terrible thing, and I don't know how much longer I can last. Dear Lord, I have their ashes right with me, in my bag. No time for a proper burial – the hospital cremated them for me. But I don't know what to do with the ashes," she said, breaking into deep sobs again.

"It's hard," Rosa said, cautiously placing an arm around her. "You've been so brave."

"If only I'd stayed awake that night," the woman continued. "Maybe I could've stopped them before they did it."

"It's not your fault."

"I don't know. All I know is that it's hopeless. We wait for this Rosanna Day, the one that can save us all. But she is nowhere and people keep dying. I don't know whether to believe in her anymore. No one does."

That name again, Rosa thought. *What did it mean? And what can I do to help this woman?*

You know what to do, Ana's voice told her, finally emerging from within, now firm and clear inside her head.

I don't. Tell me.

Take her hands. See.

Rosa did what the voice suggested. Immediately an image came into her mind, a peaceful one. She closed her eyes to better focus on it. *Sunlight on a garden lawn, the sound of children laughing. A woman was tending to a barbecue, turning the sausages so they wouldn't burn.* Rosa made the woman sitting in front of her be this woman in her mind, made the laughing children her daughters, brought her husband into view. *'It's OK, darling,'* the husband said to his wife. 'We're safe here, my dear, happy to wait and watch over you. Take your time. Be strong for us, for everyone.' The garden started to blur, colours merging into different shades of green and brown. Rosa felt herself returning to the present. It seemed like she'd been away a long time.

"Your daughters and husband are at peace," she said, her eyes still closed for a moment. When she opened them, she saw that the woman was on the ground, kneeling at her feet.

"I saw!" the woman exclaimed. Her eyes were full of wonder, her hands were clasped together as if in prayer. "Thank God that I can see."

Rosa looked at her, astonished.Tears fell down the woman's face, tears of relief. She lifted herself up and Rosa hugged her, drawing her close, filled with love and awe.

"I am your humble servant, Rosanna Day," she continued. "Tell me what to do."

29

R osa stood on the platform, waiting for a train that would connect to Nottingham. The train was already late. Earlier, the station manager had told her they were fortunate the train was coming at all, given the latest round of strikes in London. He said how just a couple of days ago a man had fallen asleep on a train coming into Kings Lynn. Other passengers hadn't noticed straightaway since the man had been alone in a first-class carriage. But they all heard his screams.

"The delayed 12:27 train to London Kings Cross will shortly be arriving on platform one," a station employee announced over the tannoy. "Kindly let other passengers off the train before boarding. Please remember, it is strictly forbidden for passengers to fall asleep on the train. Thank you."

Rosa glanced around at the few other passengers awaiting the train. Every one of them looked nervous and tired. She picked up her briefcase and walked farther down the platform. Once again, she thought about the woman kneeling in front of her in Wells Town. *Did I say the right thing to her?* she wondered, even though deep down she knew the answer. The woman wouldn't accept that she was mistaken, that she was not the Rosanna Day people had been talking about. The woman was convinced she had seen a bright luminescence, what she described as a "halo of light" around her. Rosa told herself that the woman must have been hallucinating. She was on the drugs and hadn't slept for one week straight, after all.

Still, it didn't make sense. "Tell me what I should do," the woman had kept on asking, pleading with her. Rosa had stood there, unsure of what to say. She had shut her eyes to try to find a moment of calmness, waited for some inspiration. Instinctively she put her hand to the woman's head, and as she did so the garden scene immediately came back to her. She could even smell the sausages burning on the barbecue. The woman's husband came up to her and placed his arms around her shoulders. Then her two young daughters came over, each hugging one of her legs.

"I cannot offer you a miracle cure," she had told the woman. The words flowed out of her effortlessly, as if she were merely a conduit. "But I can feel your pain," she'd continued, "and I know that this pain doesn't have to be with you forever. Your husband and daughters love you very much, I can sense it, and they miss you, too. But they want you to stay strong for them. Find a peaceful place, somewhere cherished by you and your family. Scatter their ashes, and as you do so, let the tears come. Don't hold back. After all, it is only human to be devastated by such a great loss. Still, you must not despair. Life is always full of wonder, even in the darkest times. So as you stand there, bidding your husband and daughters farewell, do your best to recall their faces, their voices and their laughter. Hold them in your mind. Your love will nourish them on their next journey. And you will meet them again when the time is right.

"But that time is not now. Now you must re-embrace the

world, with all its suffering and beauty. This is what your family would have wanted. Go home and rest well. Throw those drugs away. Then once you've regained your strength, help your friends and neighbours in any way you can."

A train whistle blew, bringing her back to the present. She saw the train approaching. Her eyes glanced upon some of her fellow travellers farther along the platform. A middle-aged woman standing alone. Beyond her, a man in his twenties, smartly dressed, with closely shaved hair. He was holding the hand of a young girl, his eyes fixed on the approaching train. Suddenly Rosa felt faint, nauseated even, from an overpowering sense of déjà vu. *What is it?* she thought. *Why is this all so familiar?* She sat down on the ground, breathing in deeply, but the dizziness was still there.

The train came to a halt. Already she knew what would happen. The child turned around as the man, who may or may not have been the child's father, lifted her onto the train. The little girl looked directly at Rosa, her tiny arms outstretched as if she were reaching for her. *I must stand up,* Rosa thought. *I must get on that train and help her.* But her head was spinning, the whole platform seemed to be lurching one way, then the other. As the train doors closed, she felt herself slipping away. There was nothing she could do.

"Are you all right, Rosa?" a woman asked her gently. Rosa detected a slight North American accent. "Don't sit up just yet."

The room was pitch-black. Rosa could feel a mask strapped tightly around her face. It felt as it was made of rubber or silicon.

"What's going on?!" she asked, scrabbling at the mask nervously. The last moment she could recall was sitting down on the ground at the train station. Was it possible that she'd harmed herself then, done something permanent? She tried to open her eyes, but the mask restricted any movement.

"Try to keep calm," the woman said, dabbing Rosa's forehead with a damp cloth.

"You've locked me up again, you bastards!"

"No. We've been looking after you, but you can leave whenever you want. We're on your side, I promise. We're not the government. Now, you've been out for a good few hours. Don't worry; the mask was only a precaution. You're fine. But first you need to regain your strength."

"Where am I? Please, take this thing off my eyes."

"OK, but keep your eyes closed. Even with the lights off, the room will seem very bright."

The woman carefully undid the mask. As she did so, Rosa shielded her eyes with her hands. Gradually her eyes adjusted to the light.

"Welcome back, Rosa," the woman said, smiling at her. She was much younger than Rosa expected her to be. "I'm Kiyoko. I've heard so much about you. I'm here to help. I'll watch over you."

"Kiyoko?" Rosa said, wondering why the name sounded familiar. Was that the name the dying boy at Cloxham Manor had said to her?

"That's me."

Trust her, Ana said. *But no one else. Not yet.*

Why? Rosa asked Ana silently. *How can you be so sure?*

She is part of who you are.

"Rosa? Would you like some water?"

Rosa nodded. She was still digesting what Ana had just said. What did she mean that Kiyoko was a part of her? Kiyoko opened a sealed water bottle. She poured water into two glasses, drank from one of them and handed the other to Rosa.

"Thanks," Rosa said, sitting up in bed. Her throat was parched and she had a slight headache, but otherwise she was OK. She took a long sip of the water, felt slightly better.

"Would you like anything else? Maybe something to eat?"

"No thanks, I'm good."

Rosa glanced around the room. Other than one small print by the door, the walls were blank. Thick shutters covered the windows.

"What happened? I was at Kings Lynn train station when I blacked out. Where are we now?"

"Little Walsingham. A small village out in the countryside, about thirty miles east of Kings Lynn. We brought you here after you fell unconscious. You're safe, I promise. I know, because the government is after me, too. Fortunately, they're not so organised."

Rosa glanced at Kiyoko, then at the glass in her hands. She felt calmer. Somehow, she knew Ana was right, that she could trust this young woman.

"I need to get to Nottingham. My brother is there."

"Right."

"What is it?" Rosa asked, sensing Kiyoko's unease. "What do you know about my brother?"

"Nathan is not well," Kiyoko said. "They're looking after him as best they can. Colleagues of Shaw and Lillian, people I understand you once knew. But Nathan is unwell. He has been drifting in and out of consciousness."

"What?! Where is he?"

"Oxford."

"I need to see him."

"I know, and you will very soon. Andrew Shaw is arranging that. It's risky. Still, Oxford is probably the safest place for us right now. The government would never anticipate that you and I would go back there. We were lucky to have reached you first."

"I don't get it. Doesn't Shaw work for the government?"

"Not any more he doesn't. I had my doubts about Shaw, too, at first. But we spoke at length, and now I'm convinced he's on the right side. He's keen to talk to you. When you're ready, that is."

"He's here?"

"No, but I have his phone number. You can call him later if you want. He also left you this package. He asked that you only open it after you've spoken with him."

"Right. What about Lillian? Is she part of all this, too?"

Kiyoko looked down at her feet and then at Rosa. "Lillian is dead," she said. "I'm sorry."

Rosa stared at the solitary picture on the wall. It was a faded print of a Van Gogh painting. One of his self-portraits after he had chopped off his ear. She gazed into the painter's eyes, sensing his anguish.

"Lillian was a good woman. One of the few people I trusted. You know about Cloxham Manor, do you?"

"Only a little."

"Lillian was the one person there who was really trying to understand this thing."

How about Shaw and John Okoro? Rosa considered them. Maybe they'd ended up on the right side in the end. But they weren't brave like Lillian.

"She tried to help me escape," Rosa continued. "Did Shaw tell you that?"

"No."

"After that I never saw her again. How did she die? Was it from the Panic?"

Kiyoko shook her head. "She died standing up for what she believed in. Without her, FRJ and the government would have taken Nathan. From what everyone has told me, she was brilliant."

"She really was. Brilliant and compassionate. My god, what has happened to this world?"

Kiyoko brought her hand to Rosa's and held it gently. "You can make it a better place," she said. "And I will help you with your burden in any way I can."

30

E dith Dubois wore large sunglasses and a brilliant, scarlet-red scarf. She looked like she was in her mid-sixties. Kiyoko guided her to a scuffed armchair. Rosa noticed the dust particles as they all sat down.

Could it be her? Rosa wondered. Could she be the Edith Dubois she had dreamt about and once seen at a train station all those years ago? And was it really possible that she was her biological mother, as Shaw had claimed? It was true at least that they seemed to share certain features – their noses thin and straight; the same gently curved upper lip; similar lightly arched eyebrows. Perhaps they had once shared the same eyes, too, before Edith had cut hers out.

Shaw warned them to be careful. Last night he had described over the phone how Edith had been institutionalised for most of her adult life, a schizophrenic who had murdered a man. Almost certainly Edith won't remember you, Shaw had told Rosa, and not just because she is blind. Still, he said, I hope seeing her brings you closure.

"It's so kind of you to visit," Edith said as they sat down. "Sorry about Gully barking like crazy earlier. She's been a good guide dog in the short time we've been together. But she does have her moments. I don't have many real visitors anymore, so the poor girl has become a little unsocialised. Even Andrew hardly comes, what with the recent troubles. Not that I'm ungrateful – I appreciate the little freedoms I now have. Sorry, I'm rambling already. I understand you are friends of his?"

"Yes. Friends and colleagues both," Kiyoko said; Rosa remained silent to begin with, as Shaw had advised. "I'm Kiyoko and I'm here with Jasmine."

"That's right," she said, touching the cloth tied around her eyes. "Jasmine is the one who doesn't talk much. Andrew told me I might be able to help you both, which I'd love to do, given how much he's helped me. But first, let me potter over to the kitchen and fix you both a cup of tea."

"Can we help you with that?" Kiyoko asked.

"Thanks, but it's fine, my dears. Practice is the best way for a blind person to get their bearings."

They watched Edith stand up. With a thin white stick, she felt her way carefully to the kitchen. Rosa smiled as she passed, trying to appear relaxed, then remembered that Edith was blind. Or at least that is what Shaw had said. She had a lingering doubt that just maybe Edith could actually see, with all this an elaborate deception concocted by Andrew Shaw.

The scarf seemed too much of a coincidence, and though she thought she could trust Shaw, she still had her doubts. She wondered if he had infiltrated Alliance, or even if the whole organisation was a front for the government, with Shaw reassigned to monitor her and this woman an actress hired to play the part of Edith Dubois.

Then again, Shaw had not tried to deny that the military had monitored her as a young child. Like a good soldier, he hadn't questioned his superiors, performing his minder's role as instructed. Indeed, it was only a few months ago, after Rosa had been interned by the government, that Shaw supposedly discovered Rosa was the same young child he had accompanied to and from Kings Lynn train station all those years ago.

On the phone Shaw had also confirmed that Edith Dubois was her biological mother. There was no doubt, he said. They had completed the DNA tests, a certified copy of which he had left for Rosa in a sealed envelope. While the medical certificate with the DNA results appeared genuine, she also knew it could have been forged.

"Are you sure it's OK?" Edith asked.

"Pardon?" Rosa said. She hadn't even noticed that Edith was already back in the room. She glanced across at Kiyoko for help.

"Edith was just asking us if the tea was OK without sugar. I said it was."

"Oh, I'm sorry, I was miles away. Yes, of course."

Rosa glanced across at Kiyoko, mouthed a quiet thanks. She was glad that Kiyoko was there with her. Although they had known each other for less than twenty-four hours, already Rosa felt a strong bond had formed between them. She was certain she could rely on her. It wasn't simply because of what Ana had said. Last night they had sat talking for hours. Rosa recounted her time in Cloxham Manor. Kiyoko described how she watched over people when they slept and her plans to set up support networks in Oxford, and she shared with Rosa how she felt about Nick.

"I had everything else lined up, you see," Edith said, her voice sounding a little unsteady. "But the sugar, I have no idea where it is."

Rosa glanced at Edith, noticed how her hands were shaking. She looked at the teacups and saucers, the biscuits on matching plates, the milk in a pretty ceramic jug. Everything was perfectly assembled except for the missing sugar.

"It's no good," Edith said, beginning to sob. "It's not the same without it."

"OK. I could look in the kitchen," Kiyoko offered. "If you would like, that is."

"Would you? That's very kind, my dear. I'm still adjusting to this new apartment you see."

"I'll go," Rosa said, standing up. Edith smiled, looking a little more confident in herself. But as Rosa walked past her, she accidentally brushed her leg. Immediately Edith looked up. She stared directly at Rosa, the smile gone from her face. As if her blind eyes could sense something in Rosa, her forgotten child.

"Cold, so cold," she groaned. "What are you doing here? I thought you were dead."

Rosa froze, unsure of what to do. Through the closed kitchen door, she thought she could hear Edith's dog whimpering.

"Are you ok, Edith?" Kiyoko asked.

Edith turned back towards Kiyoko. "Over the years they came to me," she muttered. "Lost babies, their mothers dead, not fully of this world. They haunt me even now, after all these years. Trapped in the eyes of strangers. At least I cannot see them anymore. But I can still feel their pain, like wood chopped from the earth. Come to me, Jasmine. Let me read your palm. You have a story to tell and I can help you. But you must come now, whilst the feeling is here."

Rosa and Kiyoko looked uncertainly at each other.

"What about the sugar?" Rosa asked.

"Forget the fucking sugar!" Edith shrieked. "Come here, please. I mean you no harm," she said, her voice a little calmer. "But come to me now, whilst my hands are prickling and they're able to see!"

"All right," Rosa said, sitting on the carpet by Edith's feet.

"Jasmine is sitting by you now," Kiyoko said, watching closely, ready to intervene if necessary.

"My dear girl, give me your hands," Edith said, her voice

returning to normal. "Ever since I went blind I have been blessed with the gift of second sight. An Da Shealladh."

Rosa brought her hands forward, and Edith clasped them eagerly. She ran her index finger along Rosa's right palm, all the while humming to herself.

"Your heart is still strong," she said, tracing the line running across the top of Rosa's palm. "And your mind is, as I suspected, unique. See how this line almost zigzags."

"Yes."

Edith frowned, then took Rosa's left hand and gently pinched the skin beneath the thumb.

"Your life had a very strange beginning, one that reminds me of my own great loss. Borne out of suffering and love, you had two souls. They merged and became one, but whether the new soul can prosper depends on you. Not only on you, but the whole world. For now, in this strange epidemic, people are losing touch with themselves, forgetting what it means to be truly human. The human spirit, what was once unified and whole, has fractured into millions, billions of fragments. Compassion has become a word without meaning."

Rosa looked across at Kiyoko, wanting reassurance, and was shocked to see her passed out on the sofa. She pulled her hand away and went to Kiyoko, gently shaking her.

"Wait, I'm not done!" Edith shrieked. "I know who you are."

"Kiyoko, can you hear me?" she said, ignoring Edith as best she could. But Kiyoko remained unconscious. She put her ear close to her mouth, was relieved to hear her breathing steadily.

"Ana, I know it is you," Edith said, her voice suddenly calm.

Rosa glanced back to Edith. How could she know that name? Could she really be her biological mother?

"Place her on her side so she can breathe more easily, let her rest a while. Your friend will be fine, I promise. Now, please, come back to me so I can finish reading your palm. I will be quick, five minutes max. Once I am done, Kiyoko will come to. I swear on my daughter's heart."

Rosa put Kiyoko into a side-lying position. It didn't make any sense, but at least she was breathing steadily. Best to let her come around naturally, she decided.

Rosa looked again at Edith, sitting there with her back perfectly straight, waiting patiently. She is an old blind woman, Rosa reminded herself. What harm can she cause?

"OK," Rosa said. "Five minutes, that's it."

"Fine."

Rosa offered both her hands to Edith, who took them eagerly. She started humming again, moving her lips in circles so that the murmur undulated up and down. Once again, she ran her index finger across each of Rosa's palms, then over her fingers and thumbs. She sighed and gently let go, raising her hands up to remove her sunglasses.

Instinctively Rosa looked away, afraid. But then she forced herself to look, not flinching when she saw the empty eye sockets. Two dark, shrunken holes that seemed to see through her.

"Don't be shocked by what you see," Edith said. "I have come to terms with my condition. Like you must. You are Ana, the most important of all my lost children. I can see you clearly, despite my blindness. Like a halo of light in darkness. The good part of you is permanent, shining through the evil, but still you must be vigilant. Cloxham Manor..."

Edith paused, pulled away slightly.

"Go on," Rosa said.

"Pitch black, no hint of light," she said. Her voice was shaky. "You couldn't control it. Worse will follow, a second wave stronger than the last. Nothing can stop it. But from this devastation life can start afresh."

Edith took her hands away from Rosa, put them together as in prayer. Kiyoko was beginning to stir.

"Don't judge us too harshly," Edith said, bowing her head.

"We are lost, broken creatures, we have forgotten what is right. Your new soul is truth, relentless in its judgement. You are the one who can show us the right path. Guide us out of this wilderness and keep us whole."

Kiyoko and Rosa had left Edith's house. They walked side by side, both still shaken. The street was deserted.

"I don't understand it," Kiyoko said again. "I was out for, what, almost ten minutes, right?"

"Yes. Edith must have spiked your drink."

"It's possible. But I feel completely fine now."

Suddenly they heard a scream. It came from a narrow alleyway just ahead.

Help him, Ana's voice instructed. *But be very careful.*

Rosa broke into a run.

"Rosa!" Kiyoko shouted. "Wait!"

Rosa went to the man lying prostrate on the floor. He was twitching. She noticed that his hands were raised to his face.

"What is your name?" Rosa asked gently, crouching down. "Can you hear me?"

"Leave me alone!" the man shrieked.

"Listen to me, please, come back. I am with you."

"Rosa?" Kiyoko said uncertainly. "We should go, find help."

But Rosa hardly heard. "I will help you," she said. "The burden is too great for anyone to carry alone."

Like before, with the woman at the bus stop, the words flowed out of Rosa effortlessly. She didn't try to stop it. "This world is full of suffering," she continued, "yet that does not mean you should lose hope. We hurt because we are hurt, we push our pain onto others. Do you hear me? Do you hear what I'm saying?"

The man grunted but remained prostrate.

"Let me help," she said. "I'm going to place my hands on your head, nothing more than that. Is that OK?"

"Yes," the man whispered.

"Rosa, be careful," Kiyoko said, bending down next to her.

The street was deserted. Rosa put one hand on the back of his head, closed her eyes and concentrated. At first, she felt nothing. But then it came to her. Not images, only sounds. A man shouting, this man, she was sure. What he was saying she couldn't tell, but she could feel his rage. Then she heard the child whimpering.

She let go of the man's head. It was too much for her to bear.

"Help me," the man said. "Please. I'm sorry. I have done so much wrong."

She opened her eyes, took Kiyoko's hand for support.

"What is it?" Kiyoko asked.

"I don't know."

Go on, Ana instructed. *Do what is necessary.*

Rosa placed her hands on the man's head and shut her eyes once again. She heard another voice, a woman's, urging the man to stop, pleading with him. But the man was already lost, all the anger within himself, at his own deficiencies, directed at his young son. She sensed the man's fist being clenched, heard it come down hard on the poor, defenceless child.

"We all make mistakes," Rosa whispered into the man's ear, so only he could hear. "But what you did was unforgivable. I see hate and anger: you are blind to the beauty of this world."

The man moaned quietly, as if in agreement. She heard his hands scrabbling at his face, didn't try to stop him.

"Some things are too much to bear. But even in the worst of us there are chinks of light. Strive for that light, cut out the rest, even if it leaves you blind. You will suffer, but it's your only chance of being saved."

Rosa let go of the man's head, then stood up. She felt faint. Kiyoko, sensing it, quickly supported her.

"I'm sorry," the man sobbed. "Please forgive me."

"No. Only your son and wife can forgive you," she said without emotion, then walked away, feeling a sickness deep inside.

QUARANTINE

September

31

The sun edged up above the horizon; scattered birdsong carried in the breezeless air. Nick muttered to himself, shook his arms and legs vigorously, doing whatever he could to quieten the moaning inside his head. It was worse than usual today. Nonsensical images kept appearing in the corner of his vision, abstract structures that constantly twisted and turned. He pushed them aside, muttering aloud again, desperate for some clarity.

PANIK

The misspelt graffiti was still there, the once bright red paint now dull and mottled. September 25. Tomorrow it would be the first anniversary since the epidemic had begun. According to official records, at least. *Hadn't Lillian talked about it building up over generations?* A psychological illness turned physical, she'd said, or something like that. Already millions had died. How many more would be taken?

Nick looked away from the wall and to the street in front of him. The tarmac was potholed; fallen leaves gathered in stagnant water. Autumn had barely begun, yet already the trees lining the roads looked withered and old.

He sat down on the pavement, praying that Kiyoko would show. It seemed so long since they'd last met. Thirteen weeks, if he had counted it correctly. Not that he could be certain. His memory was too hazy these days: he'd not had a proper night's sleep in all that time. But it was today that they had agreed to meet, he was sure of that.

On the phone, Kiyoko had told him she would be here. He couldn't remember what time, but he knew it was early morning and on this particular street. The same street they had met on last year, when the Panic was still in its infancy. He didn't understand why they should meet in Oxford, especially after his failed stay at Mantle Hospital. But Kiyoko had insisted. He remembered she had her reasons, he just couldn't recall exactly what they were. Could it relate to Rosanna Day, he wondered, half-recalling something Kiyoko had said. He still clung to the possibility she was out there somewhere.

At least there were no longer any travel restrictions in and out of the city. Elmore Facility had closed, the military had left, too. It was as if the government had given up on Oxford. Not just Oxford, but pretty much all of England and Wales. A blockade across the north of England was now complete, and Northern Ireland had successfully negotiated a temporary separation from the rest of the United Kingdom. Neighbouring countries had become increasingly vigilant, patrolling their coastlines to stop boats carrying British refugees from making land. It felt like life under quarantine.

The moaning in his head became louder, the abstract images formed into jagged mouths, screaming at him. He shut his eyes and clasped his hands over his ears.

Anything to drown them out. Finally, they were quiet. He opened his eyes, and for a moment he couldn't remember where he was. How long had he been sitting there, and how much longer until Kiyoko showed? The sun was bright now and had risen above the buildings. The street was deserted.

"Hello, Nick," a man said, appearing from nowhere.

It was Harold. *This doesn't make any sense,* he thought. He rubbed his eyes and Harold was gone. But moments later he was back again, sitting next to Nick on the floor, combing his hair carefully to one side. He seemed so real.

"I'm imagining it," Nick whispered to himself.

"Really? Then why am I answering you?"

Nick touched the apparition, watched his hand permeate through Harold's shoulder.

"Go away," he muttered, clamping his eyes shut and trying to picture Kiyoko instead.

"You should never have come back to Mantle Hospital."

"I had to."

"But you failed, didn't you? Don't worry, I don't hold it against you. I understand – under hypnosis, you told me everything. I have my doubts, too, sometimes. Yes, even cynical Harold Stone."

"Leave me alone."

"We're still friends, aren't we?"

"What are you talking about?" Nick shouted out. "We were never friends."

Silence. Nick opened his eyes. Harold's apparition had gone. Nervously he glanced around, relieved that no one had witnessed him talking to himself. Not that they'd do anything. It was no longer a rare occurrence. People all over were talking to themselves, slowly going mad.

Kiyoko, please come soon, he thought. *I don't know if we can go back to how it was, but I need you now. The hallucinations are getting worse all the time. If they keep up like this, I don't know what I'm going to do.*

Nervously he scanned the street: still no sign of Kiyoko. Litter was scattered all over. He looked east towards Headington, where Mantle Hospital used to be, and where he had resided for a short time.

His mission had been a failure. After just two and a half days in the hospital, Harold had discovered him, despite his forged papers and carefully altered appearance. During that time, Nick couldn't recall being hypnotised or the doctors doing anything more invasive than take urine and blood tests. And he never came across Vincent Davies, Shaw's other contact in the hospital.

"Listen, we may disagree on the best way to combat SED," Harold had told him. "But that doesn't mean I'm heartless. We were once friends, after all. I also regret what happened to Lillian, sincerely I do. If I could turn back the clock..."

Nick looked at Harold, unsure of what to say. He knew he should appear grateful, but he also wanted to tell Harold why he was mistaken, why the drugs developed by FRJ caused more harm than good. In the end, though, he said nothing, and not long after, one of Harold's staff was there at the door to escort him out of the hospital.

"Nick? Hello, is anybody in there?"

It was Kiyoko. Her smile looked radiant in the morning light.

"Hi," he said, his voice shaky as he stood up. "It's so good to see you."

"You too," she said, hugging him close, and then patting him gently on the back. "How have you been? Managing to sleep any better?"

"A little. Well, you know how it is." He looked into her eyes, wanting to kiss her, but unsure if she still felt the same way. It seemed like it had been such a long time. "How about you?"

"I'm good. Let's walk into town. Bishop's Cafe is still standing. How about a coffee there for old times' sake? You wouldn't believe it, but it's much better than it used to be."

"Sure."

"Afterwards, there's someone I'd like you to meet. If that's OK?"

Nick nodded absently.

"You know, we're making a real difference here," Kiyoko told him as they walked. "Now that the government has left Oxford, people can do what they want. There's a real sense of community. People come together to share their fears, and take turns to watch over others."

Nick nodded again, doing his best to listen, but then he stumbled on something. A huge branch, the bark dried and rotting. *At least it wasn't a corpse,* he thought grimly.

"You OK?"

"Yep."

"Good. Listen, it's not perfect. But there are pockets of hope dotted around the city. Cowley Park is once again a safe space to wander. Many people have come off the drugs. Even those still taking them seem less dependent. You know, you'd be welcome to stay here, too, if you wanted. Try it for a few days, see how you like it."

"Thanks, but I can't."

"If it's Mantle Hospital, don't worry about that. They've scaled down loads."

"Maybe."

"Give it some thought. You are staying at least for the speeches and music tomorrow? One year since the first official death from the Panic. We're expecting a decent turn-out."

"Huh?"

"Nick!" she exclaimed, stopping on the street. "I told you about this. Don't you remember?"

"Um, maybe. I don't remember. I'm sorry. Let's keep walking, all right?"

"Sure," she said. He noticed she was biting her upper lip.

"I'm OK, Kiyoko. Yeah, my memory has gotten pretty bad. It's the insomnia. I have other problems, too, but deep down I'm OK."

"Good."

"Will Rosanna Day be there?"

"No," Kiyoko replied, a little quickly.

"The word on the street is she saved someone from the Panic. Somewhere east, on the coast. Norfolk or Suffolk, I think."

"I've heard that rumour, too. Maybe there is this great healer out there. I hope so, but I don't know."

Nick looked at Kiyoko as she brushed a loose strand of hair from her face. If only everything could be simpler. "This event tomorrow," he said. "Isn't it risky? The government, surely they won't like it."

"It'll be fine. They've been fully informed, and we have promised it will be peaceful. We are trying to make it a positive experience. Respecting the dead, yes, but looking forward, too. To a potential cure, to the end of this quarantine. Anyway, who do we have to riot against? There are no police or military in Oxford. We govern ourselves."

"But wouldn't the government bring in the military for an event like this?"

"I doubt it. Even if they did, what does it matter?"

They walked in silence for a while, stepping over fallen trees and past burnt-out houses. The streets were deserted. Up ahead, Nick noticed a large billboard advertising Calm, the latest FRJ drug. A smartly dressed male model stared at the camera, arms folded, eyes focused and with a hint of a smile on his lips. His handsome, angular features were further emphasised by a bokeh background of blurry rain droplets in the night sky. It was one of a series of adverts found in almost every town and city, even the ones abandoned by government. Whether it was a man or woman, a couple or a family, the models would always be staring confidently at the camera. Each time there would be the same catchphrase:

When the going gets tough, you stay Calm©

"You're not on the drugs, are you?"

"What? No, of course not!" Nick said angrily, stopping on the street. "Not after what they did to me."

"I'm sorry."

"But how could you think that?"

"I don't know," she replied, looking momentarily at Nick, then down at her feet. "It was a stupid thing to say. I wasn't thinking straight."

"It's OK, forget about it."

"I'm sorry. It's only... it's just that I've no idea what you've been up to all this time. I mean, I know you have been with Shaw for some of that time, somewhere in Wales. But that's it. Didn't you want to see me?"

"I did, Kiyoko, really I did. I've been thinking about you all the time. I still remember, you know, our time together in Nottingham. Before I went to Mantle Hospital."

"So do I," Kiyoko said, taking Nick by the hand and leading him to a nearby bench. "I've missed you so much."

He looked at her, at those beautiful hazel brown eyes. She understood his suffering better than anyone else. "I didn't want to be a burden, that's all," he said, wanting to kiss her but holding back. "You know how bad I was the last time we met. Hearing voices, the hallucinations. It's only gotten worse. That's the sad truth. On top of that, Shaw has told me how much you've been helping people here. You have a unique talent. But with me around, I don't know. I would be in the way."

"No, you wouldn't."

"Sometimes my mind gets lost, Kiyoko. I hardly can tell where I am. The moaning, these horrible images, they're always there at the edge of my mind, threatening to take me. I'm not well. I don't understand how I'm still alive."

"Don't say that. You're strong. And I've missed you," she said, looking directly into his eyes.

"I've missed you, too; so much. But I don't want to be a burden," he said, looking away. "At least by staying at the clinic, I can be useful. Shaw's doctors can run their tests on me. Shaw's plan for Mantle Hospital may have failed, but they might not be that far from a vaccine."

"Maybe. Look, I do appreciate Shaw in some ways. He was the one who helped set us up safely here, in Oxford. This vaccine, though. I just can't see how it would work."

"You can never know, I guess. His doctors are pesky little shits at times, what with all their injections and endless questions. But they are on the right side. It's not like Mantle Hospital at all. They're trying to help me, really they are."

Kiyoko took his hand and squeezed it. He waited for her to say something, but she remained silent. She moved closer on the bench so their legs were touching, looked up into his eyes. He gazed back at her, let her draw him close, but suddenly the moaning came back. Loud, desperate cries that filled his head. Louder than ever before. He pulled away from Kiyoko, stood up, frantic, clasping his hands over his ears.

"Stop, please stop!" he muttered, rocking back and forth. The abstract shapes appeared again in front of him, jagged lines forming into faceless mouths. The moaning intensified, a piercing cacophony of lost souls, seeming to tell him that everything was lost.

He fell to his knees and shut his eyes. A panic rushed up

inside of him, harsher and more intense than any time before. He fought it, as he always did, by trying to picture Kiyoko in his mind's eye, no longer aware that she was right there in front of him.

"Nick! Nick, can you hear me?"

He couldn't hear her. The moans were deafening. He opened his eyes and there were flames everywhere, burning up the ground. Smoke billowed out of the buildings. The fire reached the advertising board, flames ripping at the canvas. The eyes of the model advertising Calm became two blackened holes, staring blindly at him. "When the going gets tough," the model shouted at him, "I rip out my eyes."

Silence. Everything had been burnt. Blackened tree trunks, charred carcasses of farm animals, their legs pointing upwards. Then, somehow, he could see it happening everywhere, the world over, as if he were floating at a great height and looking down. Plants and trees withering, sickly animals lying on the ground. The moaning returned, a deep, low sound spreading outwards. He sensed his body floating down, and as he approached the ground, he saw it. A mass of legless humans swarming over the land, their mouths open, consuming every-thing as they continued to groan.

Far away, he heard Kiyoko's voice, calling out to him. He couldn't make out what she was saying. He tried to move in the direction of her voice, but his body seemed frozen.

"Nick! I'm here. Listen to me, listen! Relax, try to be calm. I'm here, watching over you. I won't leave you, I promise. I'm by your side. Do you hear me? I'm here, and I love you with all my heart."

32

Rosa could sense them approaching. Kiyoko and Nick Parry, they would be coming through the door any minute now, somehow she knew it. She was glad to be finally meeting this man, particularly given what he had done for her brother. If Nick hadn't procured the medication, she knew Nathan would already be dead. Nathan's condition seemed to be improving now, ever since they had been reunited. Still, he was far from being fully recovered. She glanced across at her unconscious brother and smiled.

Yet still she felt uneasy. It wasn't that she distrusted Nick Parry, despite knowing that he used to peddle drugs. Now he was part of the resistance, working with Shaw. More important, Kiyoko vouched for him, and Lillian had surely trusted him, too. So what was it that made her feel ill at ease? It didn't make any sense.

It's not him, Ana murmured. *It's what's inside him.*

"What do you mean?" Rosa whispered. Ana spoke to her frequently now. An insistent voice, one that Rosa no longer tried to suppress.

You fear his illness. He is unwell, overcome by suffering and anger. The Panic should have taken him already, but he fights it. He is strong and a good man. Remember that. You shouldn't fear his sickness. You can save him.

Ana, I can't, I don't know how. These people here in Oxford. Kiyoko is the one who persuades them to stop taking the drugs. She watches over people when they sleep, keeps their emotions in check. I just sit and talk, I look after the children who have lost their parents. Anyone could do these things.

It's more than that. You know it.

Maybe. I hold their hands, I try to offer them some kind of solace. Sometimes when I listen, it seems like I can physically feel their suffering. But isn't that just being empathetic?

Rosa, you are being modest to a fault. There are many degrees of empathy. These people here, they would have slipped over the edge if it weren't for you. You know it, and deep down they know it, too. Not only that. Not so long ago you saved two people. Don't forget that.

The woman, maybe. But not the man. Maybe I helped him understand, but at what cost?

It was the right thing to do, Rosa. Cut out the evil. How else could he have been saved?

Does it have to be that way?

Yes! What you have achieved is already important. But you can do so much more, if you choose. Shaw spoke the truth when you last met.

Probably. What he had said about my childhood, it could make sense. At least Shaw believed it did.

It's not only Andrew Shaw. Kiyoko saw what you did. She knows you are the Rosanna Day that people have been waiting for. So tomorrow, stand up. Let everyone know who you really are. Speak and they will listen to you.

What could I tell them?

There was no response. Rosa waited, but she knew Ana had

gone. She drew the curtains and opened the windows. The sun cast rays of light across the room, showing up the dust and the ragged bedcovers. It was warmer than it had been for a while. Perhaps summer would last a little longer. For a moment, Shaw came into her mind, requesting her forgiveness. Without fuss, she pushed the memory to one side.

She came away from the window, sat back down next to Nathan and took his hand. "It's almost midday, Nathan," she said gently. "Don't you want to wake up?"

His breathing was steady. Looking at his peaceful face, she wondered how long it would be until he next awoke.

She cherished the good days, when he was lucid. Even days like today – where he drifted in and out of consciousness, dazed and not really knowing where he was – were special. He was still the little brother she had always loved. He was getting better, she was sure of it.

When he was awake and clear-headed, they would go for long walks around the University Parks, chatting along the way, recollecting happy memories from their childhood. Like Sunday roasts and board games. Or sitting cross-legged by the fireplace, watching the logs spark and crackle. The long summer days when they would cycle for hours on end, through woodland and pretty villages, the whirr of their bicycles' pedals and each of them happily lost in their own daydreams.

She had also tried to talk to Nathan about the present, but when she brought it up the conversation always became awkward and tense. They were like two elderly friends reminiscing because they feared what the future held.

A few days ago, Nathan had brought up their biological parents. He wanted to know who they were, why they had given them up for adoption, and whether they were still alive. Issues they had talked about many times in the past without ever finding an answer. Rosa didn't tell him about Edith Dubois and Andrew Shaw. It seemed better to protect him, at least until he made a full recovery, particularly as Nathan believed he and Rosa were biological siblings, whereas she had never been sure. Not that it made her love him any less.

———————

She heard Kiyoko calling to her from the street below. Rosa came to the window and saw Kiyoko struggling to support a man around her shoulders. It must be Nick Parry. She ran down the stairs and opened the front door. Together they lay Nick down on the sofa in the main room. His eyes were open but seemed unable to focus. He muttered incomprehensibly; moments later, he closed his eyes and fell silent.

"I can't believe we're finally here," Kiyoko sighed.

"What happened?"

"I don't know. Nick just flipped out. I thought he was going to... you know. My god, it was so terrible!"

"Sit down," Rosa told her, gently leading Kiyoko to one of the dining chairs. "Try to relax."

"I managed to calm him a little. Eventually I got him back on his feet. He wasn't making any sense; he hardly seemed to see me. At least he could walk, just about, that is. Still, it took us forever to get here. We weren't far away but he could barely support himself. I didn't know what else to do. All I knew was that I couldn't leave him alone. If I had, he would've done it. He would've killed himself, I know it."

Kiyoko started sobbing. Rosa went to her. She brought Kiyoko's face to her chest, comforting her as best she could. She glanced across at Nick. He was fast asleep.

"Kiyoko, listen to me. He wouldn't have done it. The Panic doesn't take you like that."

"Maybe. Oh, I don't know. I don't know. What are we going to do?"

"Don't worry. Rest a moment. I'll get you some water, OK?"

Kiyoko nodded. She looked exhausted. Rosa could see the beads of perspiration on her face. She went into the kitchen and ran the tap. The water came out a rusty brown. How long before everything falls apart, she wondered, as she waited for the water to clear.

That depends on you.

Quiet, Ana, please.

You can cure him.

No, I can't. I don't know how.

It's not something you learn. It's inside him and inside you. You just have to reach for it.

"Rosa? Are you OK in there?"

"I'm fine. Just waiting for the water to clear."

Rosa came back into the lounge. She sat across from Kiyoko at the small dining table. They both looked across at Nick, sprawled on the sofa.

"What should we do?"

"We wait for him to wake."

"And Nathan? Is he still asleep?"

"Yes. Why don't you rest, too, for a little while? After all, you didn't sleep much last night, did you?"

"I suppose not."

"I'll keep an eye on your friend while you lie down."

"OK. But wake me up if he stirs. Promise?"

"I promise."

Rosa watched Kiyoko walk up the stairs, then looked across at Nick. She watched his chest heave up and down, waiting for him to wake. Her heart beating fast, she willed herself to be ready.

His mother was there, standing next to him as he tended to the sausages and beef burgers on the barbecue. She was silent, gazing at the smoke rising from the burning meat. He wanted to check that she was all right, but he seemed unable to turn his head. It took all his concentration to simply flip the sausages and burgers over. When he finally managed it, he was relieved to see that they weren't too badly burnt.

"They're burnt," she said, sadly shaking her head.

"It's not so bad," he replied, still staring at the meat, the words coming out more nervously than he expected. "They're only charred, and we all prefer them like that anyway."

"My dear son, can't you see? Every day I search for your sister and father, but even when I find them, they are still lost."

"What are you talking about?" he asked. The sun had set; the light was fading fast. "They're just inside, preparing the salad. Isn't it great that Susy has nearly finished her PhD? She told me she's already working on her second journal article."

Nick turned away from the barbecue, ignoring the smell of burning meat as best he could. He looked at his mother and she was as he always remembered her: wearing an apron, her long brown hair tied in a bun. Except this time, there was no smile on her face, and he could sense the tears welling up in her eyes.

"I loved them both, like I love you," she said, putting her hand on his shoulder. "But now they are broken. I try to find them, but at best I find tiny remnants of who they once were. Their souls have shattered and it breaks my heart."

"I don't understand. They're just inside. Probably right there by the kitchen window, watching us chatting."

"Come with me," she said, taking his hand. "I don't want to show you this, but you have to understand."

She led him away from the smoking barbecue and back towards the house. Suddenly he sensed an unbearable foreboding.

"Stop, Mum, stop!"

It was too late. He whimpered, a wounded animal, for he knew what he was about to see.

Nick woke up, but inside his head, they were still screaming. His mind was a blur of harsh, jarring images. He glanced down nervously at his wrists. He didn't know where he was, but he knew what he had to do. He needed to find something sharp. Propping himself up on the sofa, he scanned the room, and as he did so he noticed for the first time a woman sitting in a chair right next to him. She had deep grey-green eyes, just like his mother. For a moment, the panic subsided.

"Nick," Rosa said, "can you hear me?"

Her words hardly registered. He saw his dead sister again. She was by the kitchen table, blindly cutting at something circular with a jelly-like texture. The knife slipped. She moaned, a coarse inhuman moan, and as she did so, her arms and legs bent backwards. They seemed to be splintering, like dried-out shards of wood. He shut his eyes and screamed.

"Nick! Listen to me. I saw what you saw. Your dream."

"Who are you?" he shouted, retreating to the far end of the sofa. "Leave me alone!"

"Your mother, she was there, wasn't she? Let me try to help you, please. If I can't, I promise to leave you alone. OK?"

Nick grunted. At the top of the staircase, Kiyoko watched them. Rosa glanced up, and Kiyoko nodded silently.

"Thank you," Rosa said, noticing Nick's shaking hands. "Now stand up straight, open your eyes."

He did as he was told, and Rosa came close to him. She brought one of her hands to his forehead, looked deep into his eyes. She could sense his agitation, like a butterfly trapped in her hands.

"Try to be calm, keep your eyes focused on mine. This might feel strange, but whatever you do, stay with me."

He nodded, a little calmer now, and she started to reach inside. He felt a tingling sensation. It was as if he were floating. She focused on his eyes, on the black pupils and the lighter shades of brown surrounding them. She let her own vision glaze until she could sense the depth behind his eyes. Putting her mind into that blackness, she felt herself turning in tight, constricted circles. *Where am I going?* she wondered as she started to feel the intensity of Nick's pain.

She sensed someone standing there, someone dear to Nick. It was his mother, it must be. She was beckoning him to follow her.

"What does your mother want to show you?" she asked Nick gently.

"She wants me to go inside."

"Why?"

"Don't make me, please!"

She was about to ask him why not, but then Nick's anguish and despair hit her. She managed to stay upright, no longer sure where she was. His sadness coursed through her veins, threatening to overcome her. As she stood there, she recalled how Kiyoko had told her that Nick's father and sister had died from the Panic. But what exactly was it that was making Nick crack today, after all this time? And what could she do? *I know,* Ana told her. *Let me take over now.* Rosa silently agreed.

This is not how your sister is, Ana murmured to Nick. *Yes, she suffered greatly, and your father, too. But that does not mean they will be forever in pain. You will be reunited with them, don't worry about that. And when you do it will be a joyful occasion. But now is not the right time, for you or for them. So come back with me. Feel my hand on your forehead. It is just an instrument, connecting you to me, to the world around us. Yes, this world is far from perfect, yet we can all find happiness here. Kiyoko waits for you patiently. Don't disappoint her. Feel the weight of your pain, dropping from your shoulders. You are floating, you are free.*

Rosa let her hand drop from Nick's forehead.

He looked at her with wonder. "Are you Rosanna Day?" he asked.

But his voice was too faint for her to hear. "It is over," she told him gently, exhausted.

Kiyoko ran down the stairs, tears running down her cheeks. She hugged them both, laughing and crying. *This is a new beginning,* she thought. *Rosa is the light that will carry us through.*

33

On several large sheets of canvas spread out across the stage, people had written the names of loved ones and the day they had died. Earlier, Rosa had stood by her brother as he wrote down their foster parents' names. Near the front of the stage, a photo collage of people smiling was projected on a big screen, with the words:

UNITED WE STAND, AT PEACE.

Now, watching Nick and Kiyoko hand in hand, Nathan entertaining some young children with magic tricks, Rosa knew she should be happy. Nathan was in good shape today. Nick too. There were thousands of people in Cowley Park, chatting easily to one another as they waited for the festival to begin. The Panic seemed far from everyone's minds.

The media were there, too, streaming the event live. Paul Blinker, a journalist whose weekly blog had thousands of followers, was about to speak. Some of the volunteers who had helped keep Oxford afloat would also say a few words, including Kiyoko. Later, local musicians would jam with one of the biggest bands in the country, Mad Hatch.

Still, she felt hollow inside. Is it jealousy, she wondered. No, she knew it wasn't that. Then what is it? She waited for Ana to answer, but she remained silent. Ana had not spoken to her since Nick's recovery.

"When does the music start?" Nathan asked her. "Rosa?"

"Hey, I was miles away. In an hour or so, I think. There'll be some speeches first. How are you doing? Not too tired after all those magic tricks?"

"I feel great."

"Do it again!" the kids asked Nathan. "The one with the coin."

"But I told you, the magician only shows his tricks once."

"Please!" they all shouted in unison.

"Ah you kids," Nathan grinned. "OK, one last time. Who hasn't been my helper yet? Charlotte, your turn."

Charlotte came forward, smiling proudly. She could only have been four or five. The kids gathered around, giggling. Nathan took a coin from his pocket. He displayed it to the children, turning the penny either side to show it was just a regular coin, and then placed it behind Charlotte's left ear. Gently he pretended to rub it into her skin. Her smile became a bright beam, the other kids' mouths dropped in wonder.

"Where has it gone? See, it has disappeared right into her skin!"

For a moment, Charlotte looked nervous, but Nathan winked at her and she smiled again.

"I want you all to concentrate on Charlotte's ear, the spot just behind where I rubbed it in. Good. Now, watch. I'll rub there again with my magic hand. Watch carefully."

The children gasped in amazement as he pulled the coin from behind her ear. He gave the penny to Charlotte, who carefully placed it in her dress pocket.

"Right, you better all go to Jane over there. She has your tea waiting for you."

Rosa and Nathan watched the kids run over.

"You're great with them."

"They're good kids. How about you? Are you going to say a few words, like Kiyoko?"

"Maybe. I haven't decided yet."

"People would like it."

"Kiyoko deserves all the plaudits. She's really helped people here deal with the Panic better. If the government gave a shit, they'd ask her to visit other cities, too. Anyways, what is this band Mad Hatch like?"

"Oh Rosa! I've been unconscious half of the epidemic, and I'm not fully with it now, yet still I know them! They're great, and not just because they're one of the very few bands who've been brave enough to keep touring. Bluesy, a bit like The Rolling Stones. They really rock."

"They do," Nick said, coming over with Kiyoko. "I saw them in Birmingham. Helped people forget all the shit for a couple of hours. They'll be even better here – the atmosphere is great. Who would've thought they'd come to Oxford!"

"Oxford is where it's at!" Kiyoko beamed, putting her arm around Nick's waist. Rosa smiled.

As they chatted, Paul Blinker appeared on stage, together with one of the volunteers organising the festival. He was a good foot taller than the volunteer. A corduroy jacket hung limply on his narrow frame. His shoulders were hunched; his thin hair had been ruffled up by the wind. Yet still he had a stage presence. The crowd hushed.

"Good afternoon and welcome!" the volunteer announced, her cheerful voice echoing out of the speakers. "Thank you for coming. We are here to remember those we have lost, yes, but to be hopeful, too. We can beat this illness, and we can do it without drugs!"

A few people cheered.

"Some of you may not know this, but Cowley Park used to be the most dangerous place in Oxford. Now look at us today, milling around happily, enjoying the sunshine. We've reclaimed Cowley Park; we've made it safe again. Now before we continue with the programme, I ask you to join together for a minute's silence. One minute for the terrible year that has passed."

The crowd fell silent. Rosa glanced around, beyond Nick, Kiyoko and Nathan, to all the quiet faces respecting the dead. She closed her eyes and tried to concentrate on her parents, Lillian, on all those teenagers who had died at Cloxham Manor. But the hollowness was still there. No, it was something more than that. A sense of detachment, an unreality about the proceedings, as if this were a dream. *Am I really here?* she wondered. Suddenly she realised it could all go wrong. She didn't know how, but she feared it.

"Thank you. Today should also be a celebration. Those many lives lost have not been in vain. Together we have come so far, and we can combat this terrible illness. Now, we have a fantastic programme ahead: speakers, a short play, live music. But first, let me hand over to our main speaker, who needs no introduction. Without further ado, I give you Paul Blinker!"

The crowd clapped and cheered as Blinker came forward. He took out a sheet of paper from his jacket, adjusted the microphone. For a few long moments he stood there, staring at the crowd, as if undecided on how to proceed.

"I had prepared a speech," he said finally, waving his paper in the air. "In this speech, I would offer you a careful, balanced take on the Panic. I would talk about the difficulties of living in this time, like I do in my blog. I might have been mildly subversive, reiterating how I think the government could be doing more. Yet essentially, I would conclude that the politicians were still on our side. That is what I promised the government officials. As I promised not to say anything inflammatory about FRJ, the bloodsucking outfit that ruins people's lives."

The crowd murmured in approval; Rosa and Kiyoko exchanged nervous glances.

"You all know how it is. We struggle on, going about our daily routines as best we can. Despite the difficulties of buying food and basic supplies, despite the stench of dead bodies on the street, despite every single one of us having lost someone dear. And we all fear sleep. Many of us take the drugs. I do. It seems like the easiest option. I'm still on GreenShoots and the thirty-six-hour day, but I'm seriously contemplating something stronger. Such a life is debilitating. Slowly but surely, we are worn down. Our ability to think clearly slips – we are losing touch with ourselves. I am forty-three years old, but I know that I look and feel much older."

Blinker paused for a moment, took out a handkerchief and mopped his brow.

"This is part of a wider conspiracy," he continued, his voice booming out. "Capitalism at its worst. Big business bribing the government, a few select individuals benefitting at our expense. The politicians observe us from the safety of Scotland and Northern Ireland, calculating their profits as more and more of us rely on the drugs they've invested in. Other countries promise to help, but it's just politicians meeting politicians. Global bodies like the UN write their reports. Nothing changes. It is a disgrace. And all the time we sit tight, trying to continue on as if nothing is different."

Blinker eyed the crowd with defiance. Rosa looked at him and at the crowd around her. She sensed their fear and anger brimming at the surface, understood it, too. Yet she also knew that no good could come of it.

"What should we do?" someone behind her shouted. Others repeated the question.

Be calm, she wanted to tell them. Now is not the right time.

She looked directly at the volunteer on stage who had introduced the festival with such positivity, hoping she would intervene. But the woman remained silent.

"Rosanna Day!" someone shouted. "She can lead us."

"There is no Rosanna Day," Blinker said. "It's just a lie perpetuated by the government to give us false hope."

Rosa sensed a ripple of indignation coursing through the crowd. She couldn't tell if Blinker still had them on his side. Somewhere nearby people were pushing and shoving.

"Now listen to me," Blinker continued. "We must rise up. In every town and every village. Take control of the drug outlets. March together to the northern blockade. Only then will the government listen to us. Did you know that they are here right now, among us? Yes, undercover agents are listening in."

People started eyeing each other suspiciously. She could sense their indignation. Someone threw a bottle; people started shouting. *Don't do it,* she wanted to tell them. There are families here, young children.

"I'm going to show you a video," Blinker said, pressing a clicker. The photo collage of people smiling disappeared from the big screen. "It's only a few minutes, but long enough for you to see how fucked up the government is."

A video started to play. Music came through the loudspeakers. No, not music – rather the sound of people moaning.

"What is this?" Kiyoko asked.

"I know," Nick said quietly. "This is a mistake."

The moaning became louder. On the big screen, a huge wave of smoke and rubble approached. Rosa shut her eyes, fearing what would come. *What should I do?* she called out to Ana, but Ana wasn't there.

"Stop it!" a woman shouted, clutching her child. "There are children in the crowd."

But others drowned her out, chanting, "Show us! Show us! Show us!"

The smoke grew larger, filling the screen. Some people tried to leave, but the crowd was too densely packed. A large group, about twenty feet from Rosa and the others, started pumping their fists in the air. They were all wearing the same t-shirt emblazoned with *FRJ out!,* each letter illustrated with dripping blood.

"Show us!" they bayed again.

"We've got to do something," Rosa said, but the others couldn't hear her above the chanting crowd. Like everyone else, they were watching the video. In it, the smoke had cleared and moaning people started to appear. They moved blindly towards the camera, their eyes torn out.

"Stop it," some people muttered in disgust. Children cried. Paul Blinker pressed the clicker again, freezing the video on a close-up of a teenager sitting cross-legged on the floor, scratching at her face.

"I'll tell you what this is," he thundered. "It's the government's fault. They sold us out to FRJ."

"Yes!" people shouted, not just those wearing the anti-FRJ t-shirts.

"They turned us into lab rats. An experiment gone wrong, a monumental screw up!"

"Yes," the people roared.

Rosa glanced across at her brother, at Nick and Kiyoko. They looked as nervous as she felt. At least they didn't seem to be taken in by Blinker, she thought.

"We should leave," Nathan said.

"The government is corrupt," Blinker screamed. "Look there!" he said, pointing up the hill. Like everyone else, Rosa followed his finger and saw the line of armed soldiers stationed there.

"Where did they come from?" Nick asked Kiyoko. Rosa looked at each of them, then across at her brother.

"I don't know," Kiyoko replied.

"You told me the government would stay out of this."

"That's what I thought."

"I don't trust him," Nathan whispered to Rosa. "He's playing us. He's on their side."

"Whose side?"

"Yes, that's right," Blinker bellowed, all venom and bitterness. "The politicians are happy to leave Oxford to rot; other cities too. But when we gather together, they don't trust us. Look at them! They treat us like unwanted animals. No love or respect. So rise up now! Let's march as one to those soldiers. Let us send a message to the coward politicians watching on their television screens."

The crowd roared their approval, moving forward together. In the melee, Rosa lost sight of the others. She saw a man slip, the crowd blindly surging over him.

Someone grabbed her hand. It was Kiyoko, with Nathan by her side. For a moment, the crowd was still, as if waiting for direction.

"Where's Nick?"

"We lost him."

The crowd surged again. "Hold hands, tightly," Rosa shouted above the din, suddenly calm. "Follow me. Whatever you do, stay on your feet."

"What about Nick?"

Rosa looked at Kiyoko's face, all colour drained from it. She felt Ana's presence, waiting.

"He'll make it out. I know it," she told Kiyoko, wanting to sound more assured than she felt. "We'll meet him on the other side. But now I must speak. I have no choice."

The crowd moved forward relentlessly. They were less than twenty feet from the line of soldiers.

"Kiyoko! Rosa! Nathan! Where are you?" Nick shouted, scanning the crowd in vain.

A warning gunshot pierced the air. "Move back," a soldier yelled through a tannoy. Nick was close enough to see the sweat dripping down the soldier's face. "Move back now or we will open fire."

Still the crowd surged. Nick tried to stay still, but the people behind pushed him closer. "Be safe," he muttered under his breath. *Wherever you are, stay safe.*

The soldiers were almost within arm's reach, close enough that Nick could see the fear in their eyes. It was clear they didn't know what to do. For a moment, the crowd was still. *Duck down!* he thought he heard someone say. Quickly he crouched down. *Stay there.* He was sure it was Rosa, even though he couldn't see her. Not her normal voice, though, rather the quiet but insistent murmur she'd spoken in yesterday. Rosa is Rosanna Day; he knew it for certain then.

"Rosa?" he said, unable to see her or the others.

Suddenly there was a burst of gunfire, and all around him people were falling. A young woman tumbled into his arms, blood pouring out of her chest. He tried to hold her but she slipped to the ground. Gunshots reverberated around him. Some people ran back in the direction of the stage, blindly tramping over the fallen.

Somewhere above he heard a faint whirring sound. He looked up in the sky and saw them, large military helicopters, hovering at the top of the hill. Five, no six of them, just waiting. Waiting for orders.

You must get out now before they bomb us, the voice told him. *Run straight ahead, through the line of soldiers. It's your only chance. Do it for us all.*

What about you? he asked. *Are you safe?*

No response. He looked around, at the wounded and dying, at others running back. The air was thick with smoke. His heart beating fast, he stood up and ran forward. A young soldier stared at him in astonishment. Nick pushed past him and sprinted for the trees at the top of the park. He heard or imagined bullets whistling past his ears, but he didn't look back to confirm if they were real.

As he ran, he thought he heard Rosa's voice over the tannoy, telling the crowd to stay calm. But he couldn't be sure. He glanced back towards the stage, unable to see through the smoke, hoping she, Kiyoko and Nathan were safe. Then he heard Rosa speaking, her voice assured and kind, and he felt a flicker of hope. They would listen to her, surely they would.

Kiyoko and Nathan had tried to stop her, but her mind was set. She clambered up on stage, pushing Blinker away from the mic. She tapped the microphone and for a moment, the gunfire stopped. Civilians and soldiers alike looked up expectantly, waiting for her to speak. Nathan and Kiyoko frogmarched Blinker off the stage.

"Be still," she said, gazing out at the crowd. The words were there, clear in her mind. "Be still and calm. Soldiers, stop shooting, I beg you. What good can come of this? Nothing, I tell you. So be heroes, and hold fire."

She looked down at her hands, at her dusty shoes. The crowd, becalmed, waited expectantly. She knew then that they would listen. It was almost as if she could feel each and every one of them, sense their beating hearts.

"Thank you. Listen to me, all of you. Please. The Panic – let's not shy away from it – the Panic is fearsome, relentless, chilling. All these things. But what is it really? A virus? Bacteria? And how did it start, how did it spread so fast? You know the conspiracy theories as well as I do. Paul Blinker, some of what he said might be true. Still, he misses the point."

She paused. Nathan and Kiyoko were looking up at her, like everyone else.

"Whatever FRJ, the government or whoever else did, this illness has always been with us," she continued. "It is *the* primal fear, hidden inside us all, passed on from generation to generation. A fear of the evil within us. A fear that we as a human race are suffocating. We fear we have lost touch with what is right and good, now more than ever before. And when this fear gets too much, we cannot cope, we panic. But I tell you, we are being far too hard on ourselves."

The crowd murmured in agreement.

"Are you Rosanna Day?" someone shouted, then others.

"My name doesn't matter. What matters is we must try to stay positive. Recognise our faults, yes, but not be consumed by them. I'm not saying that is enough. Whatever this thing is, it has gone beyond that. But if we look inside ourselves, we can find that goodness. That can only help."

She brushed a stray hair from her face. "We try to endure," she continued, "but the oppression and unnecessary anguish – sometimes it is too much to bear. We see in ourselves and others the desire to make ourselves richer, better than others, the pursuit of the self whatever the cost.

"Yet it does not have to be that way. I am not the first to say this. Many wise people have taught us about love and compassion. But remember this – when we come into this world, the first thing we see is our mother's love. Her eyes smiling at us, even though we scream with fear and worry. An unconditional love, not weighed down by the past or the future. That is what matters. So look at me now, I beg you. I love you all unconditionally, like I love my family."

She looked out at the crowd again, stepped back from the microphone. The crowd broke into a rapturous applause. They started chanting, "Rosanna Day! Rosanna Day!" over and over, civilians and soldiers alike.

But it was a temporary respite: a loud buzzing drowned out the chants. Rosa looked up and saw them. Military helicopters. They were close enough for her to see the pilots, staring blankly ahead.

She stood there, frozen, as the first bomb dropped. The explosion shook the stage, and parts of the scaffolding fell. Nathan jumped onto the stage and grabbed her by the arm. As they ran back, a gun was shot. She saw it happen in slow motion. A man with a pistol aimed at her, Nathan throwing himself in front, people in the crowd knocking over the armed man, Nathan falling to the floor. She held him in her arms, crying, as his blood seeped onto the floor.

Nick hadn't made it very far when he heard the first explosion. The floor shook and he stumbled to the ground. It felt like his ears were bleeding. Turning around, all he could see was smoke and rubble. The air cleared a little, enough for him to make out the soldiers in their uniforms and the crowd beyond. Everything was silent. They lay on the ground, soldiers and civilians alike. He was close enough to see that some of them were crawling in his direction. One of the soldiers had made it farther up the hill than the others; it may well have been the one he'd pushed past only minutes ago. Nick looked again and noticed that the soldier's legs had been blown away.

A second bomb went off, deeper in the crowd, and then another. The ground shook, yet the deep, low sounds seemed muted. Breathing noisily, gulping in the air, Nick started crawling himself; it seemed safer that way. "Dear God," he muttered as he pushed himself up the hill, "if you are out there, save them. For what is my world without Kiyoko? And what hope do any of us have without Rosanna Day?"

THE SECOND WAVE

Hours later

34

Moonlight streamed into the room. Outside a stray dog howled. Bullet holes pierced the window, with shattered glass on the floor. Still, they had decided they were as safe here as anywhere else, in their old house. It was a miracle that she and Kiyoko had escaped unscathed. Just a few hours ago, they had been sheltering under a large oak tree as helicopters fired on those fleeing the park. *Not enough of a miracle,* she thought, bringing her hands to her face. *My brother is dead.*

Once again, she pictured Nathan lying there. She tried to hold on to the image of him smiling at her before his eyes closed. But all she could remember was his pain, a type of pain she could not heal. At least he is at peace now, Rosa told herself again, trying not to visualise the deep gash in his stomach. If it weren't for Nathan, Kiyoko and I would most probably be dead. "Part of me will always be with you," he had whispered, his voice steady despite the pain. "But now, please, you must go."

The anger rose up again, an intense beating that shook her heart. This time she did nothing to quell it. *I hate them all*, she thought. *They killed my brother and thousands of others. Why, for what purpose? Was the government really so frightened of us?* Hiding up above the blockade, they kill innocent people just because of the idiotic ramblings of Paul Blinker, a rabble-rouser who knows nothing. Or was the whole event orchestrated by PureForce? That was Kiyoko's hypothesis. For surely the government, however cowardly they are, wouldn't kill its own soldiers, let alone civilians?

It hardly mattered either way, she decided. The government, PureForce, FRJ – they were all the same. Corrupt and diseased, so fearful for their own survival that they are willing to massacre without constraint. We have become the *other* to them, something subhuman, something to fear and loathe. Simply because we live on the other side of the blockade, in the wrong country. We are a menace and therefore we must be kept at bay, whatever the cost. All they care about is their own survival. There is no pity, no compassion. Don't they realise the true cost of their actions? They disgust me. Cowards, every single one of them. Frightened of us when they should be frightened of themselves.

As for Shaw's group Alliance, are they really any better? After all, Shaw was the one who advised us to come to Oxford. He said it was the safest place, that the government would never suspect us returning here. Shaw's sources within the government had supposedly convinced the bureaucrats that Kiyoko was still in Nottingham, and I was in London or had joined PureForce in Manchester, near the blockade. Supposedly. Was it possible Shaw knew what was going to happen in Oxford? No, it didn't make sense, it couldn't.

Kiyoko started moaning in her sleep. Rosa turned from the window to check that she was OK, and soon enough she was resting more easily.

"Kiyoko has a special talent, as unique as yours in some

ways," Shaw had told her when they last met, just before she came to Oxford. "On a clinical level, no one really understood SED, despite all the funds ploughed into research. Whereas Kiyoko, in some subconscious way, she understands. I'm a scientist but I believe that. When she watches over people as they sleep, it's as if she can sense when the illness is close. Then, somehow, she can keep it at bay.

"Is that why you want her to stay with me? To make sure your precious investment isn't wasted?" Rosa had replied, surprising herself with the tone of her response.

Shaw had looked at her and she saw the sadness in his eyes was unfeigned. He told her then how he regretted not being brave enough to speak more frankly with her at Cloxham Manor, and for never having contacted her before the SED epidemic had begun.

Then he'd talked a little more about that time in their past, when he had accompanied her between Kings Lynn train station and the hospital. He admitted that this hospital was a military facility, and that its purpose was to treat illnesses that could potentially be a public health threat. He never understood why they sent Rosa there. However unusual her heart condition, it could hardly be infectious.

"You were almost like a daughter to me," he had said. "During that time, I was often by your side. Four years old and you had already been through so much. It didn't seem fair, but I was too naive to question. That day at the train station, when you were just five years old, and I thought I'd never see you again..."

He hadn't been able to finish the sentence. Rosa watched him mopping his tears away with a handkerchief, unable to comfort him. Although later, as she and Kiyoko were packing their bags for Oxford, she'd gone over to Shaw. "I still don't know how I feel about all this," she had told him. "But thank you for finally being honest with me. And for letting me meet Edith Dubois, despite knowing the risks. I appreciate that."

She'd seen the relief in his eyes as he thanked her and told her to stay safe. Thinking about it now, she was sure his group was not responsible for the atrocity.

The moon seemed to weigh heavy in the sky. Rosa felt herself drawn up towards it. It was as if she were a counterbalance to its mass, keeping the crusty rock in place above the earth's stratosphere. The weight seemed too much to bear. It would be so much easier to let go, to float up and away from this cruel world. Leaving the moon to fall down and collapse in on itself.

The helicopters had been so close. Close enough to see the pilots seated in the air. She pictured their blank faces now, their empty, expressionless eyes as they released the bombs. Thousands of people dead, a few simple clicks of a button causing so much carnage. What cowards! Blindly following orders, treating them like vermin, a contaminant to be cleansed. All these deaths in the name of control.

She glanced across at Kiyoko, shifting uneasily in her sleep, wondered what she was dreaming.

There's no point, it's all too late. Another voice, not Ana's. *It's coming now. Don't try to fight it.*

"Who are you?" she said aloud.

All you can do is rest and wait it out. It is not your fault, Rosanna. The Second Wave is coming.

I don't understand.

All societies are false. The sun rising and falling is the only truth, and this truth in itself is meaningless. But that is not your concern. Go to sleep now. Rest. Tomorrow is a new day. Nothing else you can do.

Her eyelids felt suddenly heavy, an irresistible urge to sleep.

I must stay awake, she thought. *Until Kiyoko has rested, at least.* Once again, Nathan came into her mind, dying in her arms. She felt a dull anger deep inside, churning within her heart, consuming her. *Maybe it is better to leave this world behind,* she thought as she slipped off the chair and lay down on the floor. It all seemed too much. In the darkness, a barn owl screeched repeatedly. She put a cushion under her head and closed her eyes, unable to stay awake any longer.

35

In the dream, Nick lay alone in a muddy field. Gunfire rattled incessantly, explosions lit up the night sky. Kiyoko was there, just out of reach, her back turned to him. He couldn't lift himself up; he tried to call out to her, but the words wouldn't come. Then he heard her. She was sobbing.

"What is it?" he finally managed to say.

"Rosa," she replied without turning around.

"What about her? Is she OK?"

She shook her head. "No. She couldn't control it."

"I don't understand," he said, staring at her back. "What do you mean? She is Rosanna Day, isn't she? She is the one who can save us."

With a great effort he crawled towards her, each movement laboured. At last, he was there. He touched her lightly on her shoulder. Kiyoko flinched.

"Stop!" she said, her voice fearful. "Don't touch me. Don't come forward another step."

He ignored her. He dragged himself forward until he was facing her, but she looked away from him. Somewhere nearby an owl screeched. Gently he turned her face to him, and as he did so, he saw the blindfold covering her eyes. He screamed then, from the depths of his soul.

Someone was shaking him. Up above, he thought he heard bombs exploding.

"Nick, snap out of it! We need to get out of here."

He opened his eyes and saw Harold there, bending over him. A full moon lit up the park, bright enough for him to see Harold's face. His eyes were wet from tears. Glancing around, Nick saw bodies strewn all over the grass. He wondered if he was hallucinating again.

"Harold? Is that really you?"

"Yes."

Nick touched Harold's arm. His shirt was drenched in sweat. "What are you doing here?" he asked.

Perspiration dripped from Harold's brow. "I'll explain later. But now we have to go."

He pulled himself into a sitting position. The air was thick with smoke.

"Are you ready?" Harold asked.

"Wait. Why are you helping me? The last time we met –"

"Listen, there's no time. We have to go. The government bombed the hell out of this place. Who knows what they'll do with survivors. I'm on your side now. You're just going to have to trust me on that."

A machine gun rattled; Nick thought he heard muffled screams.

"For now," he said, standing up. "Where are we going?"

"To Mantle Hospital. I know what you're thinking. But honestly, it's the safest place right now."

The coffee tasted good. Nick put his face near to the cup so he could feel the warmth of the rising steam. He looked up at Harold sitting opposite him. Is this, finally, the man I once knew? Someone who, if circumstances had played out differently, could have become a close friend. Or is he still a man obsessed with money and his own pride?

"You're lucky to be alive," Harold told him.

"I know."

They were in a vacant office at Mantle Hospital. "If anyone else had found you..." he said, his voice trailing off. "Anyway, we are safe here. This room isn't bugged. Later, I'll find you a mattress."

"Did you know they would bomb us?"

Harold tapped cigarette ash onto his saucer. For a long while, he didn't say anything. "Not exactly, but I had my suspicions," he said eventually. He took a long puff on his cigarette, exhaled the smoke slowly.

"Go on."

"A few days ago, three to be precise, I was on the phone with Andrew Miller. Miller's the deputy CEO of FRJ. I knew him well – I was always the one who showed him around the hospital when he flew into Oxford. Anyway, during the call, he told me not to attend the one-year commemorations in Cowley Park."

Harold paused for a moment, cleared his throat. "I knew Miller was well connected," Harold continued. "So when he said he had inside information that the government was poised to make an intervention, I believed him. He warned me in no uncertain terms to keep this information to myself, to not even tell Vermel, the hospital director. Said he had an employee within the hospital watching us and that he wouldn't tolerate any information leaks."

Harold shook his head. "'We want to avoid unnecessary

hysteria,'" he muttered in a sarcastic tone. "That's what the contemptible wretch said."

Nick looked at him. He felt reasonably sure Harold was telling the truth. "So why did you risk leaving the hospital grounds?" he asked.

"Curiosity, plain and simple. There was a rumour going around."

"What rumour?"

"That Rosanna Day would be speaking there," Harold said, watching Nick closely.

Nick nodded, not revealing what he knew about Rosa, and how she had cured him. "Did you know I was there?"

"I'd heard rumours. But it was pure chance I found you. Honestly. And I'm glad I did. One in a hundred – no, even higher odds than that. You are a fortunate man."

"Am I?"

"You saw it. A massacre. Even from where I found you, up near the top of the park, I could see enough. The helicopters bombed the site to pieces. They even killed their own soldiers. Of course, the news channels watered it down. I'm surprised they showed footage of Rosanna Day inspiring the crowd."

"What do you mean?"

"I was moved. Yes, even cynical old Harold Stone," he said, sighing. "But now she's just like any other martyr."

Nick glanced across at Harold. He seemed a broken man. "Maybe she's still alive," he said.

"I hope you're right. But I doubt it."

Harold stood up from his chair, went over to the window.

"Nick, this hospital, the direction it has taken these past weeks and months. I want out. It's not the drugs. I still believe in their efficacy, that they are part of the solution. But last week I was asked to oversee another intervention. Dear God, it was awful," he said, holding his head.

Nick waited for Harold to continue, but he remained silent. "What was it?" Nick prompted.

"Vermel, the hospital director, that robotic, amoral shit of a man, he led me down a corridor of boarded-up offices. We got into a lift that took us deep underground. There, isolated from the main hospital wards, were a few patients kept in solitary confinement. Vermel told me each of them was on a standard drug regimen, with varying degrees of sleep suppression, but were otherwise healthy. My task was to inject the patients with an experimental vaccine and monitor the results. 'Any nurse could do this,' I'd said to him. 'Why me?' 'Because we need someone we can trust completely,' Vermel said."

Harold lit another cigarette, left it burning between his fingers.

"Nick, I peered through the small opening in each of those cells, observing the nervous glances of the patients. As I did, Vermel told me the purpose of the experiment. 'We are still in the early stages of development, but we need to take a risk. Developing resilience, that is what this injection is all about. An early vaccine, if you like.' Yet not one of those volunteers survived the injection."

"That's terrible."

"At least they didn't try to claw their eyes out," Harold muttered, his eyes staring past Nick and at the blank wall behind. "Before Rosa spoke, I tried to convince myself it was an acceptable cost in pursuit of the ultimate solution. Now I see it for what it is. Murder."

36

Rosa awoke from a terrible dream, her cheeks wet with tears. The pain in her chest was palpable and unrelenting. It felt like cold steel cutting through her heart. Fragments of the dream came back to her as she lay on the floor. Nothing concrete, only abstract sensations: a blur of motion; dull, washed-out greys suddenly transformed into a wall of red; moans of despair and an overwhelming sadness.

Fragments of a recurring dream. This time, though, she felt something else. A presence, absolute and unyielding, was there observing the chaos without judgement. She did not have to recollect the dream with any more precision to know something terrible had happened.

"I didn't want this," she said, her voice a faint whisper.

She opened her eyes and looked around the room, thankful that it was starting to become light outside. Kiyoko lay motionless on the bed, her eyes covered by a blanket. *Not her, too,* she thought, shivering. *She's a good person. Any faults she has are unimportant, ones we all suffer.*

Pulling herself up off the floor, she came to the edge of the bed and gently lifted the blanket. Kiyoko's eyes remained closed. Rosa took her hand, and it was icy cold. She checked her pulse, relieved to feel it.

Rosa shut her eyes and focused, listening for echoes in the darkness. Finally, she heard one, and she held it in her mind, until the faint echo became Kiyoko's heartbeat. She began to sing in a soft voice:

I see the moon
The moon sees me
God bless the moon
and God bless me

I see your shadow
And it sees me
The shadow is you
And you are me

"Rosa?" Kiyoko said, opening her eyes.

"Kiyoko!"

"I thought... I don't know. I had an awful nightmare. One I couldn't seem to wake from."

"Me too. I'm glad we made it out."

Kiyoko pushed herself into a sitting position, rubbed her eyes. "Cowley Park, the nightmare was even worse than that, if that is possible. The Panic, it was everywhere. The blind killing the blind."

Rosa remembered her dream then. She tried to block out the images, but still they came.

"Something terrible has happened," she said, shutting her eyes.

"Rosa?"

"Wait."

Keeping her eyes closed, she braced herself. The dream came back to her quickly. She was standing in the middle of a huge, empty space. No vegetation, just giant slabs of concrete, grimy and cracked, one after the other. Total silence. A flatness extending in all directions, as far as the eye could see. Like the ocean or a vast desert, but without any chance of life.

The sky darkened. Light slipped away as the sun was eclipsed. Then, in the half-light, she could sense it there, waiting. A malleable presence just out of reach. Like her, it knew what would happen.

On the horizon, a huge wave of smoke and rubble slowly approached. A multitude of bird wings fluttered, desperate to escape. Then she saw them, coming out of the smoke. Thousands of bodies. They crawled pitifully, dragging their legless torsos across the concrete. As they came closer, she heard their moans, then felt their frail hands clutching at her feet. Blind eyes stared at her with false hope.

"Save us," they moaned, one after the other. "Forgive."

"I'm sorry," she said, tears falling down her cheeks. "I don't know how."

Then the smoke and rubble were upon them, engulfing them all, and their moans turned into hysterical screams.

It was a dream she'd had before. The difference this time was that she could have prevented it. The presence was there, waiting for her instruction, something that could have stopped the coming storm if only she'd asked.

Yet she chose not to. She had accepted the destruction for what it offered: a chance to start anew. Fear was a decontaminant, a cleanser stripping away the hypocrisy and lies. So in the dream she had allowed it to happen, this outpouring of primal fears, a collective madness, for after there could be a new beginning. The Second Wave, like the voice had said. But now she knew they were running out of time.

"Kiyoko, you believe in me, don't you?" she asked, letting go of her hand. "I still don't know exactly what Shaw told you. But whatever it was, it was enough for you to stay with me all this time, wasn't it?"

"Yes," Kiyoko replied. She shifted herself in the bed slightly. "Since you cured Nick; before even. I've been sure, Rosanna Day."

"A curse," Rosa said. She felt herself on the verge of tears, held them in.

"Don't say that. It's a gift. Rosa? Rosa, is everything OK?"

"No. It's much worse now. People everywhere are suffering. Those who are still alive, at least."

"I don't understand," Kiyoko said, "but I know that you can help them."

"It's too late," Rosa replied. She gazed outside. It was raining hard. Water seeped in through the cracks in the windowpane. "Almost everyone is dead."

"What do you mean? Rosa, you should rest. You've been watching over me all through the night. You must be exhausted."

"No. I was asleep, too."

Outside there was a flash of lightning, then seconds later the low rumble of thunder.

"It's hard to explain, Kiyoko. It's like, it's almost as if I know what you dreamt. Not only you. What everyone has been dreaming. I don't mean the same dream. Yet it is the same sadness. Desperation. The same fear. This time I had a chance to stop it. But I was too scared, too weak."

Kiyoko looked at her, noticed the tears welling up in Rosa's eyes. "None of this is your fault," she said, touching her gently on the shoulder.

Rosa listened to the rain pounding against the window. "It is," she said, sighing. *If only they hadn't killed my brother, perhaps it wouldn't have happened.*

But it did, Rosa, Ana said. *Something unspeakable has been unleashed.*

"I'll make us some tea. Then we can plan what to do next. Rosa?"

Rosa, listen to me. You must get out. Pack a bag quickly, then go. They're not far away.

"Kiyoko, we have to leave."

"What?"

"Now."

Rosa was already in motion. She stuffed some extra clothes into a rucksack, pulled her mobile phone and the charger from the socket in the wall. "Where's your phone?"

"In my pocket."

"Good. Rainproofs. Are they here or downstairs?"

"There, in the wardrobe. Slow down, Rosa. What are you doing? I don't understand."

"It's not safe," she said, opening the wardrobe and grabbing the rainproof coats. "They're coming."

"Who?"

"I'll explain later. We have to leave. We don't have much time."

"Let's at least wait until the weather clears."

"Kiyoko, please. You said you believed in me. Yes?"

Kiyoko looked at her, nodded uneasily.

"Good. Then trust me now. We must go before it's too late. I don't know why, we just have to."

"All right. I trust you."

As Kiyoko tied her shoes, and Rosa scanned the bathroom. She filled a plastic bottle with water. She picked up a razor, dropped it. Better not to take anything sharp, she decided.

"Ready?" she said, coming back into the room.

"Yes. I put a torch in the bag, too. Don't know how long the batteries are good for, but..."

Downstairs, the front door rattled. Then there was a loud bang. Something heavy crashing against the door.

"Shit, they're here already!" Rosa said. "We'll go out the back door."

"But..."

"Quietly."

They crept along the upstairs landing, Rosa slinging the rucksack over her shoulder. Halfway down the stairs, they saw an axe splintering through the front door. Then they both heard it, the rain not loud enough to drown out the gut-wrenching, low, pitiful moans. They ran downstairs, rushing through the living area as the axe again crashed against the door. Then they were in the small kitchen. Rosa took the keyring off the latch while behind her Kiyoko snatched a large cutting knife from the kitchen counter.

There was a louder bang, and the sound of something crashing through the door.

"Quick!" Kiyoko said. "They're inside."

Rosa put one of the keys into the lock. It wasn't the right one. As she fiddled with the keys, he appeared by the kitchen door, blindly swinging an axe. His weapon smashed against the edge of the counter and fell to the floor. The man moaned as he tried and failed to locate the axe on the ground. Then he stood still, sniffing the air, a bloodied rag tied around his eyes. Without his weapon, he seemed becalmed.

Don't panic, Rosa told herself, as she tried another key in the door. This time the lock turned. She opened the door, but as she did so, the blind man lurched forward, towards the sound. He grabbed Rosa's arm and started pulling her towards him. As he did so, she felt a sharp, searing pain in her chest. It was Ana, she knew it, something was happening to her. Stay with me, she whispered under her breath. The pain intensified, and she wondered if she would lose consciousness.

Suddenly the man shrieked. He staggered backwards,

letting go of Rosa. She saw the knife, wedged deep into his stomach. He fell to the ground.

"I'm sorry," Kiyoko stammered, staring at the man as he lay slumped on the floor. In the hallway, they heard howling.

"Run!" Rosa said, regaining focus. The pain in her chest had receded. She pulled Kiyoko away, and the two of them rushed out into the pelting rain.

ASHES

Morning light

37

I n the driving rain, they saw the car's flashing headlights. The driver pulled down his window and shouted.

"Rosa, Kiyoko. Get in! Quick! I'm with Shaw."

Kiyoko and Rosa looked at each other, unsure. Rosa shut her eyes for a moment, imploring Ana to guide her. But all she could sense inside was the quick beating of her heart. She stood there, transfixed, and she felt in that moment she was aware of everything and nothing. How one heartbeat was not just connected to the next, but to the hearts and minds of every living being.

"Rosa?" Kiyoko said, touching her arm. "We've got to move."

Rosa nodded. It's hard to be sure of anything, she thought, looking down at her sodden clothes. Then they heard anguished howls, rising above the downpour. Hunched shapes lurched towards them from the far end of the street.

"Let's do it," Rosa said, taking Kiyoko's hand and running to the car. Before they had even closed the back door, the driver stepped hard on the pedal. He turned left, then right, swerving past someone walking unsteadily on the road, a young man with a bloodied blindfold. The driver crossed the intersection, continuing down Marston Road. With the street ahead deserted, he slowed the car down to a crawl.

"Where are we going?" Kiyoko asked the driver, wiping the rain and sweat from her face.

"Wait a sec," he said, concentrating on the road ahead. "This way is safer than Headington Hill, but we still need to be careful. Howlers may be here, too."

They sat in silence. Rosa glanced through the back window. She thought she saw some of them in the distance, wandering around aimlessly in the rain. *Why were they chasing me and Kiyoko?* Maybe for help, for someone to guide them out of this madness. But then why did the one who had burst into their house come after them with an axe?

She closed her eyes, trying to locate Ana in the recesses of her mind. *Ana,* she called, *where are you? Don't you understand that I need you now, more than ever? Tell me what's happened. Explain to me how Shaw knew Kiyoko and I would be there.* But there was no voice to answer her. She felt incomplete, as if a part of her had been ripped out.

It's not so surprising Shaw found us, she told herself, trying to distract herself from Ana's absence. It was, after all, the house they had been living in for the past month. Anyone could have worked out she'd be there. Still, something didn't quite make sense. Maybe they'd made a mistake, getting into the car. Either way, it was too late now. The driver looked strong and alert. Ex-military probably. And what choice did she and Kiyoko have? They were coming for them; they'd smashed down the door. They may have been blind, but still they knew how to find her.

"It's fine now, for a stretch," the driver said once they had passed Jack Straw's Lane, making eye contact through the rear-view mirror. "But Lime Walk, Windmill Road, once you get up there, it gets bad again. Howlers moving about in the shadows. Don't worry. We'll turn off before then. I'm Vincent Davies, by the way."

"Where are we going?" Kiyoko asked.

"Mantle Hospital."

"What?"

"It's where Shaw is. And before you ask why Mantle Hospital, I don't know. I'm just the driver. Shaw runs things; he'll explain his reasons. All that matters now is that it's the safest place in Oxford. It'll take us a while to get there, though. The main roads are blocked."

Kiyoko and Rosa exchanged glances. Rosa nodded. Something told her they had to go there. Not Ana's voice, but her own.

"We've been based there a month, before this... this nightmare. It was a big team. But now there are only three of us left."

"What happened?"

"So many people died last night. More than you can imagine. And amongst the few survivors, most are like those blind freaks we just encountered."

"In Oxford, you mean?" Kiyoko asked.

Vincent didn't respond, so Rosa spoke. "No, everywhere, all over the country. Houses filled with the dead, corpses spilling out onto the streets. It's still going on," she said, keeping her voice steady. "This is the Second Wave."

"What do you mean, Rosa? How do you know?"

"I just do," Rosa replied, staring at the rain lashing against the windscreen. "And this time it's different, the survivors I mean. They want to destroy everything."

They continued in silence. As they drove, a strange recollection came to Rosa. And though she thought it was the first time she'd ever recalled this, she felt it must have been at the back of her mind, it seemed so familiar – that they had experimented on her as a child. Did Shaw tell her about this? Or someone else at Cloxham Manor? Perhaps they'd informed her while she lay unconscious. Whoever it was, she thought she remembered them saying that she was immune from the Panic.

Was it possible? Surely, she would have remembered something about the experiments, however young she was at the time. Still, it was consistent with her surviving the Second Wave whilst so many others had succumbed. But then why had Kiyoko not been afflicted? Or, for that matter, the driver and Andrew Shaw himself?

She caught Vincent staring at her in the mirror. He quickly looked away. Outside the downpour had petered out to a faint drizzle, but the sky remained dark.

"Be prepared," Vincent warned them as they turned onto Woodfield Lane. "It's not a pleasant sight."

Mantle Hospital came into view. Vincent brought the car to a halt. They saw it then. Kiyoko gasped, and Rosa shook her head. Not far from the building's entrance were scores of dead bodies, arms reaching out in desperation. But what struck Rosa even more was the graffiti, the bright red paint standing out on the building's dull stone facade. *The Second Wave. Fear the Evil within. Panik.*

"I dreamt this," Rosa murmured. "I dreamt it all."

Kiyoko squeezed her hand. "It'll be OK," she said. "We'll find a way, like we did before."

Vincent came around and opened the doors for them.

"It's gruesome, I know," he said, ushering them forward. "But this is the only way in. All the other entrances have been locked for security."

"Wait. Is it really any safer here?" Kiyoko asked, standing her ground. Vincent took a step back, holding his hands up passively.

"How do we know we can trust you?" she continued. "Is Shaw even here?"

"Glad you asked," he said, taking out a two-way radio from his pocket. "Kind of surprised you didn't ask earlier. This might persuade you to go in."

He turned the volume dial, then spoke into the radio. "Davies to BASE."

"Go ahead," they heard on the other end. It was Shaw.

"Rosa and Kiyoko are here with me. Could you show yourself? So they know it's safe."

"OK. Clear."

Vincent turned down the radio. They waited. Within a minute or so Shaw appeared at the entrance, a young woman pushing his wheelchair. The two of them were both in military uniform. Shaw waved to them and smiled, but the sadness in his face was obvious.

Kiyoko and Rosa exchanged glances, then walked forward, hand in hand.

"It's a damn miracle you're still alive," Vincent said to them. "I thought you were dead, we all did. Except Shaw, that is. He never lost hope."

38

Nick turned to his side and retched. There were corpses everywhere. He looked away from them, focusing instead on the burnt-out cars and smashed shop windows. What had happened? And why wasn't he dead like everyone else?

A few hours ago, when he woke up, he had felt it. An unbearable emptiness in his heart, spreading across his chest and up into his mind. Just as he was beginning to lose hope, though, Rosa's voice came into his head. *Stay strong,* she'd said. *We need you.* With it that terrible feeling had passed. Now, standing in the middle of a deserted Headington, he wondered when it would return.

He walked past the corpses on the street, entered a convenience store on Windmill Road. The shopkeeper was there, lying face down near the entrance. He prodded the man with his foot – no sign of life. Struggling to keep his mind steady, he stepped over the body and walked behind the counter. A radio was on, playing an endless stream of static. With shaking hands, he opened a bottle of whisky and took a long swig. The heat calmed him. He put the bottle in his jacket, grabbed some chocolate bars and other items close to hand, then left the shop.

The thunder had started again. He looked up at the sky. The clouds were dark, ready to burst. *No amount of rain can wash away the blood*, he thought. *It's on us all now, this great evil. I just hope Kiyoko, Rosa and her brother are still alive.* He drank some more whisky. He should return to Mantle Hospital, he knew it. Something was there, some clue to why this had happened, even if Harold and all the others were now dead. But to face that carnage once again? He didn't know if he could do it.

He stepped back into the shop. Wedging the door open with a box, he dragged the dead shop owner out onto the street. Then he shut and locked the door, pulled out a stool from behind the counter and sat down. He turned his mobile phone on again but there was still no reception. His body started shaking again, so he took another swig of whisky. His head started to throb, a dull aching pain. That's enough, he told himself, putting the bottle down. I have to stay sober.

Once again, images from the morning came into his mind. When he had awoken, the hospital was completely silent. He left the office, entered one of the main wards. For a moment, he thought the doctors had given everyone powerful sedatives, as they had done a few times when he'd been a patient there. But then he noticed the open mouths, eyes glazed and vacant or hanging out of their sockets. He stepped over the dead bodies on the floor, ignoring as best he could the broken glass, the hastily used scalpels and syringes.

When he reached Harold's office, he found him lying there, dead like everybody else. Just when Harold was sounding like the man he had first met, back in those early days of the epidemic, he thought grimly. But now the Panic had taken him, too.

Nick thought he heard a rattling on the door. But there was no one there. He looked out the shop window. The rain was so heavy it was hard to make out the buildings on the other side of Windmill Road.

He glanced around the store. Tinned food, bottled water, enough supplies to last a few weeks, maybe longer. Perhaps there was a little apartment upstairs. The thought of staying here seemed strangely comforting. He walked through the door at the back of the shop, and up the staircase behind it.

The stairs creaked as he ascended. Then another noise. He stopped, and there it was again, a muffled groan coming from one of the rooms.

"Hello? Is there anyone there?" he called out.

No reply.

He listened carefully and heard it a third time. The sound of someone in pain.

"I'm coming," he said. "I can help." He opened the first door he came to, the main living area, but there was nobody inside. The bedroom was empty, too. Then he came to the bathroom door. It was locked.

"Let me help you," he said gently, putting his mouth to the door. "My name is Nick. Nick Parry. I mean you no harm. So, please, open the door."

He sat down on the floor and waited. From the floor, he noticed a thin trail of blood on the carpet, spreading from the bedroom to the bathroom. Images from the hospital came into his head. He stood up, tested the door. He didn't want to be too late.

"Listen," he said. "I'm going to force the door now. Don't be afraid. I only want to help you."

He pushed his shoulder firmly against the door, tried again. It didn't budge. He walked into the living room, quickly rifled through the drawers, found a hammer. Back at the bathroom door, he struck the hammer against it. Finally, it pierced the wood. Through the hole he saw her, sitting cross-legged on the bathroom floor. The shopkeeper's wife, he presumed. She had wrapped a white cloth around her eyes. It was soaked red.

"Don't worry. I'm going to open the door now. I won't hurt you, I promise," he said, making the hole in the door wider. He slipped his hand through, reached for the lock and turned it, felt a sudden jolt of pain. Quickly he pulled his hand back out of the broken door, and as he did so she thrust the knife towards him, not connecting this time.

"Stop!" he shouted. Blood was seeping from the back of his hand, but he ignored it. "Don't you get it?! I'm here to help."

Still the woman said nothing.

"Now listen," he said. "I've unlocked the door, I'm coming in. But if you do anything crazy, I'll leave you to rot. Understand?"

He opened the door, ready for any sudden movement, but this time she stayed still. Quickly he took the knife away from her. She didn't resist. He looked at her, at the blood crusted on her cheeks and blouse. He didn't need to see behind the blindfold to know what she had done to herself. It was a wonder she was still alive.

"It's all right, you're going to be all right," he said, not believing it. "I'm Nick. What is your name?"

She seemed to be glaring at him, even though he knew she must be blind. Fresh blood seeped down her cheeks. Suddenly she screamed. A high-pitched wail that made his heart pound.

"Quiet!" Nick said, covering her mouth. He felt her mouth open and close beneath his palms, scrutinised her face but saw nothing.

"Don't worry," he said, his hands shaking. "I won't hurt you. I promise."

She brought her hands to his, gently pulled them from her mouth. He didn't try to stop her.

"They're coming," she muttered.

"Who is?"

"I went into the bathroom so I could see the darkness," she said, her voice calm and steady. "The evil in my eyes. I had to cut it out. I flushed them down the toilet, but I fear they are still there, floating in the water. Watching me with their ungodly desire. Dear Sir, do me one favour. Make sure they are gone."

Nick looked, was relieved not to find anything floating in the water. "There's nothing there."

She sighed, visibly relieved, then slumped back against the bath. She seemed calm, almost sane.

"Thank you," she said, her voice barely a whisper. "Now I can die in peace. Still, they are coming. Can you hear them?"

"No."

"They did what I did, except they couldn't remove the evil. Now they are coming for you. Doesn't matter that they're blind, they can smell your sins. They want to cut them out, purify you. Wipe out all the sins in the world."

"Enough," he said, stepping away from her.

"Go to the window and see for yourself."

He did as she said, and he saw them coming: twenty or more. Less than a few hundred feet away, stumbling down Windmill Road, coming from the direction of Mantle Hospital. One of them carried a baseball bat, others had sticks or glass bottles. They lurched forward, knocking into lamp posts, tripping on the kerb, but they didn't stop.

"What do we do?" he asked her.

"Me, nothing. My time is almost up. But you, I see you still want to live. In the bedroom, under the pillow, there is a gun. Take it and run."

39

They sat in a kitchenette – Rosa, Kiyoko and Shaw – eating a simple meal of tinned fish and sweetcorn. Vincent and Rachel stood guard outside, at the entrance to the MX ward. Although Shaw and his colleagues had not come across any other survivors inside the hospital, he said howlers could still be lurking within, given the size of the place. The MX ward was supposedly the safest place in the hospital, hidden away in a disused annex. Once it had been a secure isolation facility.

"It wasn't just Oxford," Shaw said as they ate. "Most of England and Wales was hit."

"What do you mean?" Kiyoko asked.

"Millions are dead, whole towns have been stricken. The afflicted, those who haven't managed to kill themselves, blindly wander the streets. The rumour trolling the internet is that they seek out healthy survivors. When they find them, they bludgeon them to death."

Rosa glanced at Shaw. He looked weary, defeated. She'd never seen him like this before, not at Cloxham Manor or since.

"The government response?" she asked.

"Self-preservation," he sneered. "Soldiers at the blockade opened fire on the waves of people rushing to escape. You should've seen the BBC coverage. That renowned journalist Donald Flynn, his greying hair limply blowing in the wind, told viewers that the soldiers had no choice. The quarantine had to be maintained at all costs, he said with gravitas, from the safety of Edinburgh. Naturally, all the political parties agree with that. Other world leaders have also pledged their support, offering financial assistance to maintain the quarantine."

"It's sick."

"Look at this," Shaw said, pulling out his mobile phone and tapping on the screen. "Amateur videos posted on the internet. I downloaded them before they were pulled by the government."

Rosa and Kiyoko stared at the screen as the video started to play. Corpses were sprawled out of apartment blocks, you could hear moaning and screaming. "Shit," the man taking the footage whispered, his hands shaky. He adjusted the camera lens, focused it on a band of howlers not far away. They were attacking a young man, pulling at his arms, his legs, his face. Then they turned on each other, howling.

"My god," Kiyoko muttered.

Rosa stared at the frozen last frame, into the bloody faces of the howlers in the video. She sensed their blind anger, knew she'd felt something not so different after her brother had died.

"Why weren't we affected?" Kiyoko asked Shaw.

"It's a difficult question," he replied. He folded and unfolded his hands, turned his wheelchair one way and then the other. As if he knew the reason but couldn't decide whether to reveal it.

"For you, Rosa, you should know what I think," he said eventually. "That you are immune. I've said that before. But what I haven't told anyone is this – nothing can penetrate your mind. Its defence mechanisms are too strong. That's what I believe."

"What do you mean?"

"Cloxham. Godley, the fool. She was blinded by ambition. Literally," he said, laughing scornfully. "If only I had gone back there. She showed you the video and the SED survivors, didn't she? That was bad enough, but it's much more than that. What they did to you under hypnosis: it hurt you, but you withstood it. No one else could have."

Rosa stared at the tiled floor. "Why did they do it?" she asked, though she thought she was already beginning to understand.

"Godley assumed she could use you to somehow find the root cause. She was wrong, of course. And when they pushed you too hard..." Shaw said, letting the words hang in the air.

"What are you implying?"

"You know what I'm saying. You've always had it in you, ever since you were a child. They tried to penetrate your mind, and look what happened."

She looked at him, then at Kiyoko. Kiyoko sought out her hand under the table and held it.

It couldn't be, could it? she thought. *That all those people at Cloxham Manor died because of me?*

"No," Rosa said, staring at Shaw without emotion. "There are many things I don't get, but no. It's not possible. And anyway, what has that got to do with last night?"

"Nothing or everything. We don't know yet."

"I don't understand," Kiyoko said.

"Nor do I," Shaw said. "But it'll make sense soon enough. I lost many good people last night. There were sixty of us based here in Oxford. Our sources within government, they failed to inform us what would happen in Cowley Park. We really believed it would be a peaceful affair, even with that idiot road-house preacher, Paul Blinker. We never knew the government would be so foolish as to drop bombs on the crowd. We were doing our best to watch out for you both."

"So why all the secrecy?" Kiyoko asked. "Why not tell us you were here?"

"We didn't want to get in the way. What you were doing in Oxford this past month, it was good. We thought something positive could come of it."

Shaw fiddled with his hands. He looked down at his paralysed legs, then up at the ceiling. "We were wrong, of course. Now, most of my team are dead." For the first time his words sounded unsteady. "But it's far worse than that. Across the country, millions are dead. It can't go on."

"I'm sorry," Rosa said quietly. *If they hadn't killed my brother and all the other innocent people in the park, would it have been different?* No, she decided, stopping herself from thinking on it further.

The room was spartan: a couple of hospital beds, the hard chairs they were sitting on, some basic medical supplies piled up on a table. The small window was protected by steel bars. Everything smelt of antiseptic.

Shaw had said he would only be gone a short while. He had left with Ruth to check the control room, ten minutes' walk away, where monitors displayed ongoing CCTV footage of the hospital wards.

"I'm exhausted," Kiyoko said. "I don't know why, but I just want to sleep."

"It's all the stress," Rosa said, feeling sleepy herself. "Why don't you lie down? I'll keep an eye out. That guy Vincent is outside, too."

"All right. I know Shaw helped us before, got us safe

passage into Oxford. Still, something's different about him. Do you think we can trust them?"

"I honestly don't know. All I know is it was the best option we had. The door's ajar. It's not like they locked us in."

"I suppose."

"We'll be all right. You should rest now. I'll sleep later. We can take it in turns if you like. I'll wake you when Shaw returns."

"OK."

Rosa watched Kiyoko lie down.

"Rosa," she said, her voice a faint murmur. "I'm scared. I've never admitted this to you, or to anyone. The truth is I'm no different. I fear sleep, just like everyone else. I've taken the tablets, tried to meditate, I even joined one of those pointless dream-awareness groups."

Kiyoko was still talking but her words had become indistinct, mumblings in her sleep. Rosa was too tired to try to make out what she was saying. For a moment she shut her eyes, feeling a sudden heaviness in her arms and legs, but then forced herself awake. Opening her eyes, she saw that Kiyoko was already fast asleep.

Rosa felt nauseated. If Kiyoko wasn't asleep, she would have lain down, too. *Focus*, she told herself, standing up. But immediately she felt dizzy. She sat back down, holding her head. Slowly the nausea dissipated.

Her eyes glanced upon a piece of paper that had fallen on the floor. Picking it up, she saw it was a chart. Jagged lines of red and blue cut back and forth across the horizontal axis. It reminded her of something she had seen from Cloxham Manor, but she couldn't quite remember what. She thought again about the place, about Godley, the young teenagers in solitary confinement, the girl with straggly hair being forced to watch that horrific video. She shook her head, remembering how it was when she awoke there, alone, with everyone dead.

Other memories came back to her, from when she was semiconscious, moments that before had always been blurred and imprecise but now struck her with their clarity. She could picture it exactly, but she didn't know how: a birds-eye view of herself lying there on the bed, whimpering in her sleep. Dr Fersatan was in the room. He was lecturing her about hysteria. *Hysteria comes from the Greek word* hystera, *which translates as "uterus."* She saw his face close up, all lust and hatred. He was undressing her. Then she imagined him climbing on top of her inert body, heard the sound of his belt buckle being untied.

"Bastard!" she muttered, tears blinding her eyes.

Kiyoko stirred in her sleep but didn't wake.

"The bastard!" she repeated, hardly aware of Kiyoko in the room. She felt dizzy, her head was pounding. "Did he rape me? The sick pervert!"

She understood then the repulsive instinct in Fersatan's eyes. It was worse than lust. A deep-rooted evil, primal and fundamental. Driven by a desire to destroy anything good and pure. Then she could see it in other people's eyes. Not just the murderers and rapists, but in the smaller vices. Spreading like a virus, becoming worse with every day that passed. The playground bully hurting the smaller boy; the office manager abusing one of his subordinates; the middle-aged woman punishing her frail father, taking away his few meagre possessions. It filled her with a sudden intense anger, a rage against all that was wrong with humanity. She felt an inexorable desire to purge and destroy everything, the anger coursing through her veins like wildfire.

Don't, the voice inside her head instructed her, quietly but firmly. Ana. *You know that the world is far more than this. There is goodness, too, even if sometimes it feels bruised and damaged. Don't set it all on fire. Please.*

"OK," she said aloud, relieved to hear Ana's voice again. She breathed in slowly. The room was spinning. "OK," she repeated, trying to be calm.

But then the thought returned to her, and this time she didn't try to stop it. *Was what Shaw had been implying earlier true? That those people at Cloxham Manor died because of me? Is it possible?* She shivered involuntarily at the thought. *If so, if it was really like that, was last night the same? Both times I had been unconscious when it happened. Each time I had a dream where I could have stopped the suffering, yet each time I chose not to. Maybe I wasn't just an observer, maybe it's much worse. The Second Wave. My god, how did it come to this?*

Her head ached, the room veered one way and then the other. Tears fell down her cheeks. She knew something was wrong.

"Rosa, are you all right?" Kiyoko mumbled, awakened by Rosa's crying. She pushed herself up into a sitting position. "Where's Shaw? They've been gone ages, haven't they?"

"Oh, Kiyoko," she said, her voice breaking down. "What have I done?"

"Huh? What are you talking about?"

"All these people, dead or dying – I could have prevented it." *And I might have caused it,* she thought, without saying the words.

"No you couldn't. It's nobody's fault. You are special, Rosa. But still, there was nothing you or anyone could've done."

Rosa nodded, then shook her head, started to sob heavily again.

"Listen to me. I know it's hard..." Kiyoko said, before breaking off abruptly. She pressed her head with her hands.

"Are you OK?"

"My head, it's all over the place," she managed to say. "I can't even...," she said, sliding backwards on the bed, unable to hold her body up.

"Kiyoko!" she exclaimed, standing up, worrying for a moment that somehow she was the one hurting her, simply by thinking of all the pain endured. But then she felt it, too – a sharp, jarring jolt in her head. She lurched to the side, her head spinning, and felt her legs give way. She crumpled to the floor.

"We've been drugged!" Rosa exclaimed, unable to get up.

"Mmm," Kiyoko muttered. Her eyes were closed. "I always believed in you," she whispered, her voice vague. "I wasn't sure at first, even after I saw you save that man."

"Shh. Rest a while. I'm right here," Rosa said, wanting to go to her but unable to move.

"Thought it could be explained away," Kiyoko continued. "Then you cured Nick. A miracle. And Cowley Park, when was that?"

"Yesterday. Seems like a lifetime ago," Rosa replied, the sharp pain receding, now replaced by a deep numbness. She felt herself slipping away.

"The crowd, they listened to you. They'd have done anything you asked of them."

"Would they? I never really told you about Ana, did I?" she said.

Rosa started to shut her eyes, sensed a comforting darkness take hold. But Ana or some other instinct told her to keep her eyes open. *Who or what is this voice?* she wondered. *God or the Devil?*

"Ana is the voice inside my head," she continued. The words soothed her. "She guides me. Maybe with her I could have been this Rosanna Day that people talk about. Someone to pull us out of this hell. But I wasn't brave enough. Or perhaps it's worse. Maybe I didn't want to help."

Rosa looked up at Kiyoko. From the floor she couldn't see her properly, yet she could see how her arms hung loosely over the edges of the bed. Everything seemed wrong. Once again, she tried to stand up. But it was no good. She slumped back down, could sense herself drifting upwards. She closed her eyes. It felt so peaceful.

Rosa, she heard, a distant murmur. *Rosa, listen to me!* she heard again, closer now and more urgent. *They're going to hurt you. You must call for help before it's too late.*

"Who? How?" she whispered, barely able to keep herself awake.

In your mind, Ana told her. *The blind will hear you. They'll do anything you ask of them. Even though they have lost their way, deep down they understand.*

"Why? I don't understand."

Trust me. Your life is in danger; Kiyoko's too. So call them now.

WE ARE ONE

The coming night

40

Nick came out of the convenience store, closing the door as quietly as he could. Holding the gun in his hand, he was not sure if he could use it.

The first of them was barely twenty feet away. They walked together now, a slow stumble, each within touching distance of another. One stood at the front, a tall, gaunt man wearing a tattered trench coat. A leader of sorts. Like the rest of them, he wore a blindfold. They cannot see me, Nick reminded himself, tiptoeing away from them as quickly as he could. I just need to remain silent.

One of them moaned: a low rasping sound. The gruesome video Harold had once shown him flashed in his mind. He stopped a moment, glanced back. All of them were standing still, their faces lifted to the sky. Close enough for him to see the blood crusted on their cheeks. One of them, a young woman, standing in the row behind the de facto leader, seemed to be sniffing the air. She turned her face towards Nick. Removing the blindfold, she stared directly at him. Thick mucus dripped from her empty eye sockets. He stared back at her, frozen. Slowly she raised her hand, pointing her index finger at him. Her mouth dropped open and she howled. Then they were all stumbling towards him, somehow sensing where he was.

He turned away and ran. All of them were moaning or screaming now. A bottle smashed behind him and then another. Others appeared, coming out of houses on either side of the street. *How many of them can there be?* he wondered. *And how is it they can see me if they have no eyes?* They lashed out, blindly swinging sticks, knives, broken bottles. He sidestepped them, pushed past a stocky woman holding a meat cleaver. The woman fell to the floor. The others there were distracted, drawn to this new sound. They stopped by her, rained blows as she lay helplessly on the ground. The group that had first started chasing Nick came upon the melee, the tall man at the front. One of them slipped on the edge of the kerb, and soon they were all swinging at each other wildly.

He turned off Windmill Road and onto a smaller street, ran forward, ducked into a small driveway. From behind the fence, he looked out. No one was there; he seemed to have lost them. Gulping in the air, he tried to get his bearings. Bateman Street. Farther along were small roads leading off the street. If he remembered correctly, there was another hospital nearby, though one that had long since closed. *Nuffield Orthopaedic Centre, or was it Churchill Hospital? Should I hide there or keep on running?* As he was thinking what to do, he saw him there, frozen by fear.

The boy was standing in the middle of the road, one hand covering his eyes, the other holding a ragged teddy bear. He couldn't have been more than four or five years old. *What was the boy doing there? Had he succumbed like the rest of them?* No, children that caught SED died immediately, that's what they said. He tucked the gun into his jeans and stepped out from the driveway. Slowly he walked towards the little boy. He seemed to be peering at Nick from between his fingers.

"It's OK," he said as he approached. "I won't hurt you. I promise."

The boy dropped his hands from his face. Nick was relieved to see his large blue eyes, undamaged, staring at him with fear and hope. As he came to him, the boy grabbed onto one of his legs and wouldn't let go.

"It's OK," he repeated, stroking his hair. He glanced down either side of the road. They were alone, but he knew it wasn't a safe place to be. "I'm with you, I'll look after you. But listen, please. Are you alone?" he asked, gently pushing the boy away from him so he could see his face.

The boy nodded without saying anything.

"Right. And where did you come from?"

The boy looked up at him then pointed at one of the terraced houses ahead. It had a blue door.

"Is that your home?" he asked.

He nodded, started sobbing. "My daddy, he won't wake up! He was bleeding, like Mummy before."

Looking at him, all he knew was that he couldn't leave the boy alone. He pulled the boy close, soothing him as he tried to work out what to do next. Perhaps his house could be a good place to hide. Then again, the ones who had been chasing him were not far away, they'd probably track them down before too long. Better to keep moving, to get out of the city. He glanced again down the street, listening for movement. Nothing, though he knew it would only be a matter of time before the blind freaks stumbled down this road.

"My name is Nick. What's yours?" he asked. "It's all right. I know you're scared, but you can talk to me."

The boy hesitated, then spoke in a tiny whisper. "Christopher," he said.

"Hi Christopher," he replied, trying to sound calm. "This is a bit like a bad dream, nothing more. All we have to do is stay quiet and it'll soon be over. You can do that, can't you?"

"Yes," he said.

"That's good. Now, I need to ask you something. Does your dad have a car?"

He nodded, pointing to a red Volkswagen parked on the road.

"Where does he keep the keys?"

"Right by the front door."

"Good. What we're going to do is this. We're going to go inside your house and pick up the car keys. Then we'll drive out of the city, to somewhere quiet where there are no bad people. All right?"

He nodded, then shook his head vigorously.

"Don't worry, I'll be quick," he said, bringing the little boy with him to the front door. But the boy stood stubbornly at the entrance, refusing to go in.

"What is it?" he asked, trying to be patient, even though he knew they were running out of time.

"The big hospital. We must go there."

He thought about asking why, but then he saw them coming. Ten or more of them, led by the young woman who had pointed at him earlier. They were moaning in unison as they approached. The boy saw them and let out a whimper.

"OK we've got to go now," he said as calmly as he could, feeling for his gun. They stepped inside. Nick grabbed the car key hanging on a hook by the door, then lifted the boy and ran with him to the car.

The car wouldn't start. The howlers were all around them now, pounding on the windows.

"God damn it, start!" Nick shouted, punching the steering wheel. He turned the key again in the ignition, but to no avail.

The side window smashed. One of the howlers then

another pushed their hands through the window, unconcerned by the broken glass cutting their skin. He thought about getting his gun out but there was no time. Instead he put his arms around the little boy, trying to protect him as best he could. The blind hands grabbed at them, reaching for their faces, moaning. Once again Nick attempted to start the car, but he knew it was pointless, the engine was flooded.

He pushed the hands away but still they kept coming. *So this is how it ends,* Nick thought. He looked down at the boy, who had shut his eyes. As if he already knew there was no hope.

But then he heard it. A buzzing noise, like bees humming. The hands moved away from them, their moaning stopped.

The boy opened his eyes. "What's happening?" he asked, sobbing. Nick tried to quiet him, but the howlers were already moving back. From the safety of their broken car, they watched the blind stumble away from them.

"I know where they are going," the boy said, looking up at Nick.

"Where?"

"To the big hospital."

41

The door opened and closed. Shaw came in with Ruth, the young woman who had been with him earlier. Rosa kept her eyes closed, remained motionless on the floor. She felt his gaze on her, then heard Ruth wheeling him closer.

"If either of you can still hear me," Shaw said, "I'm sorry. Truly I am. But there is no other way."

Call them, Rosa! Only they can save you.

If that is how it must be, she thought, *so be it*. With her eyes still closed, she concentrated her mind. She searched for the shadows that could find her, listening for them in a vast space of darkness. There they were: faint at first, then their heartbeats grew stronger. She focused her mind on each heartbeat, picturing every one of them as an individual, willing them closer. It was draining, an almost physical sensation, despite the fact she was unable to move her body.

Hear me, she implored them with the little strength she had. *Hear me now. I understand your pain, I share it. But you must reach deep into yourselves and feel your heart beating strongly once again. I need you now, more than ever. When it is done, you will be at*

peace. I promise. You know where I am – Mantle Hospital, in the MX
ward. Come for me before it is too late.

She concentrated again, hard, as if she were pushing her
mind out beyond the confines of her body. She heard herself
humming and then she sensed it: the heartbeats becoming
stronger, larger and brighter as they approached. Like specks of
light merging together. She sighed, relieved but at the same
time fearful at what she had unleashed.

Rosa felt more assured now, even though she still couldn't
move. "Shaw," she said, opening her eyes. He was facing away
from her, towards Kiyoko, who still lay motionless on the bed.
"It doesn't have to be this way."

He swivelled his wheelchair round to face her. For a brief
moment Shaw looked surprised, fearful even, before quickly
regaining his composure.

"Rosa, my dear Rosa," he said. "If only it were that simple. I
wish it could be. But the government, watching safely from
above the blockade, they saw what happened. The problem is,
they don't really understand how special you are."

"What do you mean?"

"You know."

"I don't. Whatever you think it is, at least leave Kiyoko out
of it."

"Don't worry. What we gave you and her wasn't that strong.
Kiyoko will come to soon enough. You'll be fine too, I promise.
Our research programme formally closed years ago, but still
we've been watching you all this time. Ever since you were a
young child. I know how to look after you. I've always understood how unique you are."

"You don't know anything."

"Bureaucracies always have their cracks," he continued. His

voice sounded stilted and unnecessarily formal, but she could still sense a sadness behind it. "So we kept the project going. All these years you've had a tiny tracking device stitched under your skin. There, in your chest, just to the side of your birthmark. Replaced every few years during the check-ups for your rare heart condition."

"I don't believe you."

"I wouldn't either. But it's true."

He paused, motioned with his hand to his assistant, Ruth. She nodded, putting a medical bag on the table and unzipping it. She took out various items from the bag, shook something containing liquid. Then she lifted it up to the light, and Rosa saw what it was. A syringe.

"Andrew, you don't need to do this. There is another way."

"If only," he replied. "If only," he repeated, his voice sounding less harsh. Ruth handed him the syringe.

"Sadly, though, the government's inner circle thinks there is only one solution left. To quarantine the whole island. The northern blockade will be abandoned. They believe Scotland will be lost, too, in a matter of time. Patrolling the coastal waters is the priority now. They are trying to negotiate a settlement with Ireland and the EU, the fools."

He paused for a moment before continuing. "In the meantime, they are marooned on the tiny Isle of Man, hoping that a body of water can keep this madness at bay."

He motioned to Ruth, who then bent down next to Rosa. She rolled up Rosa's shirt sleeve, applied a tourniquet around her upper arm. Rosa tried to resist but her body remained inert.

"Don't do it."

"I'm sorry, Rosa. I mean it. But it is the only way."

"If you kill me, they'll come for you."

"We're not going to kill you. This is just a strong sedative, nothing more. The problem is you can't control it. If we don't act, more people will die."

"What are you talking about?" She looked at him, then across at Ruth. Both of their faces were inscrutable. "Do you really think I'm responsible?"

"Yes. I wasn't sure before, even after the carnage at Cloxham. But now I am, even if I don't understand the reasons why. The epidemic and your heartbeat, they move together as one. The scientists don't believe it, but I do. It can't be just random chance."

"No, it's not like that."

"Your foster parents, they weren't the first ones. The others before them died. They weren't kind to you. You made them kill themselves."

Rosa looked at him, said nothing.

"Lillian might have explained it like this," he continued. "You can reach people on some subconscious level, she'd say. You'd tell them of all the suffering in this world, but their minds wouldn't be able to take it. I think there is some truth in that."

"No there's not," she said, her heart beating strong. "But if you really believe that, why don't you just kill me?"

Shaw hesitated. He looked away from her, up at the ceiling and its harsh fluorescent lights. "Because I care for you too much," he said eventually. "You've been like a daughter to me, all these years."

She looked at him but didn't say anything, observing the tightening of his jaw, the eyes struggling to look back at her. She knew then there was at least some kind of truth to his words. His truth.

"You will fall into a coma once again," he said, more gently now, passing the syringe back to Ruth. "This time we won't meddle. No experiments, nothing. We'll look after you. Just a tiny prick, once a day, to keep you in a calm, steady state. When

Kiyoko comes to, she will watch over you. Together we'll look after you, as a team. Once we have found a cure – and we're not that far off – I'll bring you out, I promise."

She felt Shaw's assistant administer the drug. Her touch was tender. Rosa thought she felt a teardrop fall on her skin. But she couldn't be sure, for already her mind was somewhere else, soaring over waves, far from the shore.

"I'm a deep well," she murmured. "I am the ocean. The final point of all our suffering. Let me be strong for us all."

42

They lurched forward together, all of them blind. Yet instinctively they knew where to go, pain and anguish temporarily pushed aside as they moved forward. Sometimes they stumbled and fell, tripping on debris, over the pavement, banging into stationary cars. But each time they picked themselves up. They ran down Windmill Road, then turned left onto London Avenue, the main road connecting Headington to Oxford's city centre. More joined, emerging from side streets and houses, until there were over thirty of them. As they approached Mantle Hospital, they slowed, moving forward as one. Linking up, a hand on the person's shoulder in front, each of them knew what they had to do.

They paused outside the hospital entrance, not far from the dead bodies. At that point some of them howled, pointing their heads to the sky. It was as if they could sense the Panic once again, deep in their bones. But the man at the front, wiry and old, pushed forward, and they followed, entering the hospital. He guided them through the wards, past the abandoned hospital beds, the smashed cupboards, the medical supplies littered over the vinyl floors, the corpses splayed out at unnatural angles. On they went, until they reached the disused annex and the MX ward. Every one of them could sense it, a profound and urgent call reaching their damaged hearts, drawing them in like a magnet.

Vincent stood guard, wondering again if they were doing the right thing. He had his doubts. Protecting Rosa from herself was essential, for her and everyone, he reminded himself. That's what Shaw had said. Shaw knew Rosa better than anyone, had seen first-hand what she was capable of. As important, Vincent told himself, Shaw was a good and honest man. He was sure of it. In all their time working together, he had always been honest, never hiding from mistakes made and the severity of the situation. He was a good leader, too. No one else could have managed to keep the different factions united.

There was a clear and simple logic behind Shaw's plan. By placing her in a calm, stress-free coma, they could keep her heartbeat steady. Earlier, Shaw had shown them the results from the tracker that had been placed under Rosa's skin: a sudden surge and subsequent flat-lining in Rosa's heart rate that night when everyone at Cloxham Manor had died. Similar patterns had been noted at other times over the past year when the SED epidemic was particularly severe; and there were fewer deaths when Rosa's heart was calm. Most jarring of all, though, was what occurred last night, during the Second Wave. Then the tracker results found Rosa's heart rate first surging to almost 250 beats per minute, before flat-lining for almost a quarter of an hour. It was a miracle that she was still alive.

Vincent stood up and stretched his legs. Once again, he pictured his wife and young child. Once again, he prayed they were alive and well, even though he knew the odds were against them. He shut his eyes for a moment, trying to clear his mind. As he did so, he thought he heard something. Footsteps dragging, not far away now. He concentrated. Yes, there was someone or something approaching. Quickly he went over to room MX3 and rapped on the door.

"Shaw, it's Vincent. Someone's coming. Howlers maybe."

"OK," Shaw replied without opening the door. "Do whatever is required to keep them out."

"Right."

Vincent went back to the ward entrance. He glanced through the door's peephole, checked the lock. It was secured but didn't feel as solid as it should. He readied himself, taking the gun from its holster, making sure the extra rounds of bullets were close to hand.

And then he saw them. Howlers, thirty of them, or more. An old man was leading them, and a group of younger men behind were lifting a thick metal cylinder about six feet long. *My god,* he thought, *they're going to use it as a battering ram! Be cool,* he told himself, *the door is strong. And even if they make it through, they're blind. I'll take them out one by one if I must.*

It had been almost twenty minutes. Long enough for the car to start, he hoped. Remembering an old tip his father had taught him, Nick pressed his foot down on the accelerator and gently turned the key in the ignition. The engine sputtered, then finally caught. Carefully he released his foot. The engine stayed steady. He glanced at the fuel meter and was heartened to see that they had almost a full tank.

"We're set!" he said, patting Christopher on the knee. "We're set!" he exclaimed again.

"I'm scared," the boy said, hugging his teddy close.

"I know. It'll be OK, I promise."

Nick glanced back at the supplies that had been hastily

gathered from the boy's house. Bottled water, tinned food, a blanket and some extra clothes. Plus a pile of cash, for what it was worth.

"Are we going to the hospital now?" the boy asked.

"No, it's not safe. We're going somewhere else, somewhere nice and quiet," he said, not yet sure where they should go. To the coast maybe, and then another country. If they'll let us out, and if other countries will accept us.

"No, no, no," the boy screamed. He pounded his little fists against the dashboard. "We must go to the big hospital. Please, please, please."

"Why?"

"Because they need our help. Rosanna Day and the lady who watches over her."

Not long before Vincent had knocked on the door, Shaw and Ruth had lifted Rosa up onto the hospital bed and set up an intravenous drip. It wasn't easy with Shaw in a wheelchair, but they had managed it.

Now, with the essentials arranged, he glanced at Rosa, then at Kiyoko by her side, both sleeping peacefully. Outside they could hear the entrance being rammed. It was only a matter of time before the door gave way.

"Shaw, we have to go now," Ruth said. "Help Vincent keep them out."

"Yes. Just give me a moment alone."

Ruth nodded and left the room.

"Rosa, can you hear me?" Shaw asked, taking her by the hand. "They are outside, trying to break in. They're coming for us."

He looked at Rosa's silent face, remembered how it was

when they first brought her to him all those years ago. How was he to know it would come to this?

"Edith, your mother. She tried to kill you," he said, his voice wavering. "She also claimed you were conceived by her and her alone. Your foster parents knew all this, too. I don't tell you this to be unkind, but only so you realise how little we understand. I don't know what will become of you. In another time, maybe, you would have been a leader. The problem is the world today is not ready for someone like you. The truth can be too painful."

Outside there was a loud crash.

"Shaw," Ruth shouted, "we need you now!"

Shaw let go of Rosa's hand. "Forgive me," he said, glancing back at her one last time before quickly wheeling himself out of the room.

Outside, the three of them waited, each of them pointing their guns at the door, knowing it was only a matter of time before it would break.

They fell to the floor, one after another, but still others surged forward. Vincent loaded up another round as Ruth and Shaw kept shooting. Four of the howlers picked up the metal cylinder and ran directly into the gunfire. Ruth managed to shoot one in the leg but he continued on regardless. Vincent was still loading his gun when the cylinder hit him, pinning him back against the side wall. He groaned, bones broken, and then other howlers were on him.

"Take this, quick!" Vincent shouted, throwing his gun and the extra bullets towards Ruth and Shaw.

Ruth bent down and grabbed the gun. Together with Shaw they fired at the group surrounding Vincent. Some of them fell, but there were far too many of them. The howlers clawed at Vincent, moaning in unison as they reached for his eyes, low, guttural moans not loud enough to drown out his screams. Ruth, distracted by the screams, didn't see another one coming for her, wielding an iron rod, what was once part of a hospital bed. Shaw shot at the howler and missed, tried to shoot again, but his gun was empty. The howler's makeshift club hit Ruth on the head and she crumpled to the floor. Moments later they were all over her, too, clawing at her face.

Shaw retreated, reversing his wheelchair the few feet until he was outside room MX3. He was out of ammunition. Tears rolled down his cheeks.

"Rosa," he shouted. "Stop this! They are killing us."

But Rosa could not hear him. Shaw watched the howlers approaching, six of them now. He knew there was nothing he could do. Silently he bowed his head and waited for the end to come.

***

In the dream, Kiyoko was sitting on a pavement, alone. Refuse was scattered all over. Burnt-out cars and smashed shop windows made Oxford seem both older and younger than it was. Her eyes settled on an overturned shopping trolley. A large rat was gnawing on the metal, trying to get to whatever was trapped inside. She smelt something repugnant, worse than open sewage.

She sensed then something coming for her. A shadow by the rows of derelict houses. Covered in a dark veil, it limped towards her. She couldn't move. The shadow's veil slipped and she saw it – a distorted reflection of her own face staring back at her, its eyes, her eyes, filled with hatred.

Suddenly she was filled with a blind panic. She screamed but didn't wake.

"I've got to do it," she muttered, still asleep.

Gunfire rattled in the distance. Hundreds, thousands

moaned in unison, closer now. Kiyoko reached for her eyes. But as she did so, she saw Rosa. It seemed like they were both floating, a few feet above the ground.

"Kiyoko," Rosa said, holding her hand. "Stay strong. I need you, more than ever."

Kiyoko looked at her. Rosa's eyes seemed translucent, of another world.

"Where am I?" she asked, calmer now.

"In a dream. But now you must wake up. Open your eyes and lead us out of this god-forsaken place."

Kiyoko came to. Opening her eyes, first she saw Rosa, asleep by her side. Then she saw them, kneeling silently on the floor. They had formed a circle around her and Rosa. Statuesque, their blinded faces turned upwards, as if they were waiting for a sign. They didn't seem to have noticed Kiyoko stirring. Careful not to move, she glanced beyond them to the room's entrance, where she spotted Shaw's empty wheelchair and next to it his inert body, face down on the floor.

Be strong, she told herself. She quietly moved her fingers and toes, clenched and unclenched her fists. Her body seemed OK, her mind was clear, but still she had no idea what she should do.

Rosa moaned softly in her sleep. Only a slight murmur, but loud enough for them to hear. They shifted, pivoting a few degrees to the side. One of them turned his face directly towards Kiyoko, as if he had suddenly become aware of her presence next to Rosa. The man's eyes were covered by a blindfold. He raised his hands up, and she saw that they were covered in blood.

"Keep her safe," he said. His voice sounded dry and hoarse, as if he hadn't spoken for a long time.

She looked at him and at the others there. They were all facing her now.

"I will," she said, trying to sound strong.

"Not here; somewhere else," another said, a woman. Her blindfold had slipped slightly, enough for Kiyoko to see the pus and blood behind.

"We learnt too late," a third person said, an older man.

His voice sounded surer, more confident than the others. "For suffering is our strength," he said. "It is what teaches us compassion. And with this we are one."

PANIK

ACKNOWLEDGEMENTS

& A NOTE TO THE READER

I couldn't have written this book without Sandra. From talking over ideas, reading drafts and most of all, for her belief in me, she was the one I could always depend on. Thanks to mum and dad for their loving support. A big thank you to family and friends, particularly Jude, David, Monica and Ross, who kindly shared their views on PANIK; also to Michael McConnell; and a special note of appreciation to my brother Julian, who always encouraged me to write.

Finally, to the reader, I hope you enjoyed PANIK. If you could leave a review, that would be very much appreciated. You can also connect with me via my website: chrisselwynjames.com. I'd love to hear your thoughts.

Printed by Amazon Italia Logistica S.r.l.
Torrazza Piemonte (TO), Italy